Her Substitute Husband… His Brothers

PART TWO

SYLVIA HUBBARD

Published by HubBooks Literary Services

Copyright Office **A**gency Tracking ID:1-6Y1AX2M
Copyright case number 1-15118732871

Paperback Book Two ISBN: 979-8-9953349-0-3

HubBooks#: 206037-20250512-1209

Discover other titles by Sylvia Hubbard
SylviaHubbard.com/Books

For information address:

Sylvia Hubbard
18640 Mack Avenue | PO Box 36825
Grosse Pointe Farms, MI 48236-9998

Visit her website at:
SylviaHubbard.com

Author Note:

Yes, you are reading the second book and boy am I excited you got this far. I should warn you, that you have to read the 1st book if you want to understand what's happening. We're starting this baby at Chapter 29 where we're still in the Special Attention party. I do have a book summary but you'll have to contact me for it. I hope you enjoy this book and let me know which brother you liked? The ending? I won't be upset if you are. After over sixty books, it's hard to imagine something different but only when I focus on the characters and making them happy at the end.

Stick with me and as always, happy reading. PS Don't forget to drop your review of the first book too.

Author's Trigger Note

Dear Sensitive Reader

Let's have a quick moment of honesty before you turn the page.

If you're looking for a sweet love story where everyone communicates clearly, no one makes terrible decisions, and the biggest conflict is who forgot to text back...

You may want to gently close this book and back away slowly.

Because inside ***Her Substitute Husband... His Brothers*** Book Two you'll find:

- A fake marriage that gets very real
- Three brothers who absolutely do not stay in their lanes
- Jealousy that escalates... dramatically
- Family secrets that refuse to stay buried
- Kidnapping, threats, and a few very questionable life choices
- Illness, betrayal, and characters carrying emotional scars

• A mother who has done some extremely messy things for her family

• And a heroine trying to survive all of it while her heart refuses to cooperate

These characters are not perfect.

They make mistakes.

They react emotionally.

They love recklessly.

And sometimes they do things that will make you clutch your pearls and whisper:

“Oh... this is about to get messy.”

But if you enjoy romance that is **dramatic, steamy, emotionally complicated, and just a little dangerous**, then welcome.

You’re exactly where you belong.

Turn the page.

Just don’t say I didn’t warn you.

— Sylvia Hubbard

Thank you, & enjoy

Your author
Sylvia Hubbard

Contents

CHAPTER 1

All Night Long

Dinner was a Greek lemon-butter chicken breast with sundried tomatoes, accompanied by turmeric-ginger potatoes and snow peas. Every bite was scrumptious. Shawn kept her engaged, speaking about his job, which Tori found fascinating.

"I'm glad you like listening to him drone on about his job, Tori," Kevin sniped. "I swear he wants to talk about how much he enjoys it all the time, and it drives Duncan and me to boredom."

"The hospital was in desperate need of an administration podiatrist, according to Malea, and I'm so proud Shawn was up for the job." Reaching over and taking Shawn's hand in comfort." Despite what Norman did to you, giving your all to run his businesses has given you the practice to do so well."

"She's right," Duncan agreed. "It was practice for the main event, Shawn."

"I love how Tori has these glimmers instead of seeing the negative like everyone else," Kevin chimed in.

"I love the way Shawn's face lights up when he talks about his profession," she admitted. "It's rare that people enjoy what they do for a living. I've been an entrepreneur most of my life, and I rarely get around people with jobs or careers."

"What about Malea and Scott?" Kevin asked.

Tori revealed, "Malea and Scott took their jobs out of necessity. They needed to make a living. And that's what I mean. I see you all having jobs and careers that accentuate your passions and gifts, and I think that's so cool."

All three brothers shifted uncomfortably and flushed in some way.

"I didn't mean to make you blush," she said. "I was just being honest."

Dessert was raspberry cheesecake drizzled in strawberry sauce.

By this time, Shawn started massaging her other foot, and she was leaning back into Duncan's body, who was slowly feeding her dessert with his finger, which she greedily sucked off, loving how his shaft twitched on her back.

"Anyone can rarely make us feel anything except constantly annoyed, Tori. Be proud of yourself and all your skills," Kevin remarked, looking jealous that he wasn't on her side of the table.

"Did you choose podiatry because of your relationship with Norman?" Tori questioned Shawn.

"No. I had the interest first, and Norman followed."

"Because he could cheat off your papers," Kevin growled.

Shawn flushed. "He wasn't that bright, and yes, he did cheat. I thought it was because he wanted us to be together. His father encouraged us because his son had never had any direction in his life until he met me. His mother bought the podiatry business from someone else to encourage Norman, but he didn't know shit about running it."

Kevin added, "And barely knew shit about being a foot doctor."

"Kevin, if you don't stop, I'm going to come over there and shut you up," she snipped.

"Promise?" he asked with mirth, with a heavy lustful look in his eyes.

Tori chuckled and encouraged Shawn to continue. "And your mother. What did she say about you, Norman, and your choice of professions?"

A far-off look came on Shawn's face. "She was fine, happy. She didn't want me to be with any woman."

"If she had her way, she'd want to keep us all to herself," Kevin admitted. "She made it hard for all of us to be with anyone. With my background, I couldn't find anyone who tried to stay. And if she did, Momma would make me see she wasn't worth a grain of salt, and she usually wasn't if she was hanging around me."

Tori looked up at Duncan, and he just gave her an obvious look.

"Momma would beat the smart girls away with a stick from Duncan," Kevin explained. "When he did say something, it drew them in like flies to shit."

Looking back at Shawn, Tori asked, "And you? I wasn't the only girl looking in your direction, Shawn."

"Like I said, I wasn't into girls. So if you were looking, I wasn't noticing. She made sure of that. If I even looked at females, she would know. She'd come to my room and tell me how she watched me look at them and..." He stopped speaking, but his hands continued to move higher and higher up her legs. "She'd make sure she'd catch me jacking off with pictures of women in front of me and then beat me with a switch. I stopped looking and I stopped being attracted to women completely." By this time, his hands were under her dress, resting over her mound. "Thinking about them was bad. Touching them was bad. Wanting was bad." He looked up at her and confessed, "Last night, with you, Tori, I felt..." His chest hitched as if the words had gotten caught up in his throat and wouldn't come out.

His confession entranced both his brothers and Tori, and he hardly breathed, so they could barely hear every word.

Shawn continued after taking a deep breath. "Being with you last night changed me. You gave me access to a part of myself I thought I would never do with a woman, and I want to thank you for showing me it was possible to be with a woman, finally. I'm not that man my mother said I was, and I know I'm a better man without her voice in my head because you have shown me those things aren't bad with a woman." He kissed the back of her hand tenderly. "You've spoiled me for any other woman, but I hope to do them with you for as long as you would like, Tori."

Touched, he was asking for her consideration when she wouldn't care if he took it; Tori found herself falling in love with Shawn. She reached over and cupped his face. "You don't have to feel bad doing any of those things to me, Shawn." Spreading her legs wider to give him access, she said, "I want you to. I need you to."

Shawn's expression became serious as Duncan reached down and pulled her dress up so she could see Shawn's hands lying over her womanhood. Shawn stared intently as if he could see right through her soft pink panties. They were damp from Kevin's earlier expedition and her current arousal.

Shawn seemed to be in a world of his own as he dropped down to his knees and pulled her panties off, his eyes never leaving between her legs.

Watching him entranced, she could see there were still demons in him fighting his urges, and they were losing. His thumbs moved down between her over the covering of her clitoris, bringing her sensitive spot to light and making her take a quick, short breath.

Duncan's hand moved down the front of her dress to one

of her breasts to tenderly flick over a nipple, bringing it to hardness, and then he moved to the other one.

Shawn's face dipped down and kissed the inside of her thighs, tasting her skin like a dessert he'd desired but could never imagine tasting. Tori was mesmerized by how his mouth and tongue moved over her until he hovered over her clit using his tongue to coax it out of hiding and then circling about.

Kevin chuckled proudly. "That's it, just like I taught you, Shawn."

Yes, it was almost like what Kevin would do, but Shawn went much slower, enjoying the journey as much as she did. He then moved down using his tongue to part her lower lips, plunder her wet softness, and then swirl back up to her clitoris.

By this time, both of Duncan's hands were attending her nipples, and the double stimulation was making tornadoes explode inside her chest, stomach, and vagina. She was glad Duncan was holding her securely, because Tori would have fallen out of the chair and onto the floor.

"I think Tori's ready for her massage," Kevin said to Shawn and Duncan.

Tori was ready for anything at this point.

Shawn greedily licked her juices from his mouth, while Duncan carefully helped her to her feet. She was dizzy and was glad that her wine glass had somehow been filled. Taking the whole swig, as Duncan began unzipping her dress and letting it fall to her feet.

Kevin and Shawn moved off to the side and laid down a sheet over the shagged rug, where she assumed they were going to finish the special attention party.

"You keep that delicious mouth to yourself except for Shawn," Duncan said in a low tone.

She frowned, but teased a kiss on him. "You don't want my mouth on you, Duncan?"

Duncan growled, "I nor Kevin need that mouth making us lose our fucking mind. Do this for me?" he asked as he moved his hands around her back and unlocked her bra.

It was a strange request, but she only nodded, letting her lingerie fall to the ground. Duncan kissed her in appreciation and then picked her up, carrying her over to the blanket. His shoes were off as he lay her down in the center, and all of them stood above her.

Whatever was under the shag rug made lying on the floor extremely comfortable, and she realized this was better than the bed, where she could see all of them at once, and they would have enough room to do anything they wanted.

Tori knew this had to be Duncan's idea. There was a tray near them with massage oils, more wine and glasses, water, and even lube. A chill went through her, knowing the night to come was going to be truly exceptional.

She dreamed of extending her bedroom and adding a double California King-size bed, so they could make love and sleep together every night for the rest of their lives. However, in this reality, she knew that would never happen.

Her eyes were quickly drawn to the brothers as they started taking off their clothes together. She didn't know which one to watch because all of them looked delicious. One of her hands moved to her breasts, and the other moved between her legs. She played deliciously with herself as she enjoyed looking at every inch of light brown skin they revealed to her, and how she knew at one point in the night, she would be able to touch them.

"Fuck, Tori," Kevin said in amazement as he greedily watched her, rubbing himself from base to tip.

Shawn started to come down to her, but Duncan held him back, and Tori knew the older brothers wanted to enjoy the production she was giving them. Since she was already wet between her legs, it didn't take long to bring herself to fruition. She undulated her hips, squeezed and fondled her nipples, and delighted at the visual gorgeousness standing all around her, knowing what was to come. The orgasm came in soft, urging, powerful waves, making her gasp, hiss, and hum in gratification.

Shawn was still giving her that look like he was fighting his urges, but this time his hand was gripping his shaft just like both his brothers while they watched her.

Duncan knelt on the left side of her, holding the bottle of massage oil over her. Kevin knelt on the other side, slightly closer to her head, while Shawn knelt between her legs. Her fingers were still slowly caressing her folds, and Shawn took her hand and slurped her honey from her fingers.

Kevin took the massage oil and began drizzling it down her chest, then each thigh. Duncan started first, massaging her body, while Shawn started on her thighs. Kevin came around to the top of her, lifted her head, and rested her nape on his calf so she could see what his brothers were doing to her body, while he massaged her scalp and temples.

If she could cry out louder than the angels in heaven, she would. Their strong hands were dedicated to relieving every ounce of tension in her body, even down to her pinkie toe. Closing her eyes just made everything more intense. Six strong hands rubbing up and down her body, taking every worry and care from her mind, body, and soul.

"Tori," Kevin said quietly.

She looked up at him at the exact moment, Duncan's hand came up to massage under her neck and chin. Kevin was deeply massaging the back of her head, and if they wanted to kill her, she didn't even care.

"You trust us?"

For a second, Tori almost felt the trepidation Beck had put in her, but then it was gone the moment it arrived as Shawn was doing a technique to her feet that reverberated up her legs, shot to her spine, and spread over the rest of her body.

"Yes," she said. "I trust you."

Even as she said that, both of Duncan's hands moved around her neck and then applied pressure on each side of her carotid arteries. Meeting his eyes, she showed no fear as she moved her hands to hold his wrists as if encouraging him for more. A glint of humor pushed away the dark look in his eyes as he moved to her collarbone and then down her body. She didn't tense once, fully trusting they were not going to hurt her despite Beck's warning.

Any thought of what Beck said went out of her mind as Duncan knelt to begin sucking on her already erect nipples that had been screaming for attention. With his mouth, he worshiped every part of her breasts, and what his mouth wasn't touching, his hands were.

If it weren't for Kevin holding her neck steady, she'd have flipped up and over. Shawn's hand only pressed over her mound at the same time while he watched his brother, but that was enough for her to gyrate herself on his palm. She clung to Duncan as he mercilessly brought both her breasts together, licking, rubbing, and sucking on them until she came yet again, crying in thankfulness.

Shawn and Duncan switched, but Duncan helped his little brother, slipping a finger inside of her. He didn't move it, but it was just enough. Shawn was an excellent learner, and with his eagerness, it was just enough to send her over again. They didn't care how long it took between each orgasm. They were focused on teaching, learning, and using her body.

Tori did not mind.

Duncan lay on his back beside her, and Kevin helped her up and guided her on top of Duncan, slipping his manhood inside of her, but Shawn held her hips firm so she wouldn't move. She cried out in anguish, but Duncan only pulled her down so she could lie on his body, giving her forehead and cheek hundreds of kisses, while Kevin moved behind her and began to massage her back.

If she tried to squirm, Duncan would only hold her hips still so she couldn't move, while Kevin's strong hands started wringing all the tension out of her nape, shoulders, and back. And then he started on her coccyx. Tori didn't know she had so much tension in her tailbone until Kevin's big ass hands started pressing on and around it like he was trying to unleash an incubus inside.

A strange gurgling sound came from her lips, and Duncan cursed.

"I think you got... fuck, Kevin, she's fucking squeezing..." Duncan started to gurgle too because now Kevin had lube on his thumb and slipped his finger into her rear.

Tori didn't need to move; the massage was doing all the movement she needed from her back to her front and then back again. Her pelvic pulsated so hard, she could feel the vibrations up to her cervical and thrummed inside her skull. Duncan held her tight against his chest, stiff as a board, feeling everything she was going through and trying not to cum inside of her. Yet, it was too much for him, and she could feel him pulsing with her, and this only made her orgasm longer.

When she finally came down, she burst out in a sob, and Shawn asked tenderly, "Did you hurt her?"

Kevin chuckled. "That's sexual shock."

Tori had no idea what one would call being snatched out of her body and shoved back in again, but loving it.

"Your turn, Shawn," Kevin said.

She whimpered as she felt Duncan sliding out of her. Her body was still high, and she felt this sexual fogginess all around.

"Maybe we should give her a moment," Shawn insisted.

Kevin lay next to Duncan and pulled her limp body onto

his. His shaft was stiff as a rock, and he easily slipped inside of her. Tori gasped, joyfully bemoaning as he filled her up and kissed her. She loved Kevin's kisses and kissed him back enthusiastically.

"She's ready," Kevin urged.

Shawn began massaging her just like Kevin had done. Tori loved how his stroke was gentle and then grew with confidence, rubbing her up and down her back. She knew that, being a doctor, Shawn knew which muscles to concentrate on, and she could feel the blood flow in places she hadn't thought she had tension. And then when he moved to her tailbone, Shawn's hands were long enough to also massage down to her rear entrance, so he doubled her pleasure by getting all the good places. To change what Kevin had done to her, Shawn circled her rim, dug his fingers into each cheek, and then returned to her coccyx, as if chasing out all the stress.

"I see what... fuck, Tori..." Kevin panted.

But she was feeling all kinds of things as Shawn inserted another finger in her rear, while pressing another finger inside of her with Kevin's shaft. Since Shawn's finger was the only thing moving and the thickness of Kevin's shaft against her entire clitoris, that was just enough to make her entire vulva thump hard repeatedly in time to Shawn's motions in her rear and front.

She heard the high-pitched yipping before she realized it was her. Kevin brought her mouth to his to try to muffle her screams that followed shortly, and Tori received his thick, delicious tongue in hers, while she rode out the sexual cyclone, beating her blissfully.

Kevin's hips shot up, sending his shaft deeper in her, and he forgot he was supposed to keep her quiet as he bellowed, "GAWD FUCKING DAMN!"

Duncan rushed over to them and covered his brother's mouth, but Tori was feeling herself as Kevin came hard in her at the same time her orgasm was billowing all over her body, and Duncan kissed her until they both calmed down.

When she and Kevin could finally breathe normally, Kevin gently moved her off his body and shot up to swing at Shawn. Duncan pulled her into his arms.

"You fucking ass. It's her special attention party," Kevin snarled.

"I think Kevin liked that a little bit too much," Duncan whispered to her.

She giggled. "I didn't think I would like being double-teamed like that," she admitted.

"Do you think you want to try?" Duncan asked.

Tori smiled wickedly, licked her lips hungrily, and asked, "Could I have you all at once?"

CHAPTER 2
She's So Greedy

Duncan looked at Kevin and Shawn. They'd heard her inquiry very clearly.

"Turn the music up a little bit more," Kevin said in a deadly serious tone.

When Shawn walked away, Kevin winked at Duncan and said, "I'll get the water warm, and you clean up while little brother gets her ready."

Duncan smiled in response, gave her a quick kiss, and slapped Shawn on the ass when he returned to the mat. Duncan walked away, donning his underwear.

Kevin put on his underwear, but nodded at Shawn. "She's all yours."

Shawn knelt on the mat in front of her and coaxed her to him. Lifting her in his lap as he rested his butt on the back of his legs, he drew her mouth to his and lost her in the deepest kiss.

Whatever they were planning, Tori knew she was down for it. She barely noticed Duncan was cleaning up the table to move it away to create a larger space, and Kevin ducked behind a partition.

There was some water running, but damn if she knew where it came from, as the shed was bare the last time she checked. She wouldn't put anything past these brothers, who seemed to plan for everything, and she loved that about them.

Shawn's possessive kissing really started to distract her because his hands were all over her body. She couldn't touch him enough, loving how strong he was, sexy, and damn gorgeous all over. Each brother had their own particular build, but Shawn was like both brothers in one, strong, muscular, and with beautiful, light brown skin that brought out the Tori hairs all over his body.

She could kiss him all over every day, and she tried - gourging his neck, down his chest, and back up to his face, loving that he was doing the same.

He laid her down in a new spot on the rug because she knew the other places where she had lain with Duncan and Kevin were drenched from lovemaking. She didn't mind and was touched by his thoughtfulness. Shawn lay on top of her, and she was already aroused to receive him.

Grinding her body with him, she met his eyes and smiled tenderly at him. "Give me you, Shawn," she whispered.

"Gawd..." He expelled breathlessly, holding himself up on one arm and moving his other hand up to her neck.

Just like Duncan, but Shawn's long fingers could nearly wrap all the way around her neck, and he had a power she hadn't fathomed, slightly cutting off her oxygen supply as he pumped harder and harder in her. "Give... me... all... of....you...Sh-Shawn!" she pleaded between breaths she could barely take. Tori closed her eyes, fully trusting him, enjoying every hard stroke he delivered, taking her higher and higher to glory.

Suddenly, she could barely breathe, but at the same time, her pussy clenched around him, pulsing with his rhythm as her body struggled for air. Tori shot her eyes open to see this dark, vicious look on Shawn's face, his teeth gritted and a maddened look of hatred that tore at her soul.

How long could this go on? Did she want him to stop?

Sweet Jesus! Her body flooded in a tumultuous bliss that brought tears to her eyes, but she wanted him to know she didn't want him to stop, even if she died.

"It's... it's oh...kay..." She gasped out between the hard strokes that seemed to want to break her in half. Each one of them shooting explosions all the way up through her hair follicles. "Do... it! Don't...." She sobbed, gasped... hissed... "Don't... stop!"

Sharp blackness engulfed her, and Tori knew she had died, but damn if she didn't care.

Air abruptly rushed back into her lungs, and she cried out, hugging Shawn, thanking him as she shuddered, feeling him come into her.

"Fuck... fuck! FUCK, Tori!" he whimpered back as if he had given in to the demons she had possessed him with, collapsing on her body as he filled her womanly casm as his brothers had tonight.

Tori lay there flourishing in the evervesant of all the orgasms. Tears rolled down the side of her closed eyes, and she could barely breathe if she tried to move. Her whole body was racked with pure joy, and she knew that at this moment in her life, she would never feel anything like this. She realized that nothing truly mattered except her night with these brothers and being filled one by one by each of them.

"Did you kill her?" Kevin questioned.

She felt Shawn move above and touch his finger to her neck.

"I think I killed her," Shawn determined. "Or she's dying because I don't think I feel a pulse."

"At least she died smiling," Kevin chuckled.

"Tori?" Duncan asked with concern.

Slowly, she fluttered her eyes open to see them all kneeling around her, waiting with baited breath, and let it go when they saw she wasn't dead.

Shawn leaned down and kissed her. She giggled.

"Fuck you, Tori!" Kevin snarled and went back behind the partition.

Duncan chuckled and moved away, too.

"It's nice to know you cared," she said softly.

Shawn moved down her body with kisses, and she already knew what his mission was. He loved to savor their lovemaking, and she loved being savored.

His mouth rushed between her legs, wrangling her thighs over his shoulders and engulfing her womanhood like he was about to wolf down a ten-pound steak. Gawd, this was like a cherry on top, and she had a feeling he loved this more than she did.

His loud slurping and groaning as he gulped the night sexual essences down from her body kept Tori titillated. Soon, Duncan lay beside her, and after several kisses, he moved to her breasts again.

Lawd, they were keeping her aroused whether she liked it or not, in so many ways she didn't think possible.

Tori prayed this night would never end.

This orgasm was long, slow, complex, and pulsating. "Ohh.. oooohhh... uuuhhh....ooohhh," she melodiously trembled out. They were taking their time and somehow working together to keep her in a state that would take her to the edge and back several times until Shawn got his fill of her, smacking his lips and then using his finger to finish her off bringing more of essence to drip out of her, which he immediately lapped up and then sucked on his fingers as Tori finally could calm herself down.

"Damn you, Tori, for tasting so fucking good with us," he said, kissing her inner thighs and her stomach.

Duncan popped her breasts from his mouth and smiled down at her. "I think she's ready for aftercare, Kevin."

She looked above her to see Kevin moving the partition away to reveal a collapsible tub. A fifty-gallon water bladder had been brought in and placed beside it. When she started to get up, Kevin came over to her, lifted her from the floor as if she were just a piece of paper, and carried her to the tub.

When he let her down so she could stand in the very warm water, with red and white rose petals floating on top, she shrieked in glee.

"How did you guys do this?" she asked, flabbergasted.

Kevin answered, "Duncan knew you needed aftercare, and we'd planned to end the night like this, but you asked for something we'd love to do." While he spoke, he'd soaped up a sponge and was cleaning her from her neck all the way down her body. She could tell he'd already cleaned up.

"Was it too much to ask?" she questioned Kevin, biting her lip and unsure how they would accomplish her desirable request.

His smile was mischievous. "You've surprised us, Tori, with your wantonness. Duncan and I couldn't have imagined a woman as smart, beautiful, and vivacious as you, having such an excessive sexual appetite, and we find that damn attractive." By this time, he was rubbing the sponge between her legs, heightening her pleasure, and she gasped a little, holding onto his shoulders, trying not to get too aroused again.

When he was done soaping her up, he took a small bucket and poured water over her body, rinsing her off.

"You're spoiling me," she warned. "And you know if you start this, you'll be stuck doing this forever."

"For you, Tori, it would be worth it," he said earnestly, giving her backside a hard smack.

Tori giggled again, fighting the urge to reveal that the tap felt good.

Kevin lifted her from the tub and had a large towel to dry her off. "Duncan's going to lotion you down, while Shawn gets cleaned up." He tapped her on her rear again just as Duncan came over and led her to the area where the dining table had been, but now a new sheet was laid down. This one was red. From the tray, he picked up a bottle of lotion and returned to her.

She could tell he'd washed up as well, most likely while she was with Shawn, to be refreshed for what was in store for the night.

Kevin sat nearby and watched them as if he were enjoying a very intriguing television show. Duncan didn't need to speak.

Yet, his body language said so much as he tenderly slathered her body with a lavender peppermint lotion. Their eyes met, and she saw appreciation for her. When she frowned slightly, he looked over at Shawn and then back at her.

She wasn't sure what she had done to Shawn to deserve Duncan's appreciation, but the middle brother was grateful for something. When they were alone, perhaps she would inquire, but for now, she was enjoying the very relaxing full-body rub.

"I've never had a special attention party before," she noted out loud. "I think I want a million of these before I die."

Duncan shot a look at Shawn, but Kevin chuckled.

"You'd get exhausted of us," the older brother declared. "Either that or you wouldn't be able to walk straight."

"And you," she bravely asked, looking from Kevin to Duncan. "Would you all be able to give me this for as long as I desire?"

They both looked up at Shawn, and she followed their eyes as he came around the partition with the towel around his body. Were they looking at him because she was supposed to be married to him, and they were concerned about what people would think in the long run if they were seen together? Yet she had to wonder why they would worry when this was all a fake marriage? And everything was temporary? No strings attached between all of them.

Yet, the frown on his face was severe as he looked from his brothers to her. "Yes, Tori. As long as you desire."

Duncan and Kevin looked at each other and then back at her.

Tori rougishly grinned. "I could desire something for a long time. I'm very greedy, especially when I really like it."

"We'd better turn the music up louder, because I don't know how loud all your asses are going to get." Kevin snorted and changed the subject. "Are you ready, Shawn, to help give Tori her request? It is her special attention party, and we don't want to disappoint. Since you are the least refreshed, you should be able to handle everything the longest."

Shawn moved right next to her, and she crawled over to him, knowing she was giving Kevin and Duncan a nice view of her full, bare derriere. Instead of moving into his arms, she slithered over to engulf his manhood. Her mouth needed to be sated, sucking on someone tonight, and since she'd only promised Duncan she'd only taste Shawn, she took advantage of the moment once he was softened from their exuberant engagement earlier, but she knew her skills and was confident with what her mouth could do to him.

Starting at the base, she dragged her bottom lip for each kiss around the shaft, going up slowly, incorporating her tongue and looking up occasionally to delight in seeing him watching her.

He was trying to keep his breathing steady and look aloof, but she knew she could give a good oral show visually and physically. Leaving a generous amount of saliva on him but then sucking it off loudly, she repeated this motion until she was at the top, where she fluttered the tip around his frenulum to his slit, which rewarded her with a droplet of his excretion.

She moaned, loving how the taste of him reminded her of a roasted sweet pecan. Each brother was circumcised, but Shawn's phallus had old scars on its shaft. Tori briefly wondered if his mother had inflicted that pain with the switch. Dragging her mouth back down his shaft, she tenderly kissed each scar she saw as if her lips could heal his pain.

His breath caught in his throat, and an elongated huff of air let out from his chest as if he were releasing something. "Your mouth is beautiful," he said, his voice thick with emotion.

Gripping the base, Tori directed the tip into her mouth and shoved him all the way until he hit the back of her throat. Shawn gasped from the sharp sensation, and then growled as she enclosed her entire mouth around him firmly, while at the same time, moving her tongue in a wave around the shaft in rhythm to her lip movements, massaging him without moving.

He'd started to thicken exponentially until he was almost choking her, but Tori was relentless and sucked on him harder, gurgling her enjoyment.

"Gawd, woman!" Shawn hissed, drawing her body up his, holding her body close, and devouring her mouth.

His rambunctious kisses were infectious, and she was just as passionate. His skin was warm as she straddled his waist, loving how he hugged her to him as if needing skin-to-skin contact. Her arms circled his neck, and she ran her hands over his scalp. He closed his eyes briefly, enjoying her touch.

"As long as you desire," he promised in a whisper as he slipped himself into her again.

Tori moaned and shuddered, feeling herself succumb to the arousal she was still feeling. The more she was fucked, the more she wanted, and these boys knew how to make her want more and more.

Shawn drew her down with him until he lay flat, shoving a pillow under his ass to lift him higher, and she was again lying flat on a man's body. Shawn didn't move inside of her as Duncan came up behind her, placing a knee down between their legs and started rubbing the lotion all down her backside as she enjoyed kissing Shawn.

"Grab her neck," Kevin ordered.

Shawn's large hand wrapped easily around her neck, keeping her face over his, locking with her eyes, automatically making her spine straight all the way down to her coccyx. Duncan was still massaging more lotion all down her, and she was relaxed until... Duncan started to press into her with Shawn, who was already firmly inside.

Both she and Shawn gasped. The sensation for her was a lot of stretching, no pain, but she worried if she could take both of them and found herself tightening.

"Help her breathe," Kevin ordered Shawn.

Shawn called her name softly and took a deep breath. She held her breath until her lungs filled, then let it go when Shawn let his come out. They took three more breaths together until she gasped again, but it was as if bliss hit like a wave from her vagina to her eyeballs, making them roll to the back of her skull.

"Tori, stay with us," Duncan whispered in her ear, situating himself to the left of her, giving himself a peculiar angle, but still able to make entry and move if he wanted to, but leaving her rear slightly exposed on top. His incredible upper body strength gave him the advantage and was perfect for being in the middle because he could hold himself there using only his arms and one leg, and his manhood could squeeze comfortably with Shawn's inside of her.

His powerful voice and the intense look in Shawn's eyes

kept her focused on the task at hand, as the pleasure was overwhelming all her senses.

Shawn's phallus, which wasn't up to its full potential, started to move slowly back and forth. With him being fully embedded and Duncan pressed only a few inches inside, the double sensation all around sent cartwheels of bliss rolling through her.

"You're so fucking beautiful," Shawn whispered through the deep breaths he was taking, encouraging her to stay calm.

At the same time, Kevin pressed two thickly lubed thumbs into her rear, and his forehead pressed down on her back more. She knew this was to prepare her, but with Shawn's movements reverberating, Duncan's tip to swipe over the sides of her G-spot, Tori was in a euphoric splendor unheard of by any human entity.

"Gawd!" Duncan hissed with Shawn while Tori could only hum as Kevin made an easy entry. Initially, he teased the rim with his tip before sliding effortlessly only a couple of inches.

Shawn's hand that had been still around her neck only tightened a little, and she wrapped her hand around his wrist, trusting he wouldn't squeeze too hard, but needing him to stay there so she could keep her body still and straight, knowing what was to come.

He was still stroking inside her deeply, while Kevin waited until her body adjusted to push a couple more inches until he was all the way to the hilt. By this time, Duncan was breathing with Shawn and her. She knew they were all highly aroused, and it would only take a few more strokes between Shawn and Kevin to send them over in unison.

A tear from her fell on Shawn's cheek, but she was far from sad. Tori was feeling so revered, loved as all her men, vocalized praises to her concurrently. Each voice built the lustful explosion inside of her until she burst so hard, she was sure her eyeballs had fallen out of her head. There was a blind, rapturous detonation that set off a river of her essence coating all over her, Shawn, and Duncan. This pushed them to their breaking point, and Shawn's hips shot up hard, followed by Duncan and then Kevin.

Tori was sure she should have lifted off of them like a bullet, but with all their bodies holding her down, she joyfully endured their pulsating manhood, releasing their potent elixir deep into her.

Shawn's hand dropped away from her neck, and Tori sobbed enraptured as she was filled to the brim, loving every drop given to her.

As each man disengaged from her, Tori couldn't stop sobbing, loving that she had taken her sexuality to another level and not felt one ounce of guilt about it.

Duncan returned to her, wrapped her in a blanket, pulled her into his lap, and held her close.

"Is she okay?" Shawn questioned in concern, checking her vitals as if something was wrong with her.

Kevin chuckled. "That's called being a beautiful woman, Shawn."

"Fuck! That river of cum! I've never seen anything like that."

The older brother mumbled something, but Tori was too relaxed listening to Duncan's calming heartbeat to care.

Duncan passed her off to Shawn after a minute, and she realized Shawn had dressed and was taking her out of the shed. She tensed up a little, but he assured, "You're covered up enough to make it back to the house, Tori."

The king-size fleece blanket had been rolled around her like a burrito. Shawn entered the back door and immediately took her over to the guest bathroom. It wasn't until then that she realized she really needed to pee and wouldn't have made it up to her private bathroom. How the hell were they so considerate of her even when she wasn't thinking about herself?

Tori kissed his cheek in appreciation before going inside to relieve herself and tidied up a bit. When she came out, Kevin was standing there fully dressed and scooped her up.

"Are you guys going to let me walk anywhere tonight?" she asked with a giggle.

"I think after blowing your fucking back out, you shouldn't walk an inch tonight. You need to recover," he teased, taking her upstairs to her bedroom. "Get ready for bed while we get things back to normal," he ordered, giving her a tap on the bottom before letting her go into her private bathroom.

She took a quick shower and brushed her teeth. Of course, she did a full body check, just knowing she should feel some way after what they had done to her, but she felt fine. By this time, they were all in bed waiting for her with only their underwear on. She had a long tank top as usual and crawled into the bed with them, barely able to keep her eyes open.

Instead of wine, Duncan offered her a glass of cranberry juice, and each one kissed her goodnight. As soon as Tori lay down on Duncan's chest, she passed out completely.

CHAPTER 3
Ghosted

The effects of the previous night hit her in the morning as soon as she opened her eyes. Tori didn't even bother to know if anyone was around as she rushed out of the bed and into the bathroom.

She wasn't sick or in pain, but her stomach had brought her out of dead sleep and needed relief.

The food from last night?

The sexual activity?

She wasn't sure, but after a few minutes of throwing up and then her bowels taking a turn, she felt better. Not the best way to wake up after a night of unimaginable sex, but with everything naughty, there was a price to pay.

Looking out of her bedroom, she saw that no one was around, so she immediately jumped in the shower again, this time soaping up from head to toe. Since it was time to redo her two-strand twists, she decided to take her hair down. Once she was out of the shower, she made an appointment for the afternoon. The stylist just happened to have an opening, and Tori slipped herself in there.

When she was off the phone, she went to her office to

check her email. The lawyer received the message about the trust for her niece and nephew and then set up the financial shelter for the group home and courtyard. She sent an email about them finding Amos's body, but assured the lawyer that this shouldn't affect any of the funding.

The lawyer did let her know they were still digging around the register of deeds, but promised there wouldn't be any dust kicked up that could alert the Cosgroves or the hospital.

Tori sent emails to Scott and to Kevin after all the work she had done for them yesterday. She knew Kevin would love what she had proposed and had discovered for his start-up. And she knew Scott would be impressed by what she had initiated. Since he had so much in place, it only took a matter of hours to do what she had to do for him, and since she needed her mind occupied yesterday anyway, it helped. She was much more productive when under stress, but she hated it when things were like that.

There were emails about tenants needing minor fixes and renovations in their apartments. She addressed the fixes right away, but she wasn't going to address any renovation requests until next year, after the courtyard was complete.

In her calendar, she had a brunch schedule to network and speak with some suburban elderly organizations before her hair appointment. After washing and blowing out her hair, which was well past her breasts, she styled it in a high semi-puff to showcase its volume and healthiness.

Maintaining a protective style and taking vitamins daily preserved her length and thickness, unlike her sister, who constantly used glue directly on her hair and had no real baby hairs to speak of. Additionally, keeping her hair under wigs without maintenance for long periods resulted in Malea's hair becoming short with bad ends.

Speak of the devil, Tori's doorbell rang, and Malea was there looking none too pleased.

"Do you ever answer your phone?!" her sister shrilled. "I called all night and came by. No answer! Where were you?"

Calmly, Tori checked her phone to see that her doorbell had been pressed late last night when she was in the middle of three very gorgeous brothers, but she didn't say that out loud. "I was busy, Malea. I have a life outside of family. You don't think I sit at home all day waiting for one of you to bother me."

"Why do you look so slim? Are you losing weight? And you look so flushed out? What's wrong with you?"

"It's too early in the day for you to be bothering me with so many questions at once, Malea."

Her sister huffed in exasperation. "I couldn't reach Shawn, so I thought you'd be with him."

Not wanting to put her business out there, Tori asked impatiently as she returned to her office, knowing her sister would follow. "What do you want?"

"You know, ever since we started this shit, you've been acting more and more aloof, Tori," her sister pointed out.

"I'm a little bit busier, if you haven't noticed, Malea, but of course you haven't because the world evolves around you."

"I thought at least you would call me after the event, mad at me."

"Mad about what?"

"The wedding."

Correcting her sister, she said, "You mean the fake wedding. We aren't legally married, so there's nothing to be up in arms about. You said the board was very conservative. I would think they'd love that, and I wasn't going to make a big deal out of something that wasn't real."

"So why'd your foreman show up? Are you fucking him?"

As Tori went through her email, she coolly answered her sister, "No, Malea? We're not involved. He cares, and he knows a little bit more about those brothers than we do."

"Like what?"

"Like Kevin and Duncan used to do some underground fighting. Beck believes they still could be doing it here and there. The brothers were all in trouble when they were young on the streets. Kevin got into a lot of trouble and Duncan..." She remembered more of what the brothers had said than what Beck said and wasn't sure if she should still keep talking.

"Well, he's the weird one. Scott said he's smart and all, but he gives me the creeps. Like he's looking through you all the time."

"So you don't mind me being fake married to them. I mean, Shawn? You don't mind me involving myself with the brothers?" Tori asked. "You were demanding I don't that night."

"I was losing my head." Malea shrugged. "You know how things are. I thought you'd be a panicking mess, and you weren't, and that worried me." Her sister leaned over the desk. "I care about you, Tori."

Why did Tori's gut do a double flip-flop? "Well, thank you, sister. I'm glad you care." She finished with her emails and gave Malea her full attention. "But let's get into why you came over here, Malea?"

Her sister sighed. "I need your help. The kids are coming back in a week for the party, and well, our funds are short. I haven't told Scott about this."

"So you want me to fund the party?"

"It's only a couple of thousand dollars, Tori," Malea said as if it were no big deal.

"And that thing with Norman?"

"It's over with. You're right. I shouldn't hurt Scott like that."

Her sister spoke a little too quickly, but Tori knew she could only take her sister's word at face value... "And he understands this and will stay away?"

"Yes, Tori. Now, are you going to shove your high and mighty standards down my throat?"

"I'll stop when you tell your husband what you did and get you both some therapy. Scott loves you enough to stay, Malea."

"Of course, because you know everything. Are you going to give me the money or not?"

Tori took a deep breath and went over to her wall safe, where she had some quick money stashed. Her thumbprint was needed to get into the safe after the combination. Handing her sister three thousand dollars, she asked, "What about their room, board, and extra amenities?" She wasn't going to mention to Malea right now what she was setting up for her niece and nephews.

"We're still figuring that out."

The school must not have informed Malea that the kids' room and board were already paid for for nearly a year and a half. Tori made those arrangements because she knew this would be a great stress on the twins.

"I'm serious about telling Scott. You have until the day after the barbecue, Malea. Don't play around with me on this."

A deep voice clearing their throats from the office doorway got both of their attention. Beck was standing there with the plans for the new apartment building.

Tori only nodded to him. "I'll see my sister out and join you in the kitchen, Beck."

He walked away immediately, and Tori turned to her sister, whose eyes were still on Beck.

"You sure you haven't fucked him, Tori, cause I would have by now."

Tori urged, "Malea, I have work to do."

"Okay, one more thing. What happened across the street? I saw the police tape."

By this time, Tori was walking her sister out the door. Instead of going into the real details, she said, "During construction, they found a body in the walls. Police came out to recover it, and we have to hold off on construction until they finish their investigation."

"Whose body?" Malea demanded, alarmed.

"It's under investigation, Malea. It was an old school. It could have been anyone."

Her sister changed the subject. "Are you going to give me Dad's stuff or not? You just got it up there in that creepy ass attic all locked up."

Tori wondered briefly how her sister knew she kept the attic locked up all the time, but she also wanted to get to work, so she said, "We'll talk about it after the barbecue."

"And you'll give me all his things? I really want them. Especially that old chest."

"The chest where he kept all those old journals?" Tori questioned.

"I don't care about the journals, Tori. That chest was from our mother. It means something to me, and you know it. She used to keep all her little secret stuff in there. I know it like the back of my hand. I love it, and Dad kept it from me all these years, and now you're keeping it from me," Malea whined.

"I promise we'll talk after the barbecue," Tori promised and closed the door once Malea was standing outside.

Taking a deep breath, leaning against the door, Tori closed her eyes and took several deep breaths, but that only reminded her of last night with the brothers.

"You really do look flushed out," Beck said. "And you are losing weight."

Looking at him standing in the foyer's doorway, she asked, "You were there *that* long?"

"Long enough. She never comes by to see you, so I

thought it was going to be a quick visit, and then I knew you wanted her to go, so I made my presence known."

"You don't know me that well, Beck," she commented, walking past him to the counter, needing a big cup of coffee.

"I know you well enough that you tolerate her. I can't believe you gave her the money for the party."

"It's a traditional family event, Beck. Just because you disassociate with your family over a silly curse doesn't mean I have to ignore my own," she snapped.

He didn't respond, and she looked at him to see that those reddish-brown eyes were drawn together in disapproval. Beck growled, "If I didn't know any better, that smart mouth brother, Kevin, has leaped into your body to make you shoot off that shit."

"Well, good thing I'm a girl, cause you can't hit me," she shot back, but then immediately apologized. "I'm sorry, Beck. I don't know what's gotten into me today."

"I can guess. I saw the shed's been cleaned up. What happened in there last night? A fucking orgy?"

Tori couldn't hide the blush that spread all over her face.

"Woman! I was fucking kidding!"

Her face was hurting from how severe the blushing had become.

Beck growled, "Didn't I warn you to stay away from them?"

Trying to excuse her behavior, Tori answered, "We're supposed to be pretending we're married."

"Not to all three of them! Tori, I'm not only your foreman, but I'm your friend, and I'm warning you for your protection and peace of mind. I don't mind you being promiscuous, but can it be with anyone else but them?"

"Beck, you only know them from the past. They're not running the street anymore."

"But they are the same manipulating hot-headed sons of

bitches, and that middle one, I don't doubt he's hidden a lot more bodies around this city than I care to know. I know the oldest one is all talk and shit, but the one I worry about is that youngest bastard. He manipulates his brothers to do his evil ass bidding. He's the worst of the bunch."

Tori defensively said, "Shawn's been hurt."

"That's my point. Hurt people hurt people. They don't stay around each other because they want to; they stay around each other because they need to. They enable each other with their own toxic shit. Anyone else but them, Tori."

"It's too late, Beck," she said. "I think my heart is involved."

He rolled his eyes. "No, Tori. Please don't say that. Does your heart involve something they did to you last night in the shed?" Beck took a small object from his pocket and placed it on the counter next to where she was filling up her coffee cup. "It's a lens for a camera recording device. Fell off of something that was mounted on the walls of the shed. I saw on the exact other side of the shed something else similar was mounted, along with a shelf attached."

While picking up the lens, the blood rushed through her veins as her heart rate increased. "What do you think it could have been?"

"It was easily a two-camera with a recording device. Whatever took place in the shed, it's on record. So I hope whatever you did is not incriminating."

They recorded it? Why would they? Memories?

"Are you sure, Beck? It could be to-"

"Tori, don't delude yourself," Beck cut her off. "That lens is part of a camera system I've installed myself on construction sites. I know long-range systems when I see them. Now, are you going to tell me what happened in that shed?"

"No," She handed the lens back to him. "And the lawyer assured me the financial trust is untouchable for the projects, so you don't have to worry about anything. Can we look at the plans for the apartment tomorrow? I've had a long morning and I need to lie down."

Or more like call Shawn.

"I also wanted to speak with you about the historical status. The electrician wanted to come by in a couple of days-"

"That's fine. I know you can handle all that. Just keep me up to date," she said wistfully as she walked out of the kitchen and went upstairs to her bedroom. As soon as she knew Beck was out of the house, she called Shawn.

Her call immediately went to voicemail. She didn't have Duncan's number in her phone, but she had Kevin's email. She sent an electronic message. There was no reply, and when she called Shawn again, her call was forwarded to voicemail again.

Her alarm went off to remind her she needed to get to her appointments. Grabbing her purse, Tori left the house and jumped in her car. An immense foreboding feeling started to envelope her, but she had so much to do today that she didn't have time to reflect on this.

It was evening by the time Tori had returned. When she walked into her home, she stopped instantly, noting something had changed. Looking around everywhere, she saw that nothing looked damaged, but there was still something different.

She looked in her kitchen and then looked at her phone. Shawn hadn't responded to any of her calls or texts. By the time she had headed to her hair appointment, she decided not to make an effort anymore. He could be busy.

At her brunch, the elderly woman had shown up at the brunch spot with other guests and briefly said, "I'm sorry you won't be joining us tonight. Shawn told us you would be occupied with some matters regarding the building with the police. That must be terrible."

Tori was his fake wife, and she had to know what Mrs. Cosgrove implied.

Setting her purse on her counter, Tori went up to her second floor and went over to where the attic door was. Why? Because her sister had specifically mentioned it.

The lock was still on there, but why did she have a feeling that it looked tampered with? Getting a close-up look, she could swear someone had tried to use a tool to break it off, but she couldn't be sure.

She made a mental note to get another lock for the door and take a picture to know if anything had been tampered with. Beck always had extra construction locks around, and she could get him to bring her a couple instead of making an extra trip.

Why would Malea need to get to their mother's chest so urgently?

Since she still had her keys in her hand, she unlocked the attic and went straight inside to the chest.

She remembered being young and their mother showing them that this chest had been given to her by her grandmother.

Hiding your business as a woman was of the utmost importance, her mother had said as she showed them the secret compartments.

Kneeling to open the chest, Tori felt around the top and gasped, sensing something was there. At the same time, she heard her phone ring.

She closed the chest, locked the attic, and ran down to where her phone was in the kitchen, making another mental note to inspect the chest.

The phone stopped ringing by the time she picked it up. It was from Sinclaire.

Although it was after hours, there was some urgency to the call.

Before she forgot, Tori sent a scheduled text to Beck for the morning to bring the lock for her attic and the chest inside, just in case Malea got that far. The construction locks were hell to get off, and whatever tool her sister could use would likely be worn down from the first lock before she reached the second one.

When she was done, she immediately listened to Sinclaire's voicemail.

"Call me... No, COME to my office tonight! I'm still getting information in, but as soon as you get this message, get to my office now, Tori. This isn't good. This is really bad."

CHAPTER 4

They Made a Fool Out of Her

Tori could barely think, let alone get dressed in anything appropriate. She chucked on a pair of yoga pants and a long, flowing peach top. She was glad her hair was done because she would have barely been able to manage it while trying to look decent as she got out of the house.

Sinclaire had followed her voice message with a text of the address to the law offices out in Southfield, a suburb of Detroit that wasn't that far. Getting inside and then being ushered into Mrs. Sinclair Bowman's offices was like a dream or a nightmare.

The lawyer was a beautiful black woman about Tori's age, and instead of the welcoming smile from the video just a few days ago, there was a grim expression on her face. "Let's start at the beginning. Is this your signature?"

Tori looked down at the marriage certificate and nodded. "Yes, but I signed it knowing we weren't registered as a couple."

"This is your signature on the registration of marriage, as well," Sincalire said. "And a copy of your license was shown at the time of registration, which means he went down there and registered you to be married. Did you give a copy of your license to him?"

"Yes, but it was for a security thing for his apartment. He said we..." Her brain was so fuzzy that Tori could barely remember. "I'd need to come there and park my car, and there were some high security protocols."

"So this is all on the wrong pretense. I could go to court, and we could fight this whole thing. Get this whole shit annulled and sue him for forgery. I don't mind pushing for state charges against him and the hospital for participating-"

"No," Tori said, thinking of Mrs. Cosgrove and all the contacts that she would lose if this got out in public.

Her project would be decimated. Everything she had worked for —the networks, connections, and the community —but most of all, her reputation, and finally... the video coming to light.

"No? Tori, are you insane? This man lied and tricked you into a marriage, and now he could have control of all your finances and projects. I barely got things in the financial trust, but he could still have rights to it and strip everything away from you! Everything!"

Tori slowly sat down, remembering Beck's words about how the brothers had stolen other people's lives. And now they had done it to her.

Payback?

Could they actually harp on the past and hurt her?

Hurt people, hurt people, came Beck's words.

And she had not listened.

How could this be? Not after last night? How could they have made her feel that way without feeling a thing? Hating her? Not last night, but what Sinclaire was laying out to Tori was a diabolical, slow, meticulous, well-thought-out plan.

"Do you need a moment?" Sinclaire asked after calling Tori's name several times.

Coming out of her thoughts, Tori looked down at what Sinclaire was pointing at—the divorce decree.

"Explain to me how he could have gotten the marriage certificate past he deacon and the register of deeds if it was a fake," Tori demanded.

"It wasn't, Tori. Anyone can go down with a copy of your license and your signature and file the paperwork. Let me take care of this. I can get an annulment in and sue him-"

Tori knew that couldn't happen. Suing meant everything, getting out in public, and all she could think about was that they had a video of her being a straight-up, greedy slut. If that were released to the public, she could lose not only her life but also her prominence. That tape could follow her in anything and everything she did.

"What if we go with the divorce?"

"Tori, that's insane! You can't agree to that when you had no idea you were married! And the terms of the divorce are ridiculous. He wants to take apart everything you've done and demand half. As your lawyer, I can't allow you to agree to this."

"Will the group home and courtyard be protected?" she asked.

"Tori!"

"Just let me know this."

"Only if you are not on the board or the head of the trust, and that goes with your niece and nephew trust. I would need to appoint someone as head of those trusts if you agree to this, but Tori, you can't."

Tori closed her eyes. "And the apartment? Where do I live?"

"I have a feeling you already know."

"Tear it down, piece by piece."

A shudder filled her, and she closed her eyes briefly to get her thoughts together.

"What would happen if I lost everything?"

"You'd be starting back over. You'd walk away with whatever is in your pocket. They even included that once you sign these papers, you can't even return to the apartments. That's how cruel they are being. Tori, in my good judgment, you need to fight."

She felt sick to her stomach. "I need a moment."

Running to the bathroom, she remembered passing when she came in, Tori threw up what little she had eaten. With her hands still shaking, she stood at the mirror staring at herself.

This is the price she was paying for what she did in the past. She knew there was nothing else to blame but herself, and she was stupid to believe the past could be forgiven so easily.

Texting Beck hurriedly, Tori asked him to remove as much as he could from her apartments, including giving him the emergency alternate passcode to access the safe and then store everything. If she couldn't return, Beck would help her get at least all her stuff.

Beck texted back that he was across the street at the site and promised to do what he could. Amazingly, he didn't ask questions or demand details, and she was grateful for this.

Rinsing her mouth out while also pushing away the tears, she took her time getting out of the bathroom and returning to the lawyer's office.

As soon as she walked in, Sinclaire stated, "There is one thing saved. That weird thing you did with the Cosgroves. Since it was set up before you were married, that's how you could start over."

"But it wasn't for me," she said.

"The best revenge is being successful. This could be your opportunity."

Deep down inside, Tori didn't want to get revenge or be manipulative. She was so tired of that.

What was the point of anything if she constantly had to worry that every time she was successful, people would hate her because of who she used to be?

"No," Tori said. "I don't want it. Not anymore."

Sinclaire looked angry but calmed herself down and asked, "So what do you want to do?"

"I will set up terms around theirs and go from there, but I'll only sign in front of him. And only him. I don't want his lawyers around."

"I'll come-"

"No."

"Tori, this is insane. You're just giving everything up. All the work you've done. For two days of marriage?! This is ridiculous!"

Two days of the most incredible days of her life that she knew nothing could ever come close to experiencing again. That could be enough for her. Tori could leave after she signed, but she wanted to look Shawn in the eyes and see if he really hated her. She wanted to hear him say it to her face if he was brave enough because she was brave enough to face the real enemy.

"Show me the terms, Sinclaire. I want to see them, and we'll go from there. You'll draw up the papers and then send them over to his lawyer. I'll go where they want me to go and sign, but only if he is there without his stupid lawyer."

"And that thing?"

Tori took a deep breath, holding back the enormous sob welling up in her chest, and declared, "We'll figure it all out, but I'll agree to most of their terms. I'll lose everything."

As soon as Tori left the law offices, she walked to a small cafe nearby with an outside patio and sat down. She couldn't even leave Sinclaire's office with her car. *They even took her vehicle to sell off!* Tori had to leave her keys with the lawyer. At least Sinclaire allowed her to get her personal items out, which were her laptop, essential papers, an overnight bag, a gym bag, and her purse.

A waitress came over to ask for her order, and Tori calmly said A water until she could think straight.

"You'll have to start over," Sinclaire's voice said in Tori's thoughts.

Why did Tori always feel she didn't deserve the nice life she had built for herself, and why was this loss not that difficult to walk away from?

You'll survive, she told herself.

Putting her hand over her stomach, feeling it rumble, Tori didn't know if she was hungry or going to be sick again.

The waitress returned and asked, "Would you like some crackers? I was stuffing them down in the evening, too, when I was pregnant."

"What?"

"You look like you're about to throw up," the young waitress said, looking down at Tori, holding her stomach, "I just thought... I'm sorry, ma'am. I didn't mean to assume. I'll come back for your order."

Tori looked down at her stomach as if something had landed there. No! She couldn't be! Not now!

True, they had unprotected sex, but she was on birth control!

Next to the cafe was a drug store, and she walked over there to get two pregnancy kits. This couldn't be happening to her. Not after she was going to walk away from this life.

Getting back to the cafe, Tori went into the bathroom and tore open the test. Just as she finished peeing on the stick, Beck called her.

"Where are you?!" he growled. "Some fucking sheriff just

handed me these papers that I'm not supposed to talk with you about the projects anymore until further notice. What the fuck is going on?"

She could barely keep her voice from shaking when she spoke. "Beck, it's a long story.

"Tori, they're saying you can't come back to the property. I need to know what the fuck is up? Where are you?"

"I'm in Southfield." Tears started to run down her face. "I-I don't know where to go."

"I'm sending you my address. Drive to the back and park. I'll see you this afternoon." The line clicked, and she looked at the text message Beck sent. It was an address even further outside of Detroit in another suburb, with an access code.

She didn't call and tell him she'd even lost her car, so she used a car service to get over to his place.

Without looking at the results of the pregnancy test, Tori shoved everything in her purse and drove to a beautiful yellow colonial home. There was a gate in the front to prevent any vehicle from moving close to the house. After getting out of the car service and tipping the driver, she went around to the rear, where a three-car garage was located. She used the code to access the garage doors. The garage was completely bare except for an enormous, updated truck and a thick wooden door that needed an access code to enter. The digital key she was given unlocked this door, leading to concrete steps descending to a fully renovated basement beneath the house. The lights came on automatically, practically leading her through a large room with baseball cages, several other game rooms, and then more stairs leading into a beautiful home right out of a magazine. The stairs came up to a large pantry and then the kitchen.

She wondered if this was a house Beck was working on and had given her illegal access while the owner was away. Did he do this to her home?

There were cameras here and there, and she found a front room where she could sit down on a couch and relax.

Lying her head down, she just wanted to nap. With everything going on with her, Tori didn't want to think, and sleeping was the only way to keep herself from thinking. Mentally exhausted, she didn't need drugs as her body sank into darkness, hoping that when she awoke, maybe all this was some ugly nightmare and she was back in her peaceful life, lonely and rubbing out orgasms every night in her bathtub with her toys.

~

The sound of keys giggling near her brought Tori awake.

"I'm shocked you don't snore," Beck said, perched on the coffee table in front of the couch, still in his work clothes, looking down at her with displeasure.

Tori noticed the sun was setting as she sat up and stretched, hoping she didn't look like the hot mess that she felt like.

Beck reached over where her purse had dropped on the floor, and the contents had spilled out. When he raised the used pregnancy stick, tears immediately welled in her eyes because he pointed the results at her.

"What's the hell, Tori?"

"You were right," she said after letting out a big sob. "They ruined me, Beck. They ruined everything just like you said."

He viciously cursed and put the stick down. "You want to start at the beginning so I can understand what's going on?"

Tori needed to tell someone because she was going to go insane keeping it all to herself.

Two hours later, after Beck ordered them something to eat, she was sitting in the Home and Garden-designed kitchen finishing up what had happened at the lawyer's. By now, Beck knew about the Cosgrove's deal, what she had done with the brothers, and how they seduced her, the illegal way they got her to get married, and then the divorce.

"You can't go along with this plan, Tori," Beck insisted. "You can't go along with the divorce. Sue them. Sue the hospital. Sue the lawyer. Hell, sue that damn deacon that married you!"

"You sound like my lawyer.

"You're just going to let them win like this? You're not going to fight? And what about that stick? The results?"

"I can start over. Somewhere else and... a long way from here with the results of my failure." She hugged her waist. "No one knows about that except you, and don't you dare tell anyone."

"Tori, are you insane?! Have they fucked the intelligence out of you?"

"No, Beck, but I'm not fighting him. He's fucked up, and I just want to show him how sorry I am that I took their father away. The only happiness they could have had, my selfish actions destroyed what life they could have had."

Beck angrily pounded the table. "Are you listening to yourself? You've lost your mind! Tori! You're not responsible-"

Cutting him off, she said, "Beck, you know it would be bad if I fought. They have a video of what I've done. Who I really am, so I can't claim I'm a victim. I'm not fighting. I've made up my mind."

"Was this before or after you discovered you were pregnant?!"

"It doesn't matter. I'll go away from here with whatever you were able to salvage from the house and then start over somewhere far away from here, where no one knows me. That's what I should have done. I was stupid to think I could live a life here after what I did to them."

"How about I go beat the shit out of the two older ones

and wring that younger motherfucker's neck until he piss blood before dying, get the video, so you don't have to go anywhere?"

Tori laughed. "You really know how to make a girl feel nice, Beck."

"That's a fucking lie, but I'll take the fucking compliment." Beck huffed out a lungful of air, knowing he couldn't change her mind. "I have a brother who has a lot of land in the Upper Peninsula. I could make arrangements. After this lawyer lady gets you to the meeting with him, and I'm going with you whether you like it or not, you can go up there with my brother. Where he stays, it's pretty much off-grid. His skin condition is worse than mine, so he stays to himself with a bunch of damn dogs."

"I could work," she offered. "Do some small business administration stuff for him in return, until I can get some online work. By the way, how much did you salvage from my house?"

"Every fucking thing," Beck said.

Frowning, confused, she asked, "How?"

"When the crew knew what I had to do, they got into action. One of my crew was returning a U-Haul after work, and it was empty. While we were stuffing the first floor and the basement, two other crewmen had vans, and everyone else used their trucks to tow away what we could strap down. It ended up being the whole damn apartment in less than an hour. Including the attic and the safe was locked from someone trying to access previously, so I drilled that whole damn thing out of the wall and took it with us."

Tori was shocked. "Why'd they do all that?"

Beck spoke as if it were obvious. "Tori, you're good to the crew. They see you're good to them, and they, just like me, would help you at the whisper. We don't give a shit what you did in the past. I did some fucked up shit. Why the fuck do you think I'm sitting in this damn beautiful ass house by myself instead of a wife?"

"I thought this was someone else you were utilizing while they were away. This doesn't look like your style, Beck."

"It's not. It was my wife, but she's dead. This was her dream home; she spent every dime she had to buy it, and I killed her."

Flabbergasted by the confession, Tori cautiously asked, "How?"

"She had cancer. She didn't tell me. I'm a rough man, and well, I cracked her cervix. It grew into an infection. She never said shit to me. She didn't want me to know she was dying. I fucking hate her for that, but I'm too much of an asshole to give this house to her no good family, so I sit in here every night fucking finishing off all the repairs little by little until I'll sell it or give it fucking away just to piss them off."

Remembering her sister had tried to steal from her, Tori questioned, "They're greedy?"

"No, they tried to run up murder charges on me for killing my wife," Beck answered. "The charges were dismissed, but it still doesn't stop the guilt of me hurting her and not knowing." He drummed the table for a moment. "Tori, I'd kill them all if it made you happy and then hide the bodies."

"No, Beck. You know I won't let you do that."

Beck took out his phone and opened an app. "It would make fixing things easier for me, especially that fucking Hummer driving up and down the block since nightfall." Turning the camera around to her, she saw a view of the front porch camera clip capturing Kevin's Hummer slowly driving past the house.

Why were they looking for her?

"They must've had a tracker on you somehow, but as soon as you entered my garage, they lost the signal. I'll have someone check your bags. Most people don't know I live here, and others wouldn't believe I do. That garage was designed specifically to be enclosed, so no one can find anyone if they pull in."

She remembered all the times the brothers had been in her home. Any one of them could have tagged her items easily and was now using tracking software to try to find out where she'd gone since she couldn't go home.

"Where'd you store all my stuff?" she questioned.

"One of my inner city storage containers I have for backup equipment and tools for when I open up my own construction management business. After I complete these large jobs for Thaddeus Newman, I'll have all the money I need, get the certification from the city, and be able to operate my own business, hiring the best of the best. I'm grateful for you putting that business plan together. It really kept me focused, Tori."

She smiled. "I enjoyed doing it, Beck." A yawn escaped her.

"There's a bedroom on this floor, and if you hear something walking around tonight, it's just my cat. She's been locked up all day and probably pissed as hell."

Again, she was shocked by some information about Beck, but she appreciated the distraction. "What's your brother's name?"

"Everyone calls him Oscar, but just like me, he's got a girl's name. Orsica. Unless you want to gum your meals for the rest of your life, I wouldn't call him that."

"Why do you have girl names?"

"My mother thought it'd make us tougher to bullies. Sometimes it was that, sometimes it was because we were fighting for no one to touch us. Either way, it made us stronger, alright," Beck growled, showing her the first-floor bedroom. "Too tough and strong to know they cracked their wives' cervix."

There was medical equipment against the wall, a large

queen-size bed in the middle of the room, and a dresser. At least it had a full-size private bathroom. There were a lot of questions Tori wanted to ask him, but she decided to keep them to herself. Beck was a complicated man, and she understood he stayed distant from people because he could hurt them—physically harm them.

"You're taking this shit way too calmly, Tori," Beck said.

"I know, but walking away is easier and less energy than fighting. I organized things for you, the projects, and my niece and nephew. Those are the things that matter, and life goes on."

"They didn't deserve you in the first place."

Tori felt her phone text go off and saw it was a message from her lawyer with a time and place for the final meeting. "Well, I'll tell Shawn when I see him tomorrow night. You'll be on your best behavior, won't you, when you come with me?" She showed him the text.

"I'll try," he growled. "I'll put a shirt and some shorts outside the door so you can at least change out of those clothes. And I'll swing by the storage container to get some stuff out of your drawers that we yanked out of your bedroom. We didn't empty anything. We just tied it down and took it."

"Thanks, Beck. Good night."

He only nodded and walked back in the direction of the kitchen.

She confirmed the meeting with the lawyer and then lay face-first on the bed and cried.

Tomorrow, Tori would sign those damn papers, looking Shawn in the eyes to show him he may have won the battle, but not the war. She was going to come out stronger, better, and those brothers would never know about the baby!

CHAPTER 5
The Rub

Lots of mouths and hands were all over her body, playing, teasing, delighting her senses. Tori cried out, trying to reach out for something, anything to hug and hold on to, but there was only darkness. She could feel a mouth. Who was there? As much as she strained her eyes, she could not see.

Kevin's. Not thick enough. Duncan... not tender... Yes, Shawn... just leaving her clit and vulva just perfectly. She ground her womanhood against his mouth, hard, knowing she was going to come soon. Knowing she'd see her essence just dripping from the corner of his lips and she could lick it away... Almost there... almost-

Fuck!

She was going to tear up Beck's sheets, grinding on them like she was trying to start a fire. Ripping the covers off of her, she took a deep breath, remembering where she was and what was happening to her.

Jumping out of bed, Tori realized she hadn't showered, but at least she slept through the night. Checking her phone for messages, her lawyer was delivering the papers she needed for the meeting tonight, and Beck had said he'd be back by four to take her to the storage unit where she could pack what she needed before heading to the meeting at seven. And then her new life would begin.

He'd receive a fax in the kitchen from his brother because it was the only way Oscar received messages. She had almost smiled, knowing that once she was out there with Beck's brother, it would be so rural that no one would be able to find her or contact her.

Starting over wasn't that bad if she didn't think about them... She worked hard to forget what they did to her body and how she felt like a queen.

You knew that relationship wouldn't have been sustainable.

Tori wanted to sleep all day and not think about the past or the future, yet hunger was driving her to get up and find something to eat.

Opening the door, she gasped, seeing a huge fluffy main coon staring up at her as if she owed it some money. Scooping up the clothes, the feline stayed outside the bedroom as Tori went into the bathroom to wash up. Before stepping into the shower, she did another pregnancy test just to be sure. The hot water was good for her body, the spray all over her body was like a massage, but she still thought about her night with them in the shed...

When she opened the bedroom door again, the cat was gone, and Tori made her way to the kitchen. Beck had left-overs from the food he ordered the night before, but she mostly saw lunch items, some fruit, and only water to drink.

She imagined that with Beck's sensitive skin condition, everything he digested affected him, so he wouldn't have anything fancy or unnatural in the house to irritate him more.

On the counter, Beck had left a map folded over so she could look at the Upper Peninsula of Michigan. He'd drawn over where his brother owned a vast acreage of land for a large dog sanctuary and even a small town nearby. Thousands of acres secluded from anything and anyone.

It would be perfect to start over and not have to think about her former life or the three men who had done so much good and bad for her.

She knew Beck would keep her abreast of everything because she had written him in the financial trust to be the construction manager over the project. She would spend the rest of the day giving Beck access to all her plans and projection reports to literally walk him through the project's completion. She'd take her name off the digital folders so Beck wouldn't get into trouble if there was an audit of his digital traffic.

Beck had given her access to his laptop so she could get everything done while sitting at the kitchen counter, as if it were her office again.

While randomly checking her phone, she saw an email from an unknown address with the subject line: *Don't come.*

Her heart raced, but her finger hovered over the spam button. Did she want to know what this was about?

Taking a deep breath, Tori opened the email, bracing for her heart to be crushed.

I'll start this off and warn you, I'm not good at putting my words on paper, which is my Achilles' Heel.

You'll never understand what happened. You'll forever wonder, but there is no way to explain this. You were a child, but the damage you caused hurt so many - it hurt us to the core. All the times Keir promised us we could be family if only you would accept us, yet no matter what he did, you wouldn't let it happen. You wanted him all to yourself, and all we knew was that Tori got what she wanted.

So, we devised a plan to take whatever Tori had and ensure she walked away with nothing. And you made it easy and very pleasurable for us.

Tori had to stop reading because the words dug into her soul, making her ashamed of her vulnerability and how they had used it to get what they wanted.

Be strong, she ordered herself, forcing herself to continue reading.

You shouldn't come because once you give him what he wants, he'll think he's won and that everything will get better, but I know it won't. Only you made it better. Out of all the people in the world who I thought would heal my brother, I never imagined it could be you.

Tori, you changed us. We may not have told you enough or let you know what you did for us. No human being, let alone a deity, could have done it for us.

I may not say much, but I will say now that what we did to you, we thought it would heal us.

And we will probably never be able to heal what we have done to you, but I can at least stop you from making the biggest mistake of your life.

Don't come. Fight this. Please. I would rather suffer in this hell than live a life knowing we've created a hell for you.

Don't come.

The email wasn't signed, but she knew it was sweet Duncan.

Why did he have to be anonymous? Did Shawn have some hold over him?

Guilt! They didn't save him; most likely, Shawn had devised a plan to hurt her and used his brothers, but in turn, Kevin and Duncan got what they wanted out of the plan by getting Shawn to participate in their sexual fantasies using her.

Tori refused to believe that in the moments of sexual high reached, it was all fake? No, those moments had been real. There was no way all three of them could have pretended all that.

Yet, the revenge they'd inflicted was done, and she was going to let them get what they wanted.

Picking up the pregnancy test that showed positive again, she patted her stomach and said, "I'm not walking away empty-handed after all, but they will never know."

Going over to where Beck had put the safe he'd dug out of the wall in her office in the pantry area, Tori used the emergency code. As soon as she entered the code, the whole device died, but the door popped slightly. Since it wasn't wired to the electronic system, it was only on a backup battery. Otherwise, they would have probably needed a jackhammer to open the damn thing.

The lockdown only happened when someone tried to open it too many times. She knew from experience, without checking the cameras, that it had to be her sister. From all the clips she reviewed throughout the night, none of the brothers had stolen anything from her home.

Speak of the devil, her phone rang with Malea's name coming on the screen. She looked at the safe again, spitefully, and answered the phone. "Yes, Malea?"

"Where are you? I'm at your home. I heard. Are you okay?"

"What did you hear?"

"The divorce. He sent a message to the board to explain that due to irreconcilable differences, he's filed for a divorce. Tori, he's accusing you of having an affair with his brothers."

Destroying her reputation painfully and slowly seemed to be their plan. The Cosgroves and the conservative board would see a man in pain and want nothing to do with her.

And her sister? What would her sister do to save her reputation?

"Is this true?" Malea demanded to know. "Did you sleep with Kevin and Duncan? Shawn said he had proof."

The videos for the night. He could probably edit and

produce a whole hour of her fucking with just his brothers and take him out of the video.

Without shame, knowing she would have to leave, Tori admitted, "Yes, it's true. I fucked them both."

"Oh gawd, Tori," Malea said disgustedly. "How could you? I mean, I understand. Shawn is gay, but did you have to fuck his brothers?"

"The reason doesn't matter, Malea. What does this mean for you? For your job? For Scott?"

"Well, I told them Scott and I will no longer associate ourselves with someone with such low morals. Family or not, my job is important. You understand, Tori. I couldn't have them thinking I approve of something like that."

Incredulously, Tori exclaimed, "Are you serious? You're fucking your ex right under your husband's nose."

"But that's not in the pubic and there's certainly no proof of that. You knew from the beginning how important it is for me to keep my job. I had to do what I had to do. You should understand, Tori. And that also means you can't come to the barbecue. People from the board are scheduled to come. I can't have you showing up-"

Cutting her sister off, not wanting to hear anything else, Tori said, "That's fine, Malea. I won't come to a party that I paid for." She'd find another way to announce the apartments to her niece and nephew.

"Is he really taking you for all you've got?" Malea asked. "Are you going to fight him in court for everything?"

"I'm not going to fight him, Malea. I'll lose everything."

"And what about Dad's stuff. I want his things. I went over, and the whole fucking house was cleaned out. Someone even yanked the damn safe out of the wall. Who did that?"

Not wanting to implicate Beck, Tori snipped, "I'll have all of Dad's stuff dropped off immediately. You're right. I was just being selfish, holding on to his stuff. I've changed. I'm done."

"I'm sorry it has to be this way, Tori. What are you going to do?"

Tori wiped away the tears rolling down her cheek as she realized her sister wasn't going to offer a place to stay or even some type of support in any way. Glaring at the safe, Tori knew she was deluded to think Malea cared. Most likely, her sister probably secretly hated her as much as the brothers had hated her. "Don't worry about me, Malea. I'll leave town and never come back here. So kiss the kids for me. I'll try to stay in touch." She hung up the phone on Malea, knowing she never wanted to speak to her sister ever again.

The safe's lockdown mode only returned to normal after twenty-four hours, making it a waiting game. Since Tori knew that time had passed, entering the emergency code would open the safe right away.

Inside was her emergency stash of seventeen thousand dollars. It would have been twenty, but she'd given the three thousand to her sister. There were also expensive jewelry, bond certificates, her passports, shot records, and other emergency paperwork. She doled out what Beck would need, including insurance papers, building certificates, and other necessary documents. At the very back of the safe was a set of keys. It took her a moment to remember what those keys belonged to. She recalled getting them from her father's chest a long time ago, but wasn't sure what they belonged to. Why she had put them in the safe was a mystery to her.

Tori was almost tempted to give them to her sister, but decided against it. Being a little selfish made her feel a little good. Malea couldn't have everything from Keir. Yet, since she wasn't staying in town, the keys had no significance to her.

Holding up the key ring with ten various keys, she decided she would give them over to the boys this evening as another parting gift. Duncan would be smart enough to figure out what they all belonged to.

That reminded her to leave Beck a note to give all her father's things from the attic to the brothers later, long after she left without violence. He could drop it off on their front porch with a parting note from Tori.

She remembered feeling something in the lid, but there was too much going on in her life to care about what her father had hidden behind that compartment. Duncan could figure it all out.

Was she giving them this to make up for what she had done, or a dig to remind them of the hurt they had caused her?

Either way, she'd rather give it to them than her sister.

Tori put everything from the safe that she knew Beck didn't need into her messenger bag, which held her laptop, extra keyboard, and other business files.

By the time Beck returned home, he had spent only half an hour changing. Then, he drove to the storage units in the newer truck he had parked in the garage. "I caught wind of that prick Kevin coming by the house twice today on the camera. It was probably more. He's still looking around the neighborhood for you."

"I guess traveling in your truck will definitely throw him off."

"Damn punks if you ask me, and all of them need their teeth punched out of their mouth." He cracked his knuckles.

"Beck," she implored. "I'm just going in for a second, talk with Shawn, give him the envelope, and then we're going straight to the bus station."

Beck only grumbled something to himself, but she could only pray he was on his best behavior.

At the storage area, Tori showed him all the items from the attic he needed to take over to Malea's house tomorrow, except for the chest, and then showed Beck everything he could sell off. He knew someone who could take all her furniture, and the rest he promised to ship up to her when he knew she was settled at his brother's house. She instructed him to carefully hand-deliver the rug pieces she had finished to Mrs. Cosgrove as a donation to her charity. She also mentioned leaving word for the remaining rugs at the gallery, with the profits to be sold to Mrs. Cosgrove's charity.

Whether the woman had liked her or not, the rugs and the donation would be cherished. Perhaps Tori would find her muse again to make more rugs, but for now, she didn't feel like it at all.

That still didn't deter her from having Beck ship her tufting, matching materials, and the supplies to her final destination.

After Tori packed up a suitcase with enough clothes for a week, Beck put it in the back.

"It's going to take about eighteen hours to get over to where he lives, including the boat ride," Beck said. "You should probably take a day bag?"

"I stuffed an empty bag inside my messenger bag. We make a stop in Lansing, and I can pick up some snacks and any sundries that I need," she said. "I'm not tied to any of this stuff. The rest of everything can be donated or sold."

"Are you ready?" Beck asked, getting in the driver's side of the truck's cab next to her.

She took a deep breath and said, "Yes, I'm ready. I hope they are."

Beck started driving toward the address her lawyer had given her for the meeting place. From what she researched, it was an address in the Historic Boston Edison district, not Shawn's apartment across from the Caesar Arena.

Boston Edison was a division established in the seventies that consisted of beautiful mini mansions for the wealthy, complete with servant quarters, apartments above two-car garages, and palatial homes spanning three floors.

Some of the homes were so large that they were divided

into three- and four-family units, and she figured that's where they were going to end up.

Wrong.

Beck drove to what looked like a castle. Stone brick high walls, brown accents, a massive, neatly cut yard with solar lights all over to guide guests up the long walkway to the enormous oak door. No lights were on in the front house, and she couldn't see any vehicles in the driveway, which led to a large, brown painted iron gate.

"Are you sure this is the address?" Tori questioned.

"Very sure," Beck said, opening her door and helping her out of the truck. "This looks like a damn fortress. The windows are double-paned, and all the lower-floor windows have iron bars on them. That fence looks wooden, but I bet my ass it's steel, and not even a battering ram could get through that damn front door. Whatever goes in that house could get locked in there forever."

A chill went through her, and she was glad she had asked Beck to accompany her.

"Are you really ready for this, Tori?" Beck asked. "I could get you to the bus station early, and you can say fuck them."

"If I don't, the projects will be in litigation forever, you'll never get paid for all the hard work you've put in, and everything could go to ruin. I can't have that. The project still means a lot to me, you deserve every dime coming to you, and I'm glad I have you to take the reins." She gently placed a hand on his jacket, careful not to put any pressure on his body, knowing how sensitive he was. "You've been a friend I didn't know I needed, Beck."

Tori left her messenger bag in his cab and only took the envelope her lawyer had given her. After putting Keir's keys in the envelope, she sealed it up and walked behind Beck to the large oak door.

The neighborhood was quiet. All she heard was the night

summer bugs of the city, a dog barking in the distance, and some police or fire sirens going down the main streets that were nearby.

The house didn't look as if anyone was home, but as soon as she knocked and rang the doorbell, the door opened immediately.

Duncan stood there with a look of disapproval, looking Beck up and down as if trying to see where to cut him the fastest to kill him.

Dammit, why the hell was he wearing the gray outfit she had just seen him in only a few nights ago?

"Are you going to stand there and stare like a teen girl drooling, or can we get on with this shit?" Beck growled.

Duncan started to reach behind him, but Kevin slid up beside his brother to hold his arm. He was also dressed in his gray attire, and she was almost shocked that neither one had given her flowers. "We promised the lawyer we'd be on our best behavior," Kevin said, but he looked viciously past her at Beck for a moment before his eyes lustfully fell on her.

She was so glad Beck was behind her because Tori would have damn sure suggested they could put the tip in before she decided to erase herself out of this city. "I'm not here to see either of you," she snipped, remaining strong. "Where's Shawn?"

"You're supposed to be alone," Kevin said, not moving from the doorway so she couldn't step inside without brushing past him.

"I said no lawyers. I didn't mention support systems, which I guess is why you're here—for your little brother. So if he can have you, I can have Beck."

"And you don't touch her, and I won't touch you," Beck added in a vicious growl.

Duncan started forward with his hand still behind his

back, but Kevin pushed him away from the door and muttered something viciously.

She walked in very glad Beck was there because internally Tori was a hot ass mess. One part of her wanted to strip down to her skivies and beg for a repeat of their last night together, and another part of her wanted to scream at the top of her lungs about how all this is so fucked up.

The one standing in front of them, looking all calm and cool, was a cold-hearted woman she had known for so long, but she was barely holding it all together.

Shawn came into the large, welcoming hall that connected the foyer to the rest of the house. Dressed in his grey getup from the night before, he looked just as deliciously gorgeous with a triumphant smile on his lips.

There was a small table with a fresh dozen red and white roses in the middle. Yes, they were trying to drive her crazy on purpose. Next to the roses was the final divorce decree and a pen for her to sign.

Taking a deep breath, she met those golden eyes beaming victoriously.

"I'm shocked you asked for this, Tori. I thought for sure you'd sign whatever I wanted and slither away," he said.

The cold coming off of him gave her the chills. The look of pure hatred seared her soul, freezing the blood in her veins from head to toe.

He added with a sneer, "Or did you come to beg for more?"

More what? More pain? More pleasure?

CHAPTER 6

There It Is

Tori's tongue was sitting like a lead weight in her mouth until Beck cleared his throat behind her. His back was to her, most likely to glare at Kevin and Duncan, who stood against the walls on each side of her.

"I came to hear you say it to my face, you want a divorce, you did all this to hurt me on purpose, and you never want to see me again, Shawn."

Shawn looked at Kevin and Duncan before looking at her with a smirk of disgust. "I want the divorce, Tori," he said without hesitation. "I wanted to hurt you from the first moment I saw you again. I needed to see you looking like this, sad and pathetic. I wanted you to know what it's like to hurt, and no one who you thought cared about you could save you."

She looked at Duncan and Kevin. Both of them were hiding their emotions, showing her nothing of what they were feeling, but she understood. Kevin had been in jail, and Duncan had survived by doing Amos's bidding, but neither of them knew the horror Shawn silently suffered because of his mother.

He had grown up believing that no female would ever care

for him or love him unconditionally, and he hated Tori for what she took away.

"I've agreed to all of your terms with the written conditions my lawyer submitted, and I'll sign your divorce decree as long as you promise to do some things for me."

Disgustedly, Shawn asked, "What makes you think I'd agree to anything you want? You have no leverage here."

Putting the envelope on the table, she said, "I do with what's in this envelope."

He started to take it, but Beck hissed loudly.

"Touch it before she says you can, boy, and you won't be able to use your brain for a year," Beck threatened.

Shawn looked at Duncan, who nodded. The youngest brother took a step back and calmed himself with three deep breaths.

She remembered taking those deep breaths with him, and for a second, Tori lost her train of thought until Beck had to huff to bring her back to the present.

"You can do whatever you want to the apartments you guys were raised in. Tear it down brick by brick just like you wanted, but promise you'll give the tenants time to move out. At least three months minimum." She looked over to Kevin and Duncan. "I hope you two are taking notes for him."

Kevin sucked on his teeth, still glaring at Beck as if he were devising ways to rip the flesh off the masive, red-haired, white man's body.

Duncan was staring at her emotionless, but she had a feeling he was damn curious about the envelope and was the one really in control of the other two.

Tori finished her terms. "You won't touch the financial trusts for the group home, courtyard, and other apartment buildings. You'll allow my lawyer to set up the heads of the trusts under your terms. I will have no part of them, just as you want, and you can sell them off once they are complete, but under my provisions. The group home and courtyard must go to the interested organizations that I have named, and the other apartment building must be sold only to my nephew and niece, for the original price I paid for it." She knew by that time her nephew would easily have assessed that amount of money, and if not, she hoped to help him out once she was back on her feet.

"Is that all?" Shawn asked.

"Yes." Tori took her hand off the envelope, realizing she had been holding it down since she'd placed it on the table.

A whiff of the roses filled her nose, and she gasped uncontrollably as if something had shocked her. The memories of the night before had to be fought away mentally as she felt a slight weakness in her leg, but caught herself.

"What's in the envelope?" Duncan asked.

Beck looked hard in Duncan's direction, shocked to hear the middle brother's voice.

Before she answered him, she needed to hear Shawn agree to her terms. "Are my terms agreed upon, Shawn?" she gritted out, forcing the wave of desire crash all over her.

Shawn looked at Duncan, who immediately nodded, and he said. "Yes, Tori. We'll agree to them, but it better be worth it."

"Or what, you little fucker?" Beck snarled.

Tori turned to Beck, feeling him nudge up on her, and, forgetting his sensitive skin issue, she pressed her hands on the front of his chest.

Kevin and Shawn started to walk toward Beck, but Duncan snapped his fingers hard.

One could cut the tension in the room like a knife.

"It's worth it!" Tori hissed. "Beck, let's go." She needed to get out of there before she lost her mind, and Beck lost his temper.

When Beck started to move, she followed him, but

stopped at the doorway and turned to all three of them. Looking at the envelope, Shawn had picked it up and was tearing it open by then.

"It's what you wanted. It's all yours. I worked out a deal, and it's all paid for." She looked at all three of them, ending at Shawn, and said, "You got everything, Shawn. Everything you desired, including a legacy for your children, and I hope you are finally at peace in exchange for the hell you have given me." With that, Tori hurriedly walked to the truck and got inside.

Beck went to the other side and immediately took off. She noticed he didn't even stop at the corner; he only slowed down after looking in the rearview mirror and then took off at a high rate of speed. "Whatever was in that envelope has got them fools running down the street after you?" he snarled, suddenly slowing down.

Tori looked out the back window to see Shawn running towards the truck with Duncan and Kevin behind him.

"Do you want me to stop?" Beck asked.

She could feel her heart crying out to jump out and run back, but she turned away. "No. Go, Beck."

He gleefully snickered, putting his foot down on the accelerator, leaving all three of them in his dust. The farther he drove away, the less she could feel them calling out to her.

Holding her stomach, Tori prayed she could get out of town and never see any of them ever again - except in those beautiful brown eyes she knew her child would have.

Beck was still chuckling when they arrived at the bus stop.

"I'm glad I could make you so damn happy since this will probably be our last time seeing each other, Beck," she snipped.

"Oh come off it, Tori, if I weren't there, you'd have probably got run like a train for a week up in there."

Amazingly, no one heard them, even though they were around a crowd of people. This kept her quiet until they were standing in line about to get on the bus. Beck had given the driver her suitcase to put underneath the bus, while she held onto her messenger bag with all her essential information inside.

"I'm sorry," she offered, knowing this really was going to be the last time they saw each other.

"Tori, there's no need to be sorry. We've always been fucking honest with each other, and yeah, I was a little tender from you grabbing me on my chest like that."

She couldn't remember if she had just placed her hands on him or grabbed him. "I was pretty out of it."

"You would have stayed."

Admitting her weakness out loud, she said, "I would have."

"That's why you turned your phone off, too, so they couldn't track you either."

Tori still had her phone and tablet off in the part of her messenger bag that had a Faraday lining. It was just a coincidence that her messenger bag did have this, but she had a feeling that if Duncan were desperate enough, he would try to track her communications devices.

Beck had almost torn the lining out of her bag last night to find a small tracker on the side pocket, but she was very sure the brothers couldn't track her anymore.

Beck sighed. "I still hate you for giving in to their demands. And fuck Tori, a whole legacy? Fuck!"

"I don't hate myself. I'm glad I can walk away like this."

Pulling out a small mirror, she checked her face for any makeup running. Outside, she looked cute, but inwardly, she was torn up from the floor up.

"Can I know what exactly was in that envelope to make them bastards run out of the house like that?" he inquired.

Tori didn't care because the secret she'd been holding off on with Mrs. Cosgrove would be out by tomorrow.

"The hospital wants to open several free and low-cost clinics around the city, but they don't want to be in charge of running them; they need them to meet requirements to send patients through. With my business administration knowledge, I was given the task of auditing them and setting them up properly. I work with another friend who can finish this up, but the buildings themselves also can't be owned by the hospital. This was so they could funnel nonprofit and government assistance through them. They needed someone to buy the buildings who wouldn't charge the hospital an arm and a leg and would also work with the hospital. The owner just needed to ensure the buildings were maintained, and the accompanying fleet as well. The hospital would take care of the rest. Staffing and so forth."

What buildings?"

She smirked. "Norman's mother was putting all his buildings up for sale. She didn't want to sell the business to Norman, knowing he'd run it into the ground, so she offered it to the hospital instead of Shawn, who'd tried to buy it. Mrs. Cosgrove was so appreciative of the donations I gave, but felt it earned a lot of money, and she secured the building with my money, but I gave them to Shawn."

"You what?"

"He owns them. Free and clear."

"Tori!" Beck exclaimed. "You didn't. Why the fuck would you give that valuable business to him?"

"Because he and his brothers wanted it and I was able to secure it for them, so I did it, and I was going to give it to them anyway."

"Tori-"

She cut him off. "I know what you're going to say, how stupid I am, but it doesn't matter. The money Mrs. Cosgrove makes from the donations you give her will be divided among the financial trusts. Please stop worrying about me, Beck. I'm starting back over and yes, I know I'm pregnant, but I have faith my sacrifices will..." She was lost for words because she wasn't sure what her sacrifices would do for her. "Well, I'll just have to wait and see, but at least I know I got the last lick. It was pretty cool to see them running after me."

"And if they had caught up, apologized, and begged you to come back?"

"I wouldn't. I couldn't. Not after what they did, Beck. How can I trust them again? Fool me once, shame on them. Fool me twice, shame on me. I'm tired of manipulating and being manipulated. I just want peace. In the end, everyone gets what they want. This is my happily ever after."

The driver signaled it was time to board.

"Give me a dollar, Beck," she ordered.

He didn't hesitate and handed her a bill.

Tori handed him the spare keys to her car. "I signed all the paperwork over to you at my lawyer's office for one dollar. Sell it and when you present the paperwork to my niece and nephew at the barbecue, give them a cut of the car sale just as spending money for me."

Beck took the keys and said. "You really have no plans of coming back, because I don't mind keeping that in my garage for you to have if you visit."

"No, I don't, Beck. I'm fully committed to getting the hell out of dodge and starting my new life."

"If I see those bastards on the street, I can beat the shit out of them?"

"Only if it happens randomly, but don't hit them in the face and don't kill them." She chuckled. "I hope you know I'm just teasing with you, Beck. Don't you dare! I still need you to drop the rest of that stuff off to them without getting hurt."

Beck snorted and rolled his eyes as if that would be impossible.

Tori said, "I'll text you when I get there if the signal isn't too spotty."

"I'll take that stuff to your sister, and I'll set that shit you want me to give to them on their porch," he promised. "At least send me a postcard in a week."

"I will. Thank you, Beck." She got on the bus and waved to him from the window before settling down. Tori was on her way to her new life.

When the bus was pulling in for a one-hour stopover near Lansing to pick up some passengers, Tori decided to stretch her legs, use the bathroom, and get some snacks from the store adjacent to the bus station. The minute the bus was outside of Detroit, she found herself incredibly hungry. Perhaps it was the stress leaving her, the knowledge she was finally free, or the fact that she was away from all the people who had made her sad. Thirty minutes before arriving in Lansing, she decided she was safe enough distance away to turn on her phone. Checking the screen, she saw thirty calls from Shawn and about twenty each from two unknown numbers. She was sure those were Duncan and Kevin. She didn't bother looking through her emails or any other form of communication, because she was done with them and her back-stabbing attempt to steal from her sister.

Walking through the store, Tori took out her extra bag to prepare for putting her snacks and sundries inside. Since it was very late at night, hardly anyone was in the store, except for others who were taking advantage of the bus stopover to get supplies and the clerk.

Checking the time, she saw she had about thirty more minutes before the bus took off and turned down the sundries aisle. In her peripheral vision, she thought she saw someone quickly duck down another aisle as if trying to avoid her, but pushed off her worry because she knew there was no way anyone could find her that fast.

There was no way they could have put a tracker on Beck's vehicle, and her phone had stayed off until she was outside of the Detroit area. If they were trying to trace her, by the time they got to this stopover, she would be long gone.

That reminded her to turn off her phone again and put it inside the Faraday sleeve inside her messenger bag, which she was currently using as a purse. Yes, it was big and bulky, but it was all her valuable paperwork, laptop, wallet, and extra money. She would be a fool to leave it on the bus while she was in the store.

Gathering items to clean herself and other sundries, Tori only needed to pick up something to drink before making her way to the front counter. By this time, she was starting to feel that someone was watching her. However, she believed it was just her worry about being all alone outside the city, and she would have to get used to staying on alert.

"That'll be twenty-fourty-one," the cashier said, breaking through Tori's deep thought.

She knew she had changed at the bottom of her bag, so she dug around for a moment and found it not wanting to get her wallet out with all the money and credit cards inside.

The cashier looked past her for a moment and then back at her. "Ma'am, are you okay?"

Tori looked down her shirt to make sure nothing was on there. "I'm fine," she answered handing the exact change to the young girl, who took the money and cashed her out.

"Okay," she waved in exaggeration. "Bye!"

The cashier's sudden joviality disturbed Tori briefly, but she pushed this away and walked back to the bus. For a moment, she thought she should wait for others to walk back in the dark to the bus, but felt perhaps someone from the bus might be hanging around and if something happened to her, they'd see her or at least hear her scream.

Ten steps out of the store, she heard a hiss to her right, and stopped walking to look that way.

"Hey, Princess," Kevin's voice said behind her.

Tori started to scream turning around to see him standing there, but then something came over her mouth and nose from Duncan's hand that smelled sharp and pungent. Her eyes watered and she tried to fight it, but was engulfed in darkness watching Kevin just standing there smiling like he won the lottery.

No! No! Hell NO!

CHAPTER 7
You Can't Do This

Tori didn't know if she was dreaming or not. Her consciousness felt like it was outside her body as she saw herself being dumped in the back of an old car like a bag of potatoes.

"She's not dead," Kevin quipped. "You could be a lot more gentle, Duncan. I'm just as upset at her as you are, but damn! If you were going to kill her, you should have done it the night we planned to do it!"

The trunk door slammed shut, and all she could hear was Kevin bitching to Duncan. Rain started to hit the trunk's hood, drowning out their voices, but she heard car doors close and a thunderous engine start up. Tori fought through the fog to stay alert, but with every passing second, it became increasingly difficult.

What the hell did they try to knock her out with?

Kevin was still running his mouth until Duncan boomed, "Shut the fuck up, Kevin!"

No more talking after that.

She'd never heard Duncan so angry before.

The exhaust from the vehicle was making her sick, and Tori began to cough.

"Did you put the mask on her face?" Kevin asked.

The vehicle stopped abruptly. The trunk was opened, and Tori could almost open her eyes in the muddy night as the rain touched her face. She tried to crawl out, swinging her arms wildly to get away.

"Let me go," she protested. "You can't do this!"

Something over her face like an oxygen mask, and she weakly tried to pull it off. Air hissed, and that sleepy feeling overpowered her again.

"I don't think she's happy to see us," Kevin teased.

"Shut the fuck up, Kevin!" Duncan bellowed as the trunk slammed shut again.

Duncan was furious.

The next time she woke, Tori was no longer in a trunk but lying prone on a bed. Her head hurt, and her nipples were cold.

Her nipples.

Gasping as she looked down at herself, she knew she was naked even though it was dark. When she tried to bring her arms down above her head to cover herself, she realized her wrists and ankles were bound, and her mouth was covered.

Squirming as hard as she could, she couldn't get out of the restraints. Had they lost their ever-loving mind?!

Kidnapping?!

That was a federal offense unless they meant never to let her go.

What did Kevin say?

If you were going to kill her, you should have done it the night we planned to do it!

When had they planned on killing her?

That night in the shed?

Knocking her head back against the bed as if that would draw some attention or light, Tori moaned her frustration.

A motion light from a bathroom came on across the room. Tori stilled all her movements and looked desperately around in the dark for someone - anyone!

She couldn't see much, but she knew someone was there. There was a warm intensity crawling up her body, wrapping her up in a certainty that had her blood pounding in her veins and her breath unable to catch.

From the darkness, Shawn suddenly appeared at the end of the bed. He was still dressed in that gray outfit, and the light from the bathroom barely touched the side of his face. What she could see was a deep frown and tight lips, glaring down at her. Had he just been there staring at her? Or had he just come in?

He didn't look like he was the least affected by her nudity. The grim expression on his face seemed set in stone.

"You shouldn't have tried to leave," he said as if all this was her fault.

Tori screamed as many muffled curses as she could at him, not caring that it all came out in mumbles.

Shawn took out a cloth and came up to her face. The fabric went over her nose, and she remembered the scent from the store's parking lot. She tried to move her nose and mouth away, but being bound as such left her with very little room to escape, forcing her to inhale the chemical.

Tori should have told Beck to hurt them all!

~

The headache was even worse when she awoke this time, but

terrified to reveal her wakefulness, Tori chose to wake up in silence.

Taking advantage of what she could hear, Tori heard an air conditioner running, but nothing else. Was she even in the house? Shouldn't there be a central air system instead of an air conditioner?

Her body clock told her it was daylight - late morning, and she was still naked, but there was cover lying all the way to her collarbone this time. Her arms were still bound above her head, and her mouth was covered. At least her legs were undone.

Oh no! Her bladder. She had to go bad.

Fluttering her eyes open, she saw she was still lying on a twin-size bed with an iron headboard. That was where some black leather cuffs were locked to the bars, and there was still something over her mouth so she couldn't speak.

"We have a conundrum, Tori," Duncan's voice said quietly across the room.

She found his voice in the farthest corner where the natural light from a skylight wasn't hitting. Just as Beck had pointed out, the windows were double-paned and specially sealed to prevent any noise from escaping. The walls of this room were bare and painted brown, with the only furniture being a loveseat, the chair Duncan sat in, a slim night table, and the bed. Other than the private bathroom, which was also painted brown, there was nothing else about the room, except the heavy, thick oak door that stood out.

Tori didn't return her gaze to Duncan on purpose, not wanting to even look at him to show her anger.

In a deceptively calm voice, Duncan said, "You have every right to be mad at us. And I know you have a lot of questions, like where you are." He paused. "This is Kevin, and my house. I got this a long while ago from a man whose boat I was working on.

His wife divorced him and wanted to take everything. He gave me the house in exchange for fixing his boat, rather than seeing her live in it with the man she cheated on him with. We never brought you here on purpose. We never thought it would get this far."

The AC came on, and she frowned.

He read her mind. "You're in a special portion of the house. In the house but not connected to the house. Needless to say, the former proprietor had odd tastes, and a lot of these rooms aren't connected for various reasons. Kevin and I never changed that. The house was always too big for us, but we kept it just because." He looked her over and then said, "And no, your precious Beck isn't going to be able to find you or even get in here. This house was originally built to hide liquor during prohibition. It's got more secrets than Fort Knox."

She rolled her eyes ridiculously and then cut them at him.

He smiled. "You want to know how we found you?"

This reading mind trick was starting to annoy her.

"When we couldn't find you once you left your lawyer's office that day, we put a tracker on Beck. It seems that the concrete of the house he hid you in was very well done. After you left that night, we traced you to the bus station, and it was just a matter of deductive reasoning. If Beck dropped you off, and you didn't have anywhere else to go, I figured you'd head to his brother's place. And I knew once you got there, there'd be no way to get you back."

Tori huffed hard.

Duncan snarled, "Tori, I told you not to come. What part of don't come didn't you understand?" He jumped to his feet and accusingly pointed at her. "You brought this on yourself, and then you have to go and ... fuck!"

She squirmed.

"Tori, your bladder is not going to last that long, so you're going to have to quell your anger, or I'm going to have to go with plan B."

She followed his gaze to the night table on the side of her. There was a urinary catheter and a drainage bag.

Again, she muffled a curse through her covered mouth as viciously as possible.

"I know you're upset, but this isn't about you. It's about your bladder. I'll release you as long as you keep your word to go to the bathroom, wash up, brush your teeth, and then get back in bed, like a good girl."

She cut her eyes at him.

"Tori, if not, we're going with plan B, which I haven't done on anyone in a couple of years, and I haven't done on a woman in a decade or so. It's up to you."

Tori nodded begrudgingly as he came up to the bed, pressed something above her, and her arms were released.

Holding the sheet around her, she refused his help even though her whole body hurt from lying down for so long. Damn, how long was she out?

"I can carry you, Tori. You've been out for a couple of days. Shawn used a little bit too much of the knock-out sauce I made."

Tori shook her head but dizzily made her way to the bathroom, gripping the walls to steady herself.

When she realized the bathroom had no doors, she shot him another hard look.

"Tori, we're not stupid. You know you can't be trusted to be by yourself. Now you either pee on your own will in front of me, or we can go with plan B."

She hurled the sheet at his face and sat on the toilet, because her bladder won out over propriety. When she reached up to pull the tape off, he tsked his tongue.

"Not yet," he said.

He was kind enough to look away slightly as she wiped herself down and didn't look until she flushed the toilet.

Politely, Duncan held the blanket up, and she raised her cuffed wrists so he could wrap the blanket back around her.

Holding her cuffed wrists up to him, he pushed them away.

"No, Tori. You're not getting out of those."

She continued to glare at him.

"Tori, you have to understand-"

She turned away from him, holding her hands over her ears, not wanting to hear his reasoning. SHE WAS KIDNAPPED! What did she possibly have to understand?!

There was a toiletry bag with a toothbrush, mouthwash, and a tongue cleaner. There was also sweet-smelling soap and a brand-new mini exfoliating kit.

"I would have gotten more, but it was the last minute," Duncan explained. "I didn't want to leave Shawn alone in the house with you for too long. You may take the duct tape off now to brush your teeth."

Tori had too many questions running through her head, but decided to get this thing off her mouth before she allowed him to read her mind anymore.

It was duct tape—every strong piece that hurt to remove. Duncan tried to come over and help her, but she flicked away, not wanting any part of him to touch any part of her. There was a bottle of mineral oil on the counter, and she applied a generous amount, but it still hurt enough to bring tears to her eyes.

The tub/shower was too inviting, and she went over to turn the water on to get hot, not caring that he stood there. He could watch if he wanted, but Tori wasn't letting go of her anger about the whole situation.

Duncan stayed at the doorway watching her the entire time, and she deliberately gave him a look of annoyance.

"Okay, Tori, I understand your anger and why you're not talking, but I did warn you to stay away, didn't I?"

She rolled her eyes again, furiously brushing her teeth.

Duncan looked equally agitated and began to twitch back and forth. "Shawn is more disturbed than you know, Tori. You have got to understand. He needed help. Help that no one could give. No one but you."

Slamming the toothbrush down, she rinsed her mouth out, doing her best to ignore him.

"It was all my idea," Duncan confessed.

The bathroom began to fog up, indicating the shower was ready. However, Tori wanted to hear what he had to say and finally looked at him.

Duncan began to explain. "He'd wander the streets all night, and Norman was getting worried because some nights he'd return bedraggled, dazed, and really out of it. I started following him. Tori, the past was tearing him up unconsciously, and no matter what drugs he took or therapy he got, he was torn up from the floor up. But every night, he'd literally get out of bed, wander the streets in his pajamas or whatever he was wearing before he went to sleep, and end up in front of your address. And he'd stand there, staring at the building, mumbling things our mother would say to him. These cruel things about women and how he was dirty and nasty. It broke my heart to see my little brother like this, Tori, but then I realized something. He wasn't just coming to your address because that's where we used to live. He'd come for you."

She started to turn around to ignore the bullshit, but Duncan came up to her and forced her to turn to him.

"Tori, I'm not lying. If you weren't there at the house, he'd keep wandering the streets and come back when you were there. Only when you were there would he stay and stare up at YOUR bedroom window. I told you Kevin and I had the fantasy of incorporating Shawn, but he was adamant that he didn't like women. And consciously, it was partially true because for any other woman, he couldn't get it up, but with you, Tori, that boy was harder than the Rock of Gibraltar. I knew it wasn't the past anymore. It was you! You, Tori. You healed him!" He must've seen her face of doubt, because he declared. "We lived on the first floor of the apartment building. He stayed and stared up at YOU! I fucking started following you, obsessively, to the point I was stalking your ass. Coming into your house, smelling your fucking scents, and just watching you when you didn't know I was there. You'd grown into this giving, honest, beautiful creature that I just wanted to care for and protect. And I knew Kevin would so fucking be attracted to you, so I made them think all this could be solved if we got revenge against you. Shawn thought this plan was all his idea, but it was on purpose by me. He still thinks this plan is all his... well, the kidnapping was all his. He's confused. What he unconsciously feels is not what he thinks he wants to feel. He loves you, Tori. And he has every reason to. You're not the same little girl we knew. You're this cool as fuck smart ass woman with the sexual drive that rocked our fucking universe."

Stepping out of his grip, Tori still glared at him.

"That's why I didn't want you to come. I needed you to drag the divorce out in court, Tori. He needed time to get his head and his heart together. I thought you would protest the divorce. I didn't think you'd give him what he wanted. I thought you'd fight. I wanted you to fight for him... for us." Duncan hit his chest hard, and she thought she could feel the hit in her own. "And when you didn't, I went along with his kidnapping because I care too much for you, and I care too much for my brother. And I'd do it all over again," he declared unapologetically.

Hurling the sheet back at his face again, Tori turned around and jumped in the shower.

Duncan stood there looking as if he were debating getting

in there with her, but then he started pacing, holding the sheet down in front of him.

Tori took her time in the shower, letting the water massage the soreness in her back and the areas around her shoulder joints, knowing Duncan might put her back in that same position. Deliberately, she kept her back to him, trying her best not to even look like she wanted him to get in and take the shower with her. Would he scrub her down, touch every part of her, and she would do the same to him, and then their mouths would follow the paths their hands had touched and then...

NO! Tori reprimanded herself. *You will not give in and give them anything!*

The shower gave her time to think.

They thought she was going to fight the divorce decree. Sinclaire would have, if Tori hadn't given in. Sinclaire would have probably won, and things would have gone back to normal. But Tori wouldn't have just wanted them back in her life. The Brothers would have been out of her life, or would they? Had Duncan planned some grand gesture of love to make her fall back into having sex with them? Or were they going to wait until she was sexually weak and let the chips fall where they fell?

Sons of bitches! All of them!

So now what? Kidnapping her was only going to piss her off. And Shawn was still fucking mad at her? Or was he?

No, that look last night was deadly!

And now that she thought about it, what had Kevin said, *If you were going to kill her, you should have done it the night we planned to do it!*

Duncan was leaving a lot of things out. Was he manipulating her? Of course he was. From the very beginning, they had been manipulating her!

The water had started to cool, and she got out. Duncan

had arranged lotion and a towel near her for use. He politely looked the other way, but she could tell he was only being a gentleman and wanted to look.

Don't say a word to him! she told herself. *Don't give him the satisfaction.*

Tori snatched the cover from him, wrapped it around her, and went back to the bedroom. Duncan followed closely behind her, but when she started for the chair he had been sitting in, he blocked her, and she knew what he wanted her to do.

Stomping her foot in defiançe, Duncan responded, "Tori, we can't have you wandering around the house. I told you, Shawn's not in his right mind about everything. He's still conflicted. And we don't know when they're going to be looking for you."

Tori hit him on the chest as hard as she could, but he didn't budge. Stomping to the bed, knocking the catherer bag to the ground in defiance, she lay back down, and he took her wrists and put them back in whatever was keeping the cuffs above her head.

"I'll figure this shit out, Tori, but couldn't you help me just a little?" he asked, getting on his knees at the end of the bed.

Looking at him incredulously, not believing he had the nerve to ask her for a favor.

"I have no right to ask this of you, Tori, but once we can get through to Shawn, we'll figure out how to make up for kidnapping you."

Tori managed to give him her stupidest look and then rolled her eyes away to let him know this conversation was over.

The middle brother started for the oak door but turned to her just as he was about to go out and said sincerely, "I'm really sorry, Tori."

It took everything in her not to look his way, but once she

was alone, she couldn't stop herself from bursting out and crying.

If she didn't get out of there, they'd find out about the baby, and then they'd never let her go. She'd be their prisoner forever!

No one would find her! Beck would eventually stop looking, thinking she'd changed her mind about going to his brothers and just disappeared. She knew her sister wouldn't care.

Tori would be trapped there because she couldn't leave her baby with these monsters. They'd continue to manipulate her and use her!

The really horrible part that made her cry the longest was that she knew she'd allow them.

CHAPTER 8
Sick Sons of Bitches

Coming back to reality after a miserable nap, Tori realized crying herself to sleep was not good. The headache had returned, and she was hungry enough to eat off her arm as a snack.

Her back was killing her from being in the restraints, and the covers had been pulled off her body again.

Someone had physically come into the room while she was sleeping and unraveled the blanket around her body, and pulled the covers down to her feet. The chair Duncan had been sitting in was moved closer to the end of the bed as if someone had been sitting there watching her sleep.

It was still daylight, but she could tell it was getting closer to evening.

Since her feet were still loose, she was able to grab the sheet and pull it up her body, but only to her waist. Her chest was left out, and she was helpless to correct this matter with her arms still locked above her head. Her mouth was also covered again with more duct tape!

The door burst open, and Kevin walked in, wearing his

work coveralls and carrying a food tray with a carafe of water and a glass.

The smell of roasted garlic chicken and broccoli assailed her nostrils, and she moaned in hunger, not caring that she was half naked.

He put the tray down on the small nightstand with a wicked smirk. "Tori, I'd have brought you up some food whether you gave me a look-see or not," he noted, and like a gentleman, he pulled the covers over her chest and sat on the bed by her, leaning over her closely. "You're going to be a good girl for me, Princess?"

The urge to spit in his face was strong, but she wanted to get information out of him as well, and she knew pissing Kevin off wouldn't help. He might like it.

Turning her face away to show him she wasn't going to speak to him either, he clicked his tongue and then reached up and did something to release her hands from the bars. She didn't see a key, and she was sure there was no button, so she couldn't figure out how the leather cuffs were being held up there.

She'd spent at least an hour before she fell asleep trying to yank her arms down, but even when she pulled down with all her weight, her arms were stuck up there until they came and did something to release them.

When her arms came down, she had to moan as the blood rushed back in. Kevin stood up from the bed and let her stretch out. She noticed he had a black mini sac over his shoulder and looked as if he'd just gotten off work. The only thing that looked clean was his hands.

No, a hardworking man didn't look really gorgeous! she hissed in her head.

Tori sat up, ripped the duct tape off her mouth, and, without asking whose food it was, she pulled the tray onto her lap to begin to eat hungrily. She barely used the silverware, but stuffed the pieces of chicken and vegetables in her mouth with her fingers. The food was still hot and she could feel the burn on her fingertips, but she was too hungry to care.

Duncan pulled off his work coveralls, tossed them in the chair, and then went into the bathroom. The shower started immediately, but he didn't come out.

Tori looked at the closed, thick oak door he'd come in.

She heard the sink water running in the bathroom and wondered if she could make a mad dash to the door to get out, but she assumed it would lock as soon as they came in.

Just as she got the nerve to bolt to the oak door to check, Kevin ducked out of the bathroom. "Come here, Tori," he ordered.

Why did she stand up, wrap the sheet around her, and come to him?

Because Kevin had trained her well to obey him in the bedroom or in any bedroom situation, she felt compelled to do so. He had shaved before she came in and was now packing all his personal items in his satchel, except for a washcloth, some soap, and lotion.

"Duncan said to tie you to the toilet so I could take a shower, but I'm going to trust you'll stay in my visual field while I take a shower. He had to leave, and Shawn's not home from work yet, so you're stuck with me. One of us has to be here with you at all times."

Tori wanted to protest if they let her go, she wouldn't be such an inconvenience, but she held her tongue.

Without being asked, Tori walked over to the closed toilet, used the bathroom, cleaned up, and then returned to close the seat to sit. Her embarrassment about relieving her bladder went away with Duncan. Kevin was so raw that he didn't look bothered at all as he watched her the whole time.

Kevin put the satchel high up on a flush shelf over the mirror. Unless she jumped up on the side of the sink and carefully balanced, she would have been able to reach it. However, getting down could break her neck, so that was out of the plan.

Yet Tori wasn't thinking about going anywhere as her eyes were drawn to Kevin. And he blatantly turned to her and began to take off his coveralls. Underneath, he wore a tank, shorts, and socks. He promptly pulled that off, leaving him only with his underwear on.

Those admirable, thick shoulders, muscular arms, and big hands were delectable to her eyes. His lean, muscular body spoke power and strength, and with the humidity of the room rising, so did her arousal.

Kevin didn't step to her, though, but continued to look at her while his hand moved down to his phallus, where he gripped himself from the base to the tip. Her hands itched to help him, but she forced them on the side of the toilet, gripping there instead.

She swallowed several times because saliva was building up in her mouth.

He'd started to harden, and a tiny drop of precum teased on the tip of him.

Tori pressed her lips to stop herself from drooling and then forced her eyes to look away.

Chuckling, Kevin got in the shower. The glass was clear, giving her a full view of him as he soaped up and scrubbed himself to wipe away the day's work. He even paid attention to cleaning his nails and thoroughly washing his head and face.

Several times, she found herself dreaming that those big, strong hands were rubbing all over her body, and she wanted to go into that shower and join him too many times to count.

When he got out, Kevin used the towel she had used earlier.

"I didn't believe Duncan when he said you wouldn't talk," he said. "That's fine with me."

Tori huffed, folding her arms over her chest in a pout.

"But I know you got questions, Princess, and I'm not doing that mind-reading trick Duncan does." While he spoke, he lotioned up his skin and she greedily watched, enjoying the show. "Dunc's a grifter, so he's good at reading people. I'm good at talking to people and annoying the fuck out of them too, so either you're going to start talking or lose your voice calling me ten times a bitch by the time we're done."

He was not winning any brownie points with his threat, Tori noted as she narrowed her eyes.

After putting away his soap and lotion, he took a toothbrush out of the satchel and used her toothpaste to brush his teeth. She liked how simple he was. Kevin didn't need anything extra in his life, but he took such good care of himself.

"Since you've been good, I'll get you dessert if you obediently sit on the bed and don't try anything, Tori," he offered, wrapping the towel around his waist.

Why did she feel he wanted her to fight him? Was he itching to get his hands on her somehow, using her resistance to hold her down? And do what?

She was almost tempted to see, but decided not to. Nodding, she bounded out of the bathroom and sat cross-legged in the middle of the bed.

He didn't follow her into the bedroom but moved to the oak door and reached for something just beyond it to the right.

Taking note that there was a table outside her door, she also saw that the hallway was completely dark. No windows in the hallway?

Kevin snatched a pile of clothes and a saucer with a big slice of raspberry cheesecake into the room.

Now Tori drooled as he handed her the small plate, and then he stepped away.

She knew this was Duncan's doing, but she wasn't grateful. That didn't stop her from wolfing down the slice and even licking the plate, while Kevin dressed in some jogging pants, a white t-shirt, and white socks.

Looking at the socks longingly, she looked at him. Why couldn't she get clothes? Did they really think she would run around the house naked? Was it a precaution to prevent escape?

"Tori, I'm not playing your games," he said with exhaustion. "Ask your questions."

Pressing her lips together, she put the plate on the tray with her other empty plate and then poured herself another glass of water from the carafe.

Kevin came over to the bed, with a bottle of lotion from his bag, and holding the towel he'd just used from the shower. He put a pillow between his feet on the floor and sat down, rolling the towel out on his lap. "Stand in front of me, Tori," he ordered.

Curiosity nudged her to get out of bed and stand in front of him, noting how much room she had to jerk away if he tried anything.

"Get on your knees, Princess."

Tori frowned at his order, but when he did not explain, she debated with herself for a moment before finding herself kneeling in front of him on the pillow to see where this went. Kevin reached over and raised one of her arms and guided her over his leg so she lay her chest over his muscular, wide thigh, and then he moved the sheet down so only her back was exposed. His warm, large hands began to massage her neck and shoulders, pressing particularly hard over her tight muscles that had been stretched out due to the uncomfortable position of holding her arms up.

The heavenly feel of blood rushing into the muscles from his massage almost made her groan, but she fought letting him hear this and just enjoyed this act of kindness. He moved down her back, but didn't go past her waist. He also didn't let the sheet expose her backside or her rear.

Tori was sure she had fallen asleep from the deep tissue massage and hadn't come to until he was laying her back in the bed.

Kevin pulled her left arm above her head and locked it in place, then went around to the other side of the bed and lay down. Having her arm raised like this exposed her whole body to him, but she was too relaxed to tense up and worry about him touching her.

When he situated himself on the other side of the bed, Kevin left several inches between them and put his hands behind his head. "Tori, I tried to tear my fucking dick off masterbating last night thinking about you."

The statement made her blush, and she immediately stared up at the ceiling, trying not to show any emotion to his confession.

"Seeing you between us, connecting us..." He took a deep, hurtful sigh. "It was like we all connected on another level, Tori." He was staring up at the ceiling, too, and kept rambling. "I think all our adult lives, my brothers and I have been searching for that feeling we used to get, all lying in bed together, being close to each other, knowing all we had was each other. It's something as adults we can't get back cause we're grown ass men, except... that night... I knew for sure. Dunc and Shawn won't admit it, but I felt it when we were with you, Tori." He looked at her, but she didn't dare meet his eyes.

She was drilling holes in the ceiling, keeping her eyes shut, knowing that if she looked his way, she would say something.

"Tori, I didn't say that to make you talk. I wanted you to know. That night was fucking spectacular. I think the first fucking time on the boat, we were just consumed with lust, but this time, it was on a whole'nother level." He looked at the ceiling again. "When you took Dunc, I thought I was going to bust a nut, but damn, Tori. Your ass was so sweet. And I could feel everything they were doing and what you were feeling. Fuck!"

Kevin leaned on his elbow and looked down at her to make her look at him. "You've got the sweetest ass and pussy on a woman. You taste like a fucking sweet steak I could eat all night."

Deep breath! Deep Breath! she ordered herself.

Chuckling, Kevin lay back down, but his hand moved over his crotch to squeeze his manhood that was starting to twitch. She could see it in her peripheral vision, begging to come out. Her hand felt like a thousand red ants were crawling under her skin, desiring to wrap her fingers around his thickened phallus.

She swallowed hard because her mouth had started to water.

Kevin was quiet for a long moment before he spoke again. "Tori, I know this shit's gone sideways. I'm the family fuckup, so I know fuck ups, and there's nothing we could do to make you see you're fucking special to us, and we don't fucking want you to go away. Dunc and Shawn won't ever say it. Fuck! Shawn can't make up his mind if he wants to kill you, fuck you, or love you. Dunc says he needs time, but that doesn't mean shit to you. I know. You're pissed as fucking hell. Your submission tells me."

Again, he rolled over so he was over her, looking down into her face. "I'm not afraid to let you know, Tori, I fucking love the shit out of you."

She immediately closed her eyes.

"Open your eyes, Tori," Kevin ordered.

Damn! She obeyed, but she looked to the side so she wouldn't meet his gaze. Dusk was moving in, but the room was still moderately lit for her to see his face.

"I'll give you one time to ask me anything, Princess. Any question and I'll answer it."

Tears streamed down the side of her face, but she refused to look at him.

Kevin sighed, locked up her other arm, and got out of bed.

She closed her eyes immediately to regain her equilibrium. The blood in her whole body was rushing all over, and she wanted to scream her frustration. Love her?! Tying her naked to a bed was love?

What the hell insanity was he smoking?!

She could hear him picking up the pillow and tossing it back on the bed beside her, and then gathering the towel and lotion along with the dinner tray. He stopped briefly in the bathroom, most likely to collect his satchel.

He was leaving! The door opened. Should she let this moment go because of her anger? Could she find a way to get him to let her go?

"Kevin," she said in a whisper, looking his way.

He stopped and looked back as if he wasn't sure what he had heard.

Their eyes met, and she saw him tremble.

Tori realized she had control over her older brother—a force no one else had—which made her feel very powerful in that moment.

Kevin put the tray and satchel down outside the room, closed the door, and came to the bed to lean back over her. "Anything, Princess. Ask me anything," he demanded breathlessly.

CHAPTER 9

Who Loves Her

"You don't know anything about me to love me, Kevin," Tori declared quietly.

"That's not a question," he pointed out quickly. "It's a declarative statement."

Tori could see he was delighted to have her speak to him. His happiness seemed intense, almost suspicious, and the glint in his eyes made her uneasy, as if something else were driving his joy beyond their conversation.

Kevin continued, "And I do know about you, Tori. You want a soft life, to be spoiled ridiculously, and you want things when you want them. But you're terrified of wearing a man out. That after spending time loving him, he'll leave you, and you'll have to start all over again. So you've decided not to love or need anyone, because you believe you're a burden, a result of your past actions, and that people will hate you, just as they have in the past."

Kevin's words left her breathless, anger dissolving into a stunned silence. As the shock faded, suspicion flared within her, sharp and cold. "You didn't come to that deduction," she shot back, her voice trembling between disbelief and accusation.

He flushed. "No, Duncan did. When I came home, he was a box of frustration, and I've never seen my middle brother frustrated about anything. For the first time in his life, he couldn't fix a problem. You were the problem, Tori. It was tearing him up and down."

She kind of liked knowing she had frustrated Duncan, feeling a small sense of satisfaction, but she made sure not to let Kevin notice her reaction, deliberately keeping her thoughts to herself.

"I'm still waiting for your question, Tori," he said.

Why did her eyes move from his eyes to his lips? She wondered when she last kissed him, and whether her anger was really that valid.

DON'T YOU DARE, WHORE! Her sensible conscious yelled. *You are tied up! He tied you up! He kidnapped you!*

"Let me go," she said, forcing her gaze to his.

"I can't, Princess. Shawn needs you here as part of his plan, and he believes your presence is crucial. Duncan said helping Shawn is the priority now, even though it means taking risks for Shawn's sake."

She turned her face away, biting down on her sob as dread and hopelessness crashed over her. They were never going to let her go—her tears burned with fear and the ache of being trapped.

"Tori," he said, hurt. "I would if I could."

"That isn't love, Kevin!"

He cursed. "Ask your question, Tori!" he demanded.

"Can you go to hell?!" she spat.

"I already am in hell, Tori. All my life! Until you. This adult version of you has put a light, a warmth, a fucking solar flare in my fucking chest, and I feel it all the time. When I'm not around you, I fucking miss you. And when I am around you, I'm sweltering internally until I can touch you, or kiss you, hell, even fucking talk to you."

Tori trembled at his words, her chest aching with longing she refused to admit. But the reality of her life was a storm she couldn't weather, not with her baby—she braced herself against the pain and forced him out, hiding behind cold defiance. "Go away, Kevin," she whispered, shutting her eyes, a wall of ice between them.

The oak door opened, and Duncan stood there looking at them, and they looked at him.

"What the fuck is going on?" Duncan demanded.

"Talking," Kevin said smugly.

"You fucking liar! She's not speaking to anyone!" Duncan slammed the door with him inside the room.

Kevin got off the side of the bed as Duncan moved to the other side. Both of them towering over Tori gave her too many ideas, but she refused to look in either direction, so they couldn't read her thoughts.

"You're just jealous she wouldn't talk to you," Kevin taunted.

Tori rolled her eyes and really wanted to kick Kevin in the nuts.

Duncan glared at Tori. "Did you fucking tell her that I love her, Kevin! Is that how you convinced her to talk to you? You told her my business."

She couldn't help herself as she exclaimed, "Huh?"

Duncan leaped over the bed and punched Kevin, sending the older brother across the room against the wall. But he jumped up and charged after Duncan.

Surprisingly, they didn't approach the bed or threaten her as they began to wrestle and punch each other, venting their frustrations physically. Duncan was the better fighter, but Kevin's anger pushed him to land several solid blows.

Tori pressed her fists into the mattress, exasperation crackling through her. Rage, confusion, and an ache she hated—all tangled together, knowing the two of them wanted her, maybe loved her. It was too much to bear.

The oak door opened quietly and slowly, as Shawn's frame filled the doorway. The older brothers shoved each other away and straightened themselves up on the other side of the bed.

Shawn initially looked at Tori when he entered, with a cold, hateful glare, before settling on his brothers.

"We agreed only one in the room at a time," he said coolly, betraying what he was really feeling.

She could see the tightening in his jaw, the intensity in his body, and the tightness in his fists. She wondered if he was angry at his brothers for breaking the rules or if he resented her presence for personal reasons. Why did Shawn insist on only one brother at a time?

Looking at Duncan, who glanced at her, he explained. "Shawn's worried we'll get a pack mentality and it'll make us weak when it comes to you."

Rolling her eyes, she looked up at the ceiling so no one could read her thoughts again.

"Duncan started it," Kevin declared. "He accused me of blabbing his feelings for Tori, and I didn't. Did I, Tori?"

She closed her eyes to show she was out of this conversation. Having them in the room while she was naked was not helping her libido. Her body was responding to the level of testosterone in the room, and she had to take several deep breaths just to keep herself from squirming her hips into the bed.

The room grew suddenly quiet, and Tori opened her eyes to see that all three of them were staring at her with hungry looks, and she knew they weren't thinking of food. Those looks clearly told her they could feel her arousal and wanted to sate her hunger.

"You're right, Shawn," Duncan said. "We'd better get out if we don't-"

Kevin shoved him. "Just get the fuck out then. I was-"

Shawn ordered, "Kevin, you think we're going to let your horny ass be alone with her anymore. Your dick's barely staying in your pants!"

Tori chortled because she could see Kevin's member pressing against the front of his pants, begging to get out, and unconsciously, she licked her bottom lip.

Kevin huffed in exasperation. "I'm not the only fucking one with a hard on. I'm just wearing tighter pants," he accused his other brothers. "And I got more control than Duncan's horny ass, any day!"

It took everything in her not to laugh.

Shawn, in his deadly serious tone, said, "We need to move her tonight."

"Why?" Kevin demanded to know.

Tori wanted to know as well. Was Beck looking for her?

Shawn looked perturbed at his brother. "We can discuss this-"

"No," Duncan said sternly. "She deserves to know what's going on, Shawn."

"The lieutenant came by the hospital today looking for her. He said he'd tried to call her several times over the past couple of days to ask her about her father, but she's been avoiding his calls. He only received some push calls to voicemail with a reply that she would call him later. Good for us, because that gives us time."

As Shawn spoke in icy monotone, Tori's heart squeezed painfully. The man she thought she knew had vanished. Vulnerability had given way to a cold stranger, and now mistrust gnawed at her—was any of his warmth ever real? She hated that she had to wonder.

Shawn stated, "Keir made some police reports and had a

restraining order against Amos a long while ago, before I was born. The lieutenant wanted to know if she knew anything about it."

"What did you tell him?" Duncan demanded to know.

"I told him I'd never heard her speak about Amos."

All three of them looked at her.

Tori glared at Duncan.

"Shawn, she's never heard Keir talk about Amos," Duncan responded. "She would have never heard anyone talk about anything other than herself back then. Tori was only consumed with her needs. So why would we need to leave?"

"He's eventually going to go back to Beck and let him know he hasn't spoken to her, and get Beck to start looking earlier than we expected. We need to jump to our next step now before that bastard starts looking, or worse, get others involved, and you know what I mean." That last part was a private dig at his brothers, which made the oldest two look very worried.

Shawn instructed his middle brother, "Dunc, get the place ready. Kevin and I will bring her."

Kevin started to protest, "She can't-"

Shawn hissed, "Shut up, Kevin. Duncan, we got her." He patted his chest confidently.

Duncan looked at Kevin in a silent order before he looked at Tori almost apologetically.

This was Shawn's plan, and the older brothers intended to see it through. Duncan had told her that the family's commitment was absolute and that only she could help.

But this wasn't Shawn—this wasn't the man whose rare laughter and care comforted her. She stared, heart pounding, as a stranger stood before her: cold, distant, laced with cruelty she thought impossible.

What the hell was he pulling out of his pocket?

"We need to move her out of the house without arousing

neighbors' suspicion," Shawn announced, holding a roll of duct tape. "Our goal is to make sure she isn't harmed, so transporting her without attracting attention is essential. Get the rug ready."

Kevin moved the furniture away from the floor in the bedroom. Tori knew there was a large rug on the floor, and that must be what they were going to wrap her up in to transport her out of the house. But how were they going to keep her quiet, because she wasn't about to allow them to just drag her out here without the whole world knowing she was in there?

Shawn dragged off half of a foot in duct tape and moved over her, straddling her chest. She twisted her face away so he would avoid her mouth, but she could barely breathe because the more she fought, the more he put his weight down on her.

Shawn kept tearing tape, cold efficiency in every move as he straddled her chest. Tori twisted away, panic nearly choking her, but his weight pressed down, stealing her air and hope. When the tape finally sealed her mouth, fury blazed behind her eyes. Trapped, she glared murderous promises at the man she thought she'd known—her rage hotter than ever.

He moved off her chest but started holding down her arms. Tori fought like crazy, wildly squirming her body, and even trying to get her legs up to kick him in the head.

"Come hold her arms, so I can inject her, Kevin," Shawn ordered.

Kevin came over and easily brought her arms down with very little effort on his part, while Shawn dug a needle out of his breast pocket.

Whatever he was going to inject her with could harm her baby! Tori desperately looked at Kevin and screamed for his help at the top of her lungs. She knew he couldn't read her mind like Duncan, but he had to understand a woman's cries for help!

And if he loved her...

Shawn took the cap off the needle. "Hold her tighter, Kevin, so I don't miss a vein."

Tori screamed louder and shot everything she could at Kevin, praying he would see her desperation not to get injected. Pressing her face against his shoulder, rubbing her face hard against him, and crying as much as she could, she tried everything to get him to understand that Shawn couldn't do this to her.

"Wait," Kevin said. "She's too upset, Shawn.'

"This will shut her up for a couple of hours. That's more than enough time."

Tori shrilled at the highest pitch, feeling the prick into her skin.

"Shawn fucking stop or I'll let go of her arm. Don't shoot that shit in her," Kevin ordered.

Shawn stopped what he was doing and looked at Tori and then at Kevin. "Kevin, we have-"

"Get the needle out now," Kevin growled.

Huffing in exasperation, Shawn pulled the needle out of her skin, and Kevin pulled Tori into his arms. She sobbed in relief, pressing herself against him for comfort and safety.

"She'll alert the neighbors, Kevin. We only have your car. The tinted Bronco is still in storage. How the hell are we going to get her out of here and over to the place?" He held up the needle. "This is our only solution."

Trembling, Tori wrapped her arms desperately around Kevin, not caring that she could be almost choking him.

"Can't you see she's scared, Shawn. She's terrified." Kevin rubbed her back for comfort. "Just give me a sec. Go over there, and put that fucking needle away. You're scaring the shit out of her. Fuck, you're scaring the shit out of me."

Shawn cursed viciously and stormed to the doorway. "Do whatever you have to do, but hurry the fuck up."

Kevin dragged her face out of his neck and cupped her face so she was forced to look at him. "Tori, it's okay. Calm down."

Her heart was beating too fast, and even if she wanted to, she couldn't calm down. All she wanted to do was scream: *The baby!* Yet knew she couldn't, and it tore her up inside because she hated that she had to keep this secret in order to survive.

He pulled her against his body and held her close. "Breath deep, Princess. Breath with me."

Remembering how they'd taught her before, she concentrated on his deep, slow speech, and Tori allowed her breath to align with his. She still shuddered intermittently, but she could feel a calm come over her. Kevin's scent, musky and soapy from the shower, lulled her into a comfort, and she occasionally sobbed and shuddered.

If they were willing to do something like this so easily, the more she kept this secret, the harder it was going to be for her. What if they come in her sleep and inject her with something? Who could she trust without letting any of them know she was pregnant?

Whispering, she said, "Please don't let him put that stuff in me. Please, Kevin - ever."

"Tori, we have to get you out of here," Kevin said firmly, in a normal tone so she and Shawn could hear him. "You have to swear to follow all my commands. You won't move a muscle or alert anyone, and I'll protect you from my evil little brother and putting that shit in you. Swear!"

As a dominant over the bedroom, she knew that asking him to repeat his domain over her was asking her for a lot, and this was important. Tori trembled some more but mumbled her acquiescence low in his ear.

Kevin's arms squeezed her so hard she almost moaned in pain from the sheer strength behind the powerful hug, and then he lifted her off the bed, while she still held his neck. "She swore, Shawn."

"I didn't hear shit, and if she did, she'd say anything to get herself in a position to escape, Kevin," Shawn sneered.

Tori squeezed Kevin's neck harder, knowing he was carrying her closer to Shawn, which could mean a prick by that needle.

Moving to the rug, Kevin knelt and laid Tori down. Shawn came to stand at her feet. The needle was away, but Tori didn't want to let go of Kevin's neck with Shawn so close.

"Tori, it's okay," Kevin assured her. "You need to cup your hands over your face because the rug is heavy and the weight could suffocate you."

He tore her arms from his neck and put them where he needed them to be, above her face. She knew explaining himself was an annoyance, especially as the dominant in the bedroom, but he also seemed to understand her fear.

Kevin ordered his little brother. "Get the pair of socks in my satchel and put them on her feet."

"Why? She's going to be in the rug. It's big enough to cover her."

"I think I know more about kidnapping people than you do, asshole. It's fucking cold outside!" Kevin barked. When Shawn went out the door to dig around the satchel Kevin had placed out there earlier, Kevin said to her, "We're going to roll you up, Princess, and get to my Hummer. You swore, Tori, so don't fuck it up."

Warily, Tori watched Shawn return and put on her socks. The warmth from his hands felt good, but she wasn't going to show that she appreciated his actions.

Putting her hands back up as Kevin had instructed her, Tori waited for them to start rolling her.

Kevin had been right, the rug was extremely heavy, and she was glad for the way Kevin had told her to put her arms because it would have crushed her chest and made it difficult to breathe.

Was he a professional at rolling women up in rugs?

This question left her as soon as she felt herself being picked up and carried like a sack of potatoes down several flights of stairs. Their voices were muffled, but she could pick up conversations. Shawn was grabbing emergency bags and other items, while Kevin, who was carrying her, was headed outside.

The socks were perfect for keeping her feet warm because as Kevin stepped out into the night air of Detroit, the cool air swept inside the rug, giving her fresh air to breathe, but Tori knew her feet would've been miserable.

She could feel herself being placed down, and she assumed it was in the back seat of the Hummer because she could hear them get into the front and the back doors closing on her.

The iron gate made hardly any noise, and Kevin was driving.

"How'd you do it?" Shawn demanded. "What did you do to make her trust you like that, Kevin? And don't you dare say because she likes you? No one likes you."

Kevin chuckled proudly. "And the same for you, brother. At least I'm an honest ass. You covert your shit so well, you smell like a fucking rose. A woman obeys with limits, little brother, and you ain't been around them enough to know how to do it right."

"But I've been nice to her more than you."

"You've been faking, and now that she knows that, she's never going to trust you, no matter what you do."

"Kevin, just tell me how you did it. Why the fuck do you and Dunc make women so damn hard for me?" Shawn seethed.

"It wasn't us that did this to you, Shawn. Ma did it. She made you like this, and you're going to have to get through all the fucking noise she makes in your head to see yourself, and then you can see Tori." There was some physical altercation, and Tori felt the vehicle jerk. "Fucking stop before we have an accident," Kevin ordered.

"Then just fucking tell me!"

Kevin sighed regretfully. "I can't. Like Duncan said, to get to her, we're going to have to find our own way. You still don't know if you hate her or love her."

Shawn snorted in disgust."I don't see how you guys don't see that she did this to us. From the moment she was conceived, Tori was used as a weapon to hurt us."

"And we weren't conceived as a weapon against her mother? See, that's that Ma shit fucking with you. Ma deliberately stuffed all the shit in your head so you don't know whether you're coming or going when women are around. But Tori's the real deal, and maybe Ma knew this. Ma couldn't do it to me, so she sacrificed me to the streets, and when she couldn't do it to Duncan, she sacrificed him to Amos, but you- YOU, Shawn. She started from day one, and all the fucking therapy is not going to get you out of your own head to see what a real woman can do for you. FUCK!" A fist slammed on the dashboard, making the whole vehicle jump. "I hate Ma for what she did to all of us, but we just fucking tolerated her until her dying day like good little fucking boys. Maybe Tori did the one thing we couldn't do—she made Ma miserable and suffer while that old woman lived. All the way to her dying day, Ma cursed Tori to the ninth ring of hell. Even though it was selfish as fuck, Tori hurt Ma. We saw Ma torn up from the floor up every day, knowing Tori was keeping Keir all to herself, and there was nothing Ma could do about it. Maybe you need to see what an extraordinary woman Tori has become and appreciate what she really did and find the beauty that Duncan and I see."

"Shut the fuck up, Kevin, and drive," Shawn seethed, turning up the music in the Hummer extremely loud.

Tori strained her ears to hear anything that was said, but she couldn't hear anything above the music.

Exhaustion from expending so much stress and frustration, Tori found herself getting sleepy.

Kevin's words were sweet and powerful. Nice way to turn her selfishness into a good thing. She still wasn't going to like Shawn, but she could like Kevin even if he was an ass.

You're just horny! Her inner whore sniggered.

Tori drifted to sleep thinking about Kevin's powerful tongue and how he liked to lave repeatedly from her perineum up to her clit, tickle his tongue around her labia, and then lick her all over again before darting that big fat tongue into her.

Ummmm.

She squished her thighs together, feeling the wetness trickle down her ass.

Tori! Stop it! she ordered herself.

But she didn't, because she fell asleep dreaming of Kevin taking care of her needs, not just with his mouth, but with his hands and his body. Somehow, she was going to have to get Kevin to give her a little lickety lick without the others knowing about it.

She was still piqued at Duncan, and as for Shawn? He could go to hell in a handbasket.

All those manipulation skills Tori had stopped using were going to be put to good use if it could mean her freedom and maybe a little titillation as well.

CHAPTER 10

Oooh Ahhh Ummmm

"Tori," Kevin called out skeptically, slowly pulling the duct tape off her mouth.

Reluctantly, she opened her eyes and stared up at a skylight directly above. She frowned, trying to remember if this was the same position she'd been in before. Had they moved her? The layout and furniture mirrored the other room where she'd been rolled up in the rug.

Were they trying to trick her and make her think she hadn't been moved?

When she turned her head to the left, she spotted Shawn standing nearby. He hovered with his arms crossed, his gaze fixed on her, brows knit together in skeptical concern.

Tori pressed herself closer to Kevin, using him as a shield. She looked away from Shawn with an eye roll, then glanced back at Kevin, silently demanding answers.

"Tori, I'm not doing mind-reading shit," Kevin said.

She cut her eyes at Shawn and then back at Kevin.

"Leave, Shawn," Kevin ordered. "Most likely, she has to go to the bathroom, and she needs to take a shower. She's sweated up a damn storm in that rug. She'll do neither in front of you."

Reluctantly, Shawn walked out of the room, dragging the extra rug with him, but as she followed him, she noticed the oak door was different—almost thicker.

"We're at Duncan's house. He built it almost exactly like the other as a sick joke," Kevin explained.

He helped her to her feet, and Tori moved quickly to the bathroom, cheeks burning with embarrassment as she realized how desperate she was. Her bladder was screaming for relief, and humiliation gnawed at her.

As Tori finished wiping herself in the bathroom, Kevin leaned against the doorway, arms folded. Tori ignored him, choosing not to speak. She scanned the bathroom and noted familiar sundries, now accompanied by an extra towel; the newer tiles caught her attention. She turned on the shower faucet, let it run, and crossed to where he stood, waiting for the water to heat up.

With the cover of the water, Tori could speak without others hearing them. "Were you all really planning on killing me that night?"

Kevin gulped, guilt flickering across his face as he slowly nodded. "And then pack all your shit and make people believe you left town all of a sudden over a broken heart. Shawn would still announce the proclamation of divorce for sleeping with his brothers, showing the carefully edited video to everyone, so no one would suspect any of us, and they would have never found you."

Tori's chest tightened. She couldn't believe she'd played right into their hands. Of course, no one would look for her—everyone would assume she vanished, heartbroken, while these jokers got away with murder. The unfairness stung like a slap.

"What would it have been? Stabbing? Poison?" she pressed.

"Shawn wanted to strangle the life right out of your eyes."

The many times all of them had come in the vicinity of her neck. "And how were you going to get rid of my body?"

"The middle of the Detroit River was my suggestion. Then Duncan said, right under the shed—we could disassemble and reassemble in one night, and no one would be the wiser. The last suggestion by Shawn was to send you with other unknowns through the hospital system, in some Potter's grave, like everyone thought happened to Amos. It'd be fitting - like Father like daughter."

"Kevin, how can you say you love me-"

He cut her off and leaned over her. "Tori, we need Shawn to heal, and if it meant that, then we would have to do it. We'd have to rip our hearts out to save him." His indomitable stance on the matter chilled her to her core. "The hold he has over us is stronger than anything, even what we feel in our hearts, but that's why Duncan came to ask for your help. We don't know how to reach him, and we can't break our bond even if it means hurting our hearts."

Angry that they had removed her for their brother's sake, Tori still felt the pain in Kevin's voice. She almost offered comfort but kept her arms folded, shielding herself. "Why do you both think I could change him?" she asked, desperation cracking her voice as she squeezed her arms tighter.

"You already have, Princess. What you see now is the real Shawn, but he's different. Very different than the monster he really was. He can't fucking function unless he's in your proximity. I never saw him sleep for long hours until he slept with you -with us. He fucking takes your sheets and wraps himself in them, jerks off to your scent, but at least he stopped taking your underwear. Shawn hates what he was told to feel about you, and he hates that he's obsessed with you. He didn't kill you, Tori, when he had the chance. That means something."

She sucked her teeth, cutting her eyes at him. "I thought it was Duncan taking my underwear."

"Initially it was, and then I started stealing them and putting them under Shawn's pillow," he admitted guiltily. "Your scent stopped the nightmares he would scream out of sleep, and I believe he became addicted to your smell."

Tori swore her cheeks would explode from all the blushing she was doing. Her pulse thudded in her ears, and the memory of Kevin's lingering gaze sent tingles over her skin. Not to mention Kevin's eyes were doing that up and down visual caress to her body.

Kevin volunteered, "You know, if you need some help getting to your back-"

"No, Kevin," she said firmly, dropping the sheet on purpose, knowing his eyes were glued to her full, voluptuous body while she got into the shower.

He ran a frustrated hand over his head and turned slightly away to try not to be tempted, but Tori knew her nakedness tore him up. She felt a potent mix of triumph and longing humming in her veins—damn, despite being angry with him, she wanted him to burst in that shower, hiked her body up on his, and ground himself to the hilt inside of her.

Her shower was quick yet thorough, and Kevin had the fresh towel waiting for her.

"Will I get some clothes soon to wear?" she asked, annoyed while brushing her teeth.

"That will be up to Shawn. He's the one who felt the need to keep you like this."

"Why does the one who hates me most control my care?" she demanded.

"Princess, if it were me, I'd keep you fully naked all the time, too. Fuck a sheet."

Storming back into the bedroom area, Tori flopped on the bed, with her back to him.

"Would that mean you don't want lotion?" Kevin asked with great disappointment.

Her body completely responded, remembering the last time he'd put lotion on her skin. Tori pulled the pillow over her head in her attempt to let him know she was done with this conversation. Since she couldn't get what she wanted, she was going to act like the spoiled brat Shawn thought she still was. Kevin and Duncan would have to deal wth her, and she hoped they were all miserable.

"Guess that's a no," Kevin said and left.

Moaning loudly now that she was alone, Tori felt misery crushing her chest because she found herself sexually excited with every preferable dick around and too prideful to lower herself and get thoroughly fucked. Frustration warred with desire, and she curled herself tighter under the covers, groaning at her own predicament.

Somehow, she fell asleep, and when she awoke, Tori was still lying on the bed, but the lights were all dimmed, except for a nightlight in the bathroom. She was just glad that her arms weren't bound and happily stretched out on the bed, but realized the towel she had been wearing around her body was nowhere to be found.

A sudden motion from the darkness made her tense up. She pulled the covers tightly around her body and peered toward the far corner, where the only chair stood. Her eyes strained to adjust, searching the shadows, but all she could make out was a vague outline sitting there.

Bravely, she demanded, "Who's there?"

Shawn came in the partial light and stood there again, glaring down at her.

Tori felt immense sadness, knowing she'd never forgive him, though her body still longed for him. Tears gathered. He would continue to haunt her, and once they discovered the baby, Duncan and Kevin would make sure she was never released. The thought brought a fresh wave of despair.

Only you can heal him.

Her tears immediately returned, running down her cheek.

Grabbing her wrist, he put them back above her head to the lock that seemed the same, although this one wasn't so high. And he stayed there over her, staring down at her. The light was shadowed away from his features, and she couldn't see.

Shawn huffed long, and she could feel his frustration, but what about her?

How dare he make it seem like she was being the difficult one?!

Tori turned her face away from him and tried to cry herself back to sleep.

She remembered the scars on his lower front body, the inside of his thighs, and even his phallus. Welts and burns that had long since healed physically, but she knew mentally were still open and bleeding. She also remembered that look, so deep in pain but with a wild pleasure and joy in his eyes, when she had kissed each one of those scars without judgment.

'Don't care! Don't care! Don't care!' Tori ordered herself, but her chest heaved with thick, shuddering sobs as she cried harder, pain suffocating her resolve.

After a few minutes, she heard him leave the room, but that still didn't stop her misery.

"You're going to get it together, Tori," Duncan said firmly.

Looking at the door, she was a little surprised to see he was standing there in some jogging pants and a tank, holding a small tray with water and some fruit. There was also a large backpack slung over one of his big shoulders.

She shot him a hard look of annoyance.

Duncan crossed to the table, set down the tray, then unfastened the restraints holding her arms. He reached behind the chair to turn on a standing lamp, creating a softer pool of light between them.

Looking at the skylight, she couldn't determine the time.

"Six a.m.," he answered. "Shawn said you slept all night."

Tori frowned as she rubbed her wrist.

"What?" Duncan questioned.

Her confusion befuddled his mind-reading skills, and she looked away.

"No, Tori. What was that, dammit?" he demanded, standing by her.

She realized that when she thought about another brother directly, Duncan couldn't use his mind-reading powers on her, and his frustration with her grew.

"Dammit, you speak to Kevin, who's been an ass to you, and you won't talk to Shawn or me. I can understand you not talking to Shawn, but-" He stopped himself and moved to his knees in front of her. "How many ways can I say sorry, Tori? I shouldn't have been a manipulating asshole to get my little brother to feel he needed to hurt you in order to heal, just so I could fulfill Kevin's and mine sexual fantasy. Is that what you want me to admit?"

Tori folded her arms tightly over her chest and continued to shoot hate bullets at him. What else could she get him to admit?

"I really am sorry for all the hurtful shit we did, Tori, but I can't regret it either because you've done more for our connection to each other than anyone or anything ever has." Duncan rested his hands on her knees, but she didn't snatch away, and she could see how that meant a lot to him. The way his whole body relaxed made her realize how uptight he had been, and her acceptance of even the slightest touch from him brought him immense relief.

Yet, on her end, Tori was a jumble of nerves even though he safely kept his hands on her knees in a non-sexual manner. It was taking everything in her not to fling her thighs wide apart and order him to dive in.

Listen here, whore! Don't you dare give in to your high sexual needs! Be angry! Be really angry! she reminded herself.

She forced her brows to furrow as he spoke further.

"Tori, for years Kevin and I were in hell trying to make up to Shawn what our mother did - even in her death, we couldn't sate the monster he had become, and I knew we couldn't go on. So, when the opportunity to meet you came up, my wheels started turning, but I didn't think... I didn't know how much you'd changed." Duncan had not made eye contact with her, and it was hard to determine if what he said was coming from his heart or if he was trying to carefully lay out his words so he could hide behind something more. "Feeling your lips on mine so long ago, feeling your body buzz with pleasure gave me decades of unconscious joy, and when I knew I could make a way to kiss you again to get you out of my system, I thought that was all I needed, but you turned the tables on me. You turned the tables on all of us, Tori. And we can't get enough of you." He finally raised his face to look at her, showing her a very vulnerable man searching for some response from her. "Tori, I do love you. I knew the second time I kissed you, I would never be able to get rid of you out of my system, no matter how much I tried to deny it, and I didn't want to."

Tori couldn't breathe and started to turn her face away from him, but Duncan gently cupped her face to keep her looking into his eyes.

"I'm not ashamed to admit how much I love you, Tori. And I hate myself for asking you to give your heart to us... All of us, because it's the only way Kevin and I can be free to love you unconditionally. And we want to with every fiber of our being. And I'll swear on my soul I'll spoil the fuck out of you until time ends."

Why the hell did he have to say that?

Tori couldn't stop herself from leaning in and kissing him,

almost knocking him back, but Duncan was quick to receive the kiss and pressed her back on the bed. Her arms moved around his neck, receiving his body onto hers. The moment his tongue pressed between her lips, she knew she would lose all self-control, but she didn't care. Tori parted her lips to devour his tongue, moaning loudly and rubbing her body against him.

Duncan suddenly broke the kiss, panting, "Tori! Fuck! We can't! I promised."

She pulled him back down to kiss her, needing his mouth just as much as she needed the next breath. And he was eating her kisses like a man dying of hunger as if she were his manna. It was Duncan's turn to groan, and the reverberation only tickled her all over, spurring her on to shoot her hand down into his jogging pants to grip his thickened phallus.

You're going to hate yourself! she scolded herself in the back of her mind as she felt Duncan rip the sheet from her body and then plunge down to put his lips on her breasts.

That was pretty much the last thoughts she had because Duncan's delicious mouth licking and sucking all over her chest made her sexually high, and it only took a couple of hard nudges with her hips grinding on his body to take her over the edge from his nipple manipulation.

The man's mouth on a nipple should be put in a bottle and sold because she swore he'd make a ba-jilion dollars from his technique. Her body was pulsing with a hard need driving her past common sense. Tori curved herself to pull his rock-hard manhood from his pants, and then, shoving all her weight against him, she rolled them over until Duncan was lying on his back in the bed, and she was straddling his waist. Their mouths found each other again, and at the same time, her sopping wet womanhood nearly swallowed half of him inside of her.

His chest bucked, but he was holding her so close that this only pushed him deeper into her.

Duncan groaned louder, and she kissed him harder to muffle him so the others wouldn't hear them.

At the same moment, she started rocking back and forth, throwing a circular jerk every three to four strokes.

They were both out of their minds, loving each moment, and not caring about the past, the present, or the future. Tori was in this moment with Duncan - their moment, wanting and needing on a spiritual level unknown to many and experienced by very few.

"Gawd, I love you," he panted over and over again.

Tears filled her, and she sobbed, shoving her face into his neck, sucking his skin so hard while her inner muscles from her stomach to her knees convulsed in waves so hard she thought her heart would just burst out of her chest. She thought for sure she had torn the skin from his body, and Duncan didn't stop her. As a matter of fact, he only held her tighter until he followed her lead, but at the same time, he grabbed her hair, pulled her face back, and reciprocated at her collarbone, a considerable area to suck on as he came inside of her, pumping up into her so viciously her teeth chattered.

And since Tori was still on her orgasm high, the added bonus of feeling his essence deep into her only escalated and returned her soul back into hot bliss that left no ounce of her blood burning.

He let go of her hair, and she collapsed on his body. Immediately, Duncan rolled her to his side, panting like someone had made all the air in the room disappear.

"Damn you, woman!" he sneered.

Tori only giggled wickedly and put her hand over his semi-hardened phallus to gather their lovemaking essence on her palm. He watched as she raised her hand to her mouth and licked their juices off.

"Fucccck," he hissed and kissed her hard.

His manhood twitched against her side, definitely trying to get roused for a round two, but a knock at the door stopped them both. Duncan quickly pulled his pants up and lay his top body on her as if to cover up the mess between her legs.

She had to strain to look up as the door opened, and Shawn stood there in their compromising position.

Tori's demeanor instantly changed, seeing that it was the little brother, because she was sure that if it had been Kevin, she would have definitely tried to entice him to join in.

"I thought you were coming back down before I left for work after you-" Shawn stopped and looked at her and then Duncan. "What the fuck, Dunc?"

Duncan jumped up defensively as Tori pulled the sheet over her body. "I can explain-"

Shawn hissed, "You were supposed to come up and get the name of her birth control, Duncan, not fuck her! You know she hasn't had them since-"

"I know!" Duncan exclaimed.

Tori turned away from Shawn and smiled, feeling no guilt at all. She even exaggerated a stretch and wiggled her toes.

Shawn came to the bed. "I couldn't find her messenger bag. I'll stop at the house to look for it. Did you get the name of her birth control?"

Standing up, facing Shawn with the bed between her, Tori folded her arms over her chest as if she were getting ready for battle. The intensity in his eyes showed he was debating his own arousal, and she could almost feel him wanting to come to her and have at her. Running her eyes down his body, she could see his manhood was pressed against the front of his pants. His arousal did affect her, but she refused to show him anything.

"We didn't get that far," Duncan admitted, reaching into his jogging pants and pulling out a pencil and paper.

They both looked at her, and she sighed, snatching the items from Duncan and writing down the name of birth control. Deliberately, she passed the paper and pencil back to Duncan and then turned herself partially away from Shawn to let him know she was still pissed at him.

"I'll bring her birth control and Plan B pill when I get home from work," Shawn said with his eyes locked on Tori as Duncan handed him the paper. "Until then, keep your dick to yourself, Duncan!"

As soon as the door was closed, Duncan pulled her body against his until her back was molded against his chest. leaning close to her ears, he said, "Since he's bringing the Plan B, we could-"

She didn't let him finish, turning into his arms and kissing him.

He lifted her body, not breaking the kiss, and carried her to the shower. They'd refresh themselves, and then she hoped that before Shawn came home, they could go to round three.

Once she got away from them, Tori had eighteen years to be angry at what they did. But for now, she needed some of Duncan, and she knew she could get a lot of Kevin. Shawn could go to hell!

CHAPTER 11
Hickies

Two hours later, they were sexually sated and had taken a short nap.

Tori awoke to small light back scratches still lying on the side of Duncan. The bed was messed up, but she didn't care.

During this entire time, the only time she used her voice was to moan and cry out, because Duncan was determined to ensure she enjoyed herself. The man was a giver-in and out of bed, and it killed her to be so angry at him when her heart wanted to soothe him.

"We fucked up with you, Tori, I know it," he said quietly as his fingers drew little circles all over her back. "The moment I knew I kissed you again, I knew we fucked up, but there was no way to turn around once this plan was in motion. The change in Shawn and seeing him happy for once in his whole damn life brought us together. And you were there holding us together, and we've never felt so close, even with our mother." He was quiet for a moment as he nuzzled his face in the top of her head like a large feline, leaving his scent possessively on her. "It's going to take a lifetime to make up for what we did to you, but I still need your help with Shawn. I'd help you in any way possible."

She stiffened because she couldn't make herself want to fix things with Shawn.

Duncan gently pulled her chin so she looked down at him. "I will promise you the world if you help me, Tori. Anything you desire."

Tori harshly expelled the breath she had been holding and finally spoke, "To be left alone, and never hear any of you say my name again. And you can't tell Kevin or Shawn this promise we made."

Duncan looked as if she had stabbed him in the chest. His hand even moved up to his heart as if he were trying to stop the bleeding. "You mean you still want to go away and leave us?"

"Duncan, realistically, our relationship could never work in the real world, but if I can help heal Shawn and get him to release you two from this indomitable hold he has on you two, then you have to swear to leave me be and never bother me ever again." She knew these words hurt him, and they were difficult to say, but she knew if she wanted peace and happiness, it couldn't be with them while trying to raise a child. "If I do this, you have to help me leave from here, Duncan, and never tell your brothers where I've gone."

"You'd still walk away with absolutely nothing and never see us again?" he skeptically asked.

Without hesitation, Tori said, "Yes, Duncan. I would. And I wouldn't press any charges against any of you."

"But would you forgive us?"

"I would not only forgive you, I would forget you. It would be the only way to go on for me."

Duncan sat up in bed as if it were hard to breathe, and she could see that he was trying to think of every scenario and how he could work it to his advantage. However, his frown deepened as if he knew he had to accept her terms.

Leaning his forehead into her collarbone, where the large love bite was, he sadly responded, "You're asking me to let you go and then betray my brothers."

Tori wrapped her arms around him and pressed her face against the side of his so her lips were at his ear. In a whisper, she said, "If you love me, Duncan..." She left the statement open on purpose, and she could feel his arms move around her body to hold her close.

After a long moment, he conceded. "Yes, Tori, I will help you."

She squeezed him harder in appreciation. If she had known it would be so easy to get her freedom, she would have jumped his bones days ago, before she took her away from the main house.

To brighten the mood, Duncan offered, "What if I take you out of this room and show you the house?"

Raising her arms to look down at him, Tori narrowed her eyes suspiciously, wondering what the catch was.

"You don't have to talk to me if you don't want to, but in return, I will have to put something on you to assure you can't get away, Tori. That's the only way I can give you a tour."

With a frown, she looked away for a moment to think, and then she nodded. Oddly, he was excited to show her the house he had built, but in return, she knew she would have to pretend she wasn't that mad about being kidnapped, and whatever contraption he was going to put on her, she would have to be okay with it. This could give her an opportunity to see where she was exactly and how she could get out of there.

Gently, Duncan pulled her lips to him and kissed her as a reward. "Good. Let's eat, and then we'll go. I want to show you so much."

And she would make sure she took note of everything. There had to be a way to get off this so-called island.

The bowl of oatmeal was still moderately warm on a self-heating tray, and the mixed fruits were a good morning treat. The coffee was just delicious, and she knew it had been freshly brewed.

If there was one thing about these brothers, it was that they fed her the most delicious food, and she knew she would miss that the most.

"So when did it start? Your undaunting allegiance to Shawn?" she questioned as they ate.

Duncan answered immediately without thought, "The night Amos disappeared, or I guess that night Amos died, now that we know the truth. When Shawn crawled into bed with us and fell asleep, Kevin and I swore we would protect him and help him heal from all the shit that had been done to him. And we thought now that Amos was gone, life would get better. Well, you know that part. But when Ma couldn't have Keir to herself, well, she punished Shawn. By that time, I had joined the Army because the apartment had become unbearable, and Kevin was sent to the streets because he was tired of Ma trying to control us as well. We didn't know the extent of what she did to him."

"So it was worse once Keir made the choice to stay away," she surmised.

"Much, much worse." His eyes wandered to something horrible, and Tori decided not to press it.

He gathered all their dishes and encouraged her to freshen up, while he put the tray outside the door.

When Tori came out of the bathroom, Duncan pulled off his tank top and gave it to her.

Happily, she dropped the sheet and put on the tank. He then pulled a large jewelry box from behind him, giving her a proud peck on her cheek. Opening the box, she looked at him with full inquiry.

In the box was a John Hardy silver choker, resembling a jeweled rope wrapped around an ultra-fine pave clasp set with diamonds and four small red rubies that matched her ring.

"What's this?"

"A choker," he said, obviously.

"I know that, and it's very expensive. Why?"

"Because it's beautiful," he said, taking it out of the box and putting it around her neck. It was cool to the touch, and it didn't feel heavy, but she knew there was weight to it, indicating that this piece of jewelry was very expensive. When the clasp was in place, she heard a high-pitched beep as if something had been activated.

Tori inquired, "What was that noise?"

"That was the device that was embedded in the choker, activating. The entire island has a perimeter fence, and if you get within two feet of it, the choker activates and alerts us. We'll also be able to find you no matter where you are on the island, and if you decide to escape, you won't like it."

"What? You put a collar on me?"

He coolly corrected her. "It's a choker."

"Oh hell no," she hissed, and tried to unclasp the jewelry from around her neck, but she couldn't. The clasp was somehow locked in place. "Take it off."

"Tori, you agreed," he said.

"To wear a leash?"

"It's a choker."

"Duncan, if you say choker one more time, I'm going to knock your two front teeth out."

He snorted in amusement. "You can't do that, Tori, your hands are much too delicate. Now come on." He'd already opened the thick wooden door and extended his hand.

Huffing, she took his hand and let him lead her out. The

hallway was long on either end, and she assumed this wasn't the only room on this floor, but the brick wall in front of her felt like they were in a hidden area of the house. Just as she knew, there was a long table against the wall where he kept his phone and anything else that had been in his wallet.

He quickly stuffed everything in his pockets and then knelt down to retrieve some soft house shoes to put on her feet.

She hated to admit he was being extra sweet. And despite some cruelty, all three brothers' small acts of kindness were getting to her. Yet, she had to resist this because she needed to get out of there sooner rather than later, especially before they tried to shove a Plan B down her throat.

When she had stepped into her house shoes, Duncan took her hand again and led her to a narrow spiral staircase that took her down two floors to another thick oak door, which even he had to use his shoulder to push open.

This door opened to a very large hallway in the rear of a huge colonial house with barely any furniture.

When he closed the door, she saw that it was flush with the wall, and if anyone didn't know the house, they wouldn't know that this stairway or the bedrooms above were part of the house.

That thought gave her a chill, but she focused on Duncan showing her around, gauging where she was and how far she was from the city. Every window had a gorgeous view of water, and she noted Duncan had purposely placed the house in the perfect location. He stated that the island had about thirty acres of space, and then there were about ten acres of swamp running through it. He'd mapped it out completely so he could understand where to build the house.

Since she hadn't had a tour of the other house, she was wide-eyed and impressed with this one. Duncan received this island fifteen years ago - actually two islands, but he had sold the other one to a prominent family that had just moved to Metro Detroit. He'd taken the smaller of the land masses and rebuilt the house in Detroit because he liked the way the house there was built.

"Since we can't build a basement, a lot of things that would be in a basement were added as an addition to this house," Duncan said. "Although the family room is being used as a weight room, and then the solarium was completely off the plans, I have a small love for plants. I do plan on placing some containers on the land, but that's for a future bigger project." There was a secret twinkle in his eye, and he looked away to avoid her reading his face for too long, as he proceeded to explain. "Our bedrooms are on the third floor of this house. Each one of us has our own room." He reached into a closet to pull out a thick brown fur coat that reached all he way to the ground. “Put that on,” he instructed.

She couldn’t believe how perfectly it fit her and knew it was very expensive.

He took her past a large kitchen and out to a deck with a fenced-in backyard. On his way, he grabbed a small box she remembered he had put roasted chicpeas in before, and she greedily took it from him before he offered it to her.

"I take it you love those."

"Yes," she admitted, popping a handful in her mouth. "I think it's the crunchiness, and it keeps me away from craving all the junk food I used to eat."

"I'm shocked you haven't thought you could have gotten pregnant earlier if you've been eating them," he noted.

Frowning, she asked, "What's that supposed to mean?"

“Chicpeas have high folic acid in them. A lot of women swear it got them pregnant."

Tori instantly stopped eating them and narrowed her eyes at him. "Was that your intention, Duncan?"

"I only learned recently when a young chef was at the

restaurant where I was cooking up a second batch for you," he admitted. "I thought it was funny."

While they were on the subject, she quickly challenged him. "And what if I did get pregnant?"

He shrugged as if it were no big deal. "It'd be fine with me, and I wouldn't care who the father was. I'd raise it like my own. I think all of us wouldn't mind getting you nice and pregnant. Kevin has a breeding kink, if you didn't know. And we'd make better fathers together than apart."

That instantly gave her an idea of whether she could get to Kevin before Shawn brought the Plan B back.

Duncan continued explaining the property. There was a separate fence with a covered pool, as well as a basketball court. Past the pool, he was building a large jacuzzi, which would be next to a solar house he was adding to the island. The power grid on the island was old and often knocked out by heavy storms, but once he finished the off-grid system, he could power a small town.

Looking back at the house, Tori realized he'd only shown her the first floor. There was a secondary staircase right before the kitchen, but he hadn't taken her that way. "What's on the second floor?" she inquired.

"More bedrooms and a library. No books but the one in the city have very little. We've yet to make it a home at either place."

She hauled off and hit him in his arm, and he pretended it hurt, but there was still that wicked twinkle in his eye. "I know what you're trying to do, Duncan, and it won't work."

"What?" he feigned innocence.

"You're half crazy if you think I'm even thinking about trying to stay and be married to... to even imply or-" She hit him again on his other arm.

"Okay, now that's starting to hurt, Tori," he said, rubbing where she had hit him. "And I never implied marriage because it'd be illegal for all three of us, but a small commitment ceremony in the solarium to bring us-"

"Shut up, Duncan! No! You promised."

"I will keep my promise, but you could always change your mind."

Tori couldn't believe the audacity and how calm Duncan spoke, as if it should be her obvious choice after what they were doing to her. "Get this through your thick head, you manipulating ass! I will never! NEVER even think about staying around for you all to hurt me ever again."

"But we love you, Tori," Kevin said, dropping his work bag in a mini outside shed on the deck and closing it up. "And we know we fucked up."

She turned away from Duncan to face Kevin, trying not to be glad he arrived. "Duncan already went in about that, which makes his assumptions even more stupid!" she admonished.

Kevin moved up to her and gently kissed her on the cheek. "It's not stupid, Tori, if we want you in our lives and we're going to spend a lifetime making up for this shit. Duncan even-"

"I didn't get that far," Duncan hissed. "Why do you always open your big ass mouth, Kevin?"

Tori stepped away from both of them. "You think I'm going to get your brother's head space together, make it all right for all of you, and just forget the shit you've done and stay here with you all forever?"

They looked at each other and then at her.

"It's the obvious choice, Tori," Kevin said.

"You couldn't love me enough-"

Kevin cut her off. "I couldn't by myself. You're too much for one man, but all three of us could."

Being offended, she asked, "Too much?"

Kevin said, "Tori, don't say it like it's bad. You're deserving of whatever love you desire. You've looked inside yourself, seen the bad parts, and changed for the better. Not for someone else, not for the world, but for you, and that's got you more beautiful than you could even imagine. Duncan saw it, and I see it now; soon, Shawn will not be able to help himself and see it. And you're perfect for us."

Tori was getting overwhelmed by this verbal affection from both of them and huffed in exasperation.

"Damn Duncan!" Kevin changed the conversation abruptly in a teasing tone, moving the coat open and seeing Duncan's masterpiece near her collarbone. "Did you fucking try to eat her? She's got a hickey the size of Maine on her damn chest!"

The tank top Duncan offered, of course, was too baggy, and by now the love mark he'd left was starting to clot.

"I bet Shawn was pissed. He thought I'd break first," Kevin said triumphantly.

"He's bringing Plan B home for her," Duncan added. "And she started it."

"Oh damn," Kevin said and pulled Tori into his arms. "Well, since we're being naughty, can I start something?"

Why didn't she push away? Why did her body heat up like a damn furnace in a blaze of sexual lust, loving how his manhood pressed against her stomach? She even trembled.

Trying to distract herself, she asked, "Shouldn't you be at work?"

"Took off," he answered, dolling kisses on her face, neck, and collarbone. Long, luscious kisses that were taking away from her resolve to be upset at him. "Couldn't stop thinking about you, Tori, and I wanted to eat you for lunch." He dipped into her mouth and, hungering, plunged his tongue inside, swirling about, drawing out whatever fight she was trying to muster to resist him.

Tori sighed, wrapping her arms around his neck and pressing herself more against him as he gripped her ass cheeks.

"I haven't shown her the solarium's shower and relaxation area," Duncan mentioned, taking the box of chickpeas away she'd been gripping in her hands and then helping her off with her fur coat. With the heat vibrating from Kevin, she was warm enough. "She can help you get cleaned up, while I get a light lunch ready."

Becoming discombobulated by Kevin's kisses, Tori knew he carried her somewhere, but was so damn distracted by her own sex almost leaking from her. The solarium could be accessed from the deck and enclosed space, featuring edible and large tropical plants. There were heated floors, and the temperature was warm enough. If one continued, they would end up in the back, where there was an outdoor shower with more heated floors, and to the left, a large open space with a huge living room area with a unit to cool down or heat up.

Kevin headed to the shower, which mimicked the sound of rainfall. No walls were around them, and all the plants received the benefit from the water in some way. She could see natural castor soap had been placed out there to clean up, and a waterproof closet most likely held towels.

Before he put her down on the ground, he was pulling the tank top off of her and had knocked her shoes off somewhere along the path to where they had come.

Tori tugged at the choker. "Can it get wet?"

"Nice try, Princess," he chuckled, rapidly undressing himself and then pulling her under the water.

Showering with Kevin was like that night in the shed, but this time, she could soap him up. His well-muscled body, similar to his brothers, aroused her with his light brown skin. She loved that he had every scar from his childhood, and being a man who worked hard, he also played harder. So many guys she'd dated had lived a soft life, but not Duncan and Kevin, and that aroused her so much about their bodies. Kevin didn't hold back his roughness, and she needed that firm grip on her skin, the hard kisses, and the all-around roughness he gave her.

His mouth moved down her chest and stomach, as he dropped to his knees, so she could wash his head and back together. He pulled her thigh over his shoulder, taking his lunch while she tried to scrub his neck, shoulders, and upper back. He lingered purposely on the inside of her thigh, sucking an area bigger than what Duncan had done on her chest, and Tori knew that was going to leave an enormous mark later.

She liked how they tried to top each other, and if she did decide to stay, Tori knew she would be well sated with each of them. Yes, she needed more than one man to sate her appetite. Perhaps she'd jealously show off her hickies to Shawn later and watch as he wished he could stop hating her enough to put one on her too.

Tori was glad Kevin held onto her body hard because she could barely stand up or concentrate on her chore at hand while his tongue delved all around her lower lips, licking and sucking and then dipping inside of her greedily for more. He was determined to take all he could get, and by the end, Tori was giving him some more, forgetting about washing his back, while her nails raked over his skin, clawing in passion as his mouth brought her to a beautiful fruition.

And she just adored how he didn't stop because he'd brought her to climax. Kevin lovingly lingered between her legs, getting the remnants of her essence like he was licking crumbs from a plate. She could watch him eat her out all day and night…

But you won't! You need to get to business at hand and ask him for the favor! she ordered herself.

CHAPTER 12
The Past is the Past

Kevin stood up abruptly and, with a growl, yanked her up on his body, impaling her on his massive, hard-on. They both moaned melodiously, and somehow he made it over to the waterproof sectional where he lay her back and then plunged even deeper into her. His rough, long strokes took her back up to sexual heights she loved.

"Gawd, you're fucking gripping my dick, Tori! Gawd, I love your pussy. Gawd, I want you fucking morning, noon, and..."

Tori gripped him extra tight to shut him up because damn if her heart was about to pop out of her throat from the ecstasy exploding all through her.

Damn his words!

Kevin jammed down into her so hard, she was sure something cracked, but she didn't care because she was so far gone, feeling his body fill her up. And then he collapsed on her body with a satisfied chuckle.

Tori fought to stay conscious because she needed this moment before she knew Duncan was going to come join them.

Still breathless, she cradled Kevin's head and lightly ran her fingers up and down his back. "Kevin, can I ask you a favor?"

He only grunted with a nod as breathless as she.

"Can you help me not take the Plan B?"

Instantly, he raised his head and gave her a hard, sharp look. "Tori, what the fuck?"

"Hear me out," she said hurriedly, not stopping to rub his back, especially because she could feel the goosebumps under her nails, which meant his skin was thoroughly enjoying the touch. "Yes, I know I haven't taken my birth control pills, and I know we've had unprotected sex, but the Plan B can be taken five days from now. Can't we wait while all the time, we could be doing so much more in sex?" She made sure to give him a nice, juicy kiss to follow the temptation.

That hard look of his softened, and one inquisitive brow shot up, making him adorable as fuck.

"Shawn would never agree to that," he said.

"But does he have to know?" she inquired, giving him another luscious kiss to his cheek and neck. "No one has to know but you and me. You could tell him you gave it to me. But in truth, I promise to take it in five days." Leaning in close to whisper, "And I bet baby-making sex feels so fucking good."

His semi-hardened phallus twitched. "Four," he growled.

"Okay, fine, four days and in twelve hours after that, I will take the next one. No complaints or fights," she quickly agreed. "And we'll keep it a secret between us." Tori deliberately nipped at his lips, and Kevin started becoming aroused again.

Loving that she had gotten her way, Tori easily indulged in another round of sex with Kevin, giving her all. When she was nice and sated for the night, she would figure out a way to get out of there. She had four days!

By the time Duncan came to them, Kevin had her over the

side of the couch and was stroking her so good from the back that her eyes had rolled up into the back of her head. Duncan sat by her head, and once she knew he was there, she pulled down the front of his pants and engulfed his semi-hardness in her mouth.

The feel of him in her mouth, while Kevin indulged her from the back, was so much, and Tori found herself cumming so hard she could feel it running down her legs.

Kevin shortly followed, and she crawled onto Duncan's lap and took him inside. He was ready by then and had pushed down his pants to give them both more room.

He only held himself inside of her, but ground her hips slowly, keeping her highly aroused.

Tori shuddered and shook, while Duncan indulged in sucking on her breast. Occasionally, Kevin would stick a well-lubed thumb up her rear, bringing her again to high arousal, while he stroked himself and watched them.

She had lost count of her body, which had gone off its rocker, and by then she knew time was a construct and had no meaning in the pleasurable bliss erasing away anything she should have been angry or concerned about.

By this time, Duncan was so hard that he was gasping at each movement she made, and finally allowed her to build her own rhythm to bring them to their peak. She loved how he pulled her chest hard against his bare chest and held her close, nuzzling his face in his neck, but she could still feel his mumbles of appreciation, calling out her name over and over again.

Tori was dizzy with satisfaction like she'd been injected with a drug that was making her high, but there was something still missing, and she hated knowing that deep inside, she wished Shawn were there enjoying these moments with them.

"Does it get better and better each time?" she asked out loud, randomly.

Kevin chuckled, handing Duncan a slightly damped washcloth. "It's supposed to, Tori," he said. "Especially when all of us are together."

She hated that he pointed that out, and she was wondering if Duncan was rubbing off on Kevin with special mind-reading powers.

Duncan lifted her off of him and dabbed at her so she could at least get up without leaking. And then he cleaned himself as he nodded to another clean tank top, socks, and some trunks she could wear. "Get dressed so we can have lunch."

The older brother was already lifting a table from one of the sectionals, low enough for them to sit around and eat.

She was starting to think clothing for her would be optional, but she felt like every time she was offered some, it was a treat. Opting not to put on the trunks until she could shower again, which she would do after they ate, Tori looked around for a sink.

"Past the cabinet is a bathroom," Duncan instructed her, passing her the washcloth.

Tori darted to empty her bladder, wash her face, chest, and between her legs, before rejoining them, sitting between them as Kevin poured sparkling grape juice. Internally, she was grateful it wasn't wine or liquor because she knew she would have to make excuses not to drink it, or they could get suspicious about her condition.

In the mirror, she could see that somehow Duncan had tried to make the mark he'd made on her a little larger because Kevin had covered a significant surface on the area between her thigh. She giggled at their competition with her body, but then she bit her tongue to punish herself for enjoying their sick-sibling rivalry.

Duncan made a tuna salad with chickpeas, sweet dill pickles, and red onions, with fresh sourdough bread and colorful chard.

"I haven't eaten healthy in so long, my body must be asking all kinds of questions," she relished taking huge bites of her sandwich.

"Why did you eat so horribly before?" Duncan questioned. "When I cleaned out your kitchen, I swear you had every preservative known to man and not a vegetable to boot."

Tori shrugged. "I was never really told how to eat. My father... Keri, let me eat whatever I want. My mother didn't care and didn't allow anyone to discipline me." She sighed. "Keir never told me no, but deep down inside, I wish he had put a firm hand in my life because it was difficult to parent myself when I didn't have a good role model. He wasn't a parent to me, really. More like a guardian. I realized after a while I parented myself." That heavy guilt filled her.

"You glow now," Kevin noticed. "You have this sense of ownership over your life, and I think that's what attracted us all to you. That you changed yourself for the better, not because someone forced you to, but because you wanted to. That says a lot about you as a person, Tori."

"Thanks, Kevin, or it could be good sex," she said, trying to get the attention off her appearance. "What made the two of you realize you like having a woman together?"

The brothers looked at each other as if having a brief internal conversation before Kevin said, "Dunc didn't like approaching women, so I'd bring them back to our place, warm them up until they didn't care who gave it to them, and then watch my brother enjoy himself. It was something about being with him, in the same room, that I felt comfortable; that I could feel vulnerable and really enjoy myself." He looked at Duncan. "And then once I was so fucking horny, I couldn't wait for him to take his sweet damn time to finish and just slipped in from behind. And we both agreed that we had to do that again but found that not many women want to; we can be overwhelming. And when Duncan served and we didn't see each other, I tried others, but it wasn't the same."

She glanced over at Duncan, who only nodded in agreement.

"Being together did something for us," Kevin said. "Brought us together in a way we enjoy."

"But what does it do for you?" she pressed.

"That's just like asking what it does for you, Tori?" Duncan challenged.

Remembering the few times they'd done it, she answered, "I like how I feel connected on a metaphysical level." Remembering earlier how she felt a sense of loss without Shawn there, she admitted, "And I honestly don't think I could have that with someone else other than you all."

"And it's just like that for us, but even more," Duncan responded. "And being that we're brothers, it just brings us to those times when things were bad and we got that chance to lie in bed together, when we were little, and it gave us all comfort. It was the first time in a very long time that we've felt like that when we were with you, Tori. You connect us. You comfort us."

Why did they have to say things like that and make her chest feel funny? "That still won't-"

Duncan cut her off. "I didn't say it to convince you to change your mind or not be mad at us anymore, Tori. I said it because it's the truth, and you should be aware of the power you have over us. All of us. We crave that feeling like a drug, and we've realized only you can give us that."

Kevin cosigned, "So we're at your beck and call. You have power over us, and we don't give a damn what we have to do to make you feel safe and loved. As you can see, we lose all control when it comes to you, and we will break all rules for you, Tori."

She covered her ears, closed her eyes, and took several deep breaths. All this meant was that she would have to do whatever it took to get off the island, because they had no reason to let her go. "You have to give me a moment," she said, looking at them.

"We'll give you anything you ask for, and deep inside Tori, you know you have all of us wrapped around your finger," Duncan responded. "Now all we need you to do is harness that power and bring Shawn into the light."

"And probably lick his ass too," Kevin added. "Norman told me once he liked that, but Norman didn't like to do that."

Tori blushed, remembering the several times she had delved her lips close, but that was because she had licked around his scrotum and perineum, but Shawn had gone mindless whenever she got close. Why was she imagining pushing his cheeks apart and just delving into...

Stop! she warned herself.

"And what could I do, other than lick his ass to help him heal?" she asked them, vulgarly irritated by how they were so insistent that she was the answer to their prayers for Shawn, but Tori just couldn't understand how.

"Tori, I'm not one to take note of things," Kevin admitted. "But a blind man can see you're the first person who has ever affected Shawn. He's allowed himself to become vulnerable with you; that dark side of him disappears when I see him with you."

"How do you know it's not because we're all together?"

"No, Tori. It really is with you. Shawn's never danced with anyone except Ma," Kevin insisted. "He's made it a point to never dance with anyone after Ma passed, and even when we started this endeavor, he said he wasn't going to do it, but did you see him in that blue room? He put on his best moves out, and then at the restaurant, he was a dancing fool. And he stayed on the sidelines and watched you the whole time? He's always watching you. That's not Shawn. He never gave a fuck about anyone like he does about you, Tori."

"Maybe I don't believe you because I don't know this Shawn you speak of. Only that person who ripped everything out of my life and left me desolate," she snarled. "This Shawn you speak of, how do you even know I'll care for him like I do you two?" She covered her mouth, not believing she had said that out loud.

Duncan and Kevin smiled with their whole damn face, and her heart surged in palpitations.

The middle brother moved close to her and pulled her to him, so she leaned in his arms as he cupped her face, forcing her to look up at him. "Tori, I know you would never say this unless it hurt you, but you know deep inside who Shawn really is now."

A gut feeling started to warm in her stomach, and her eyes diverted over Duncan's shoulders to meet with Shawn's, who was peaking around the corner of the solarium. He was far enough away that he probably couldn't hear all their conversation, but he didn't make a move to come to them, yet she knew he was staring at her and looked jealous that she was in Duncan's arms.

"But there is a lot you don't know about him that he's kept from you," Kevin admitted, moving behind her and rubbing a soothing hand on her back and thighs.

"Can't you tell me what's wrong with him?" she demanded.

"No," both of them said simultaneously.

Duncan continued to answer her. "It's something Shawn has to come to terms with and allow you permission to see for yourself."

A chill swept through her, and Duncan held her closer, brushing his lips over hers. "It's alright to be scared, Tori,"

Duncan whispered. "But once he gives himself and his heart to you, he will forever be changed."

She could feel a sob building in her chest.

Kevin leaned close to her ear and whispered, "He will finally understand what Duncan and I understand."

Their voices seem to already be in her head, echoing the popular quote: *'If you love someone, let them go.' If they come back, it was meant to be.*

Tori shut her eyes tight again because she wanted to resist the pain in her heart, knowing she would leave this place and never ever come back! No matter what her body or heart wanted!

And just to make Shawn jealous even more, she kissed Duncan passionately and then easily twisted to kiss Kevin. While she was kissing Kevin, Duncan dipped down, raised her shirt, and began licking and sucking her nipples.

Yes, she enjoyed that and was in even more enjoyment knowing Shawn watched them from afar.

She moved her hands down to Kevin's jogging pants and moved her hand inside. The feel of his hardness ready to go again tantalized her, and when she leaned back more, she was laid on the couch and was able to dip down and take him down her throat.

Duncan continued his beautiful oral ministrations while his other hand moved down her body, and she could feel his finger dip into her soppiness. Filled to the brim already from their earlier lovemaking, the sloshing sound, mixed with Duncan's licking, Kevin's groaning, and her sucking, was a euphonous melody that inflamed all their senses! ALL of them.

"What the hell are you all doing?!" Shawn sneered, slamming his fists on the table.

She wasn't startled, and neither were Duncan or Kevin, but they did stop their foreplay with very amused, disappointed looks on their faces as they looked up at Shawn's angry visage. The younger brother's display of vexation sent them into chuckles, snorts, and giggles.

Kevin responded between chortles, "Enjoying ourselves, Shawn."

"Did you both knuckleheads forget she hasn't taken her pill in almost three days?" Shawn argued.

Tori's humor suddenly vanished as she saw that he was carrying a bag from the pharmacy, and she moved toward Kevin to hopefully remind him of his promise.

Kevin insisted, "So give me the Plan B and after we're done, we'll make sure she takes-"

"No!" Shawn said, hitting the table again. "She needs to take it now, and in the morning, she can take the next one. And we'll go back to the plan that WE don't fuck her for any reason."

Duncan huffed in irritation and shot a look at Kevin before raising his eyes up to the ceiling.

"You're scaring her, Shawn," Kevin said, standing up and letting Tori stand slightly behind him, while Duncan also handed her the trunks he'd given her.

"Jezzzzusssss!" Shawn exclaimed, looking at Tori's chest, and then his eyes moved down to her thigh. "What the hell did you do to-" He'd stopped yelling at the top of his lungs, and his eyes widened in initial horror and then turned into an animalistic, lustful gaze.

Tori looked down to see what Shawn was looking at and gasped. From their foreplay and gravity, the remnants of earlier lovemaking with the older brothers started running down her leg. It was almost at her knees as she slowly looked back up to see his tongue darting over his lips.

Moving more behind Kevin, she looked over at Duncan for help.

Duncan jumped up and snatched the pharmacy bag from Shawn and then tossed it to Kevin with a nod.

"I'll take her up to her room and make sure she takes it," Kevin assured his little brother, scooping Tori up and carrying her out of the room.

Tori nuzzled Kevin's neck in gratefulness, but she was watching Shawn covertly as the younger brother glared at her.

"Leave the other one!" Shawn yelled, but Kevin was taking hurried, long strides and didn't put her down until they reached the secret door. He reached up high to push at a candle affixed to the wall - too high for her to reach - and a powerful gust of air pumped, cracking the heavy door open enough for him to pull it open and get them inside.

She was holding her hand down between her legs because she was still slightly leaking, and Kevin chuckled as he lifted her again, took the steps two at a time, and didn't stop until they were inside the room and took her straight into the bathroom.

"We filled you too much, but damn if that breeding kink made me fucking hard," he said, tossing the pharmacy bag on the counter while she quickly started the shower and took off her clothes.

Immediately, Tori went to the bathroom, feeling no discomfort. Kevin stayed in the bathroom because he was pulling everything from the pharmacy bag.

"I'm such a harlot!" she declared, flushing the toilet, noting she was filled to the brim with two men-brothers! And if she wasn't so pissed off at Shawn, she'd probably have insisted he join in the fray.

Kevin firmly grabbed her chin with a disapproving glare in his eyes. "Didn't I tell you never to speak down on yourself about your sexual needs and desires for us, Tori?"

"But it's true. I should be so angry I shouldn't allow any of you to touch me, but I'm so damn-"

He reached around and smacked her butt. The blow wasn't playful and stung.

"Not another fucking word, or I'll put you over my lap and tap that ass for every horrible word you sputter about yourself. And each lick will get harder and harder, because we never want you to think you're beneath anyone, because you enjoy our touch. You're not out there on the streets just letting any man touch you, and even if you tried, we wouldn't let you. You only allow us the pleasure, and that means you're our woman, not our slut, harlot, or whore. OUR WOMAN, Tori. Do you understand, Princess?"

Why the fuck did he have to say those things?! And her butt still stung, but she was almost tempted to refute this to get some more firm smacks on her rear to see if she really enjoyed being smacked hard or not?

Tori raised on her tiptoes and softly kissed his cheek with an obedient nod.

Kevin returned to the pharmacy bag and tore open the Plan B package after he handed her the birth control. She briefly wondered how Shawn knew what pills she took but carefully watched Kevin.

He took both pills, tossed them in the shower, and stomped them down the drain. He tossed the package of the first pill away, but he put the package of the second pill in his jogging pants.

"Shawn will bring it in the morning but know it's a placebo. I know I have some aspirin that looks like that. It'll be safe to take," he assured her. "Are you going to take your birth control pill now?"

She put it in her drawer but took out one of the pills and tossed it in the shower as well. "I got four days to play around and enjoy your breeding kink."

CHAPTER 13

Tori Heals

Kevin chuckled wickedly and kissed her hard, full of passion.

Even if someone was listening outside the door, Tori knew they wouldn't have heard them over the shower, and she returned his kisses in gratefulness, with just as much passion, if not more.

Kevin took his clothes off and joined her in the shower, turning playful as they made a game of how soapy they could get each other. Tori couldn't stop herself from howling in laughter.

It felt refreshing, and she realized Kevin was only like this with her because he was letting his guard down, choosing to be vulnerable. This awareness shifted her own feelings, making her cherish the playful moment even more.

Just like they said, Shawn was different with her; Duncan and Kevin were also different with her.

Perhaps she could reach Shawn, but he was being an annoying prick, and she could wait another day to concentrate on him.

For now, she found herself having too much fun with

Kevin. After finally getting out of the shower and redressing, the mood remained playful as he chased her around the room, towel in hand as if he was still angry.

They must've made so much noise. Shawn banged on the door outside the room and demanded that Tori get some rest.

"That pill needs to fucking settle, Kevin! Stop fucking around with her!"

Kevin whispered, "That's just love talking. He sounds like a grouchy old lady."

And they both burst out howling in laughter, both knowing Shawn was clearly jealous that he couldn't be there with Tori like he wanted.

Kevin kissed her forehead and guided her to get under the covers, then lay beside her.

She remembered the tattoo on his chest and pressed her hand there. "What was that for?"

He flinched as if something had hurt him from the inside out, and then his hand moved up to cover hers. "A little girl who never had a chance in this world. I got a girl pregnant and my mother…" He paused to catch himself again as if someone had stabbed his chest. "I found her lying in the gutters. She lost the baby. Sherrie said she wasn't going to have any bastard grandkids as long as she was alive. No one could ever prove what was done, but I knew. I knew I would never have anything."

Feeling his pain, Tori kissed his cheek. "I wish I knew."

Kissing her palm and returning her hand over his heart, Kevin smiled. "She was terrified of you, Tori, and maybe if we had loved you back then like this-"

"I was a child, remember." She wrapped her arms around him and pulled his head to her chest. Kevin rested there, taking deep, long breaths, needing her closeness.

"Thank you, Tori," he barely whispered. "Thank you for taking my pain away."

She stroked the back of his head, wishing those words didn't make her want to love him so hard. At the same time, she wished she could have made Sherrie pay for hurting her boys.

"Maybe Keir was lucky you were selfish and didn't even know it, Tori," Kevin murmured, raising up and looking at her. "Maybe she knew if we liked you too, you'd have everything she wished for."

"What was that?"

"To be loved, adored, and worshipped by all of us."

Tori knew he was right—if she let herself, she could love them all, but then she'd owe love in return.

Old habits told her to use him, but the idea left her feeling sick.

"No more locking my arms?" she asked.

"No." He tapped the choker. "That's all over the island, so you can't get out of here even if you tried with damn near almost stopping your heart, or someone shuts down the system. As a matter of fact, Duncan said once he convinced you to wear that contraption, you'll have free rein around the house. When I leave, I'll make sure to leave that door slightly cracked so you can slip out if you want to go to the kitchen. Be careful because if someone trips the alarm, that door will close automatically."

"Aren't you worried I'd bash your brains in?"

Kevin chuckled again, not taking her seriously. "Our doors are locked, and you forgot that Shawn will be around.

"Yuck." She pouted.

"Tori, he's torn up inside," Kevin implored.

"Good. And you can't convince me he really likes me, Kevin. He was probably putting up with the charade to destroy me. He might not even like my ass."

A wicked smile ran over his lips. "Oh, he likes your ass. It's beautiful."

She rolled her eyes at his ridiculousness. "I'm sure Norman's ass was just-"

"Ugh... Tori, I don't fuck other men's asses, but I've fucked other women's asses, and your ass is superb."

Could her face burst into flames?

The older brother continued, grinning, "And Shawn noticed, too. He asked me why you have that perfect dent at the back like a welcome mat—"

Tori hit his chest. "That's enough!"

"I'm serious, Tori. You can't see it, but we-"

"Kevin, stop talking about the entrance to my ass!"

He chuckled. "Just know Shawn adores your ass too."

A yawn escaped, but she stiffened as Kevin grew serious, his hand on her stomach. The earlier playfulness gave way to nervous uncertainty.

"Tori," he said hoarsely. "What if you're pregnant, right now?"

Sourly, she said, "Even if I am, that's what Plan B is for, which I will take in a couple of days."

He cut his eyes, cruelly reminding her so much of Shawn. "You wouldn't want the baby?"

"Whose baby? Yours, Shawn's, Duncan's? What do I say? Remember, Shawn spread rumors about me and his brothers."

"Fuck everyone else, Tori, and we wouldn't fucking care. All of us would claim whatever baby you had. All of us would love to be the father to that baby of yours. And love you and support you-"

Tori placed a finger on the middle of his lips to stop him from speaking. She was internally screaming because her heart was about to burst. The one she knew should never be taken to heart was now spilling his heart to her, and she knew if he continued, she'd lose her damn mind.

"You, like Duncan, are delusional if you think your love can make me forget what you did to my life, my business, everything. And once Beck knows I didn't show at his brother's, he'll tear up the whole state looking for me."

Kevin lay back on the pillow and smirked with confidence. "By that time, you'll text him and let him know you're fine so that he won't look."

"Oh, really?" Tori questioned incredulously. "Will it be from all the good loving you all will be giving me?"

"Tori, we've admitted we fucked up, but you really have to know our hearts are true."

"Kevin, nothing you do will make me stay."

"And if I don't give you the Plan B in four days? What if you get pregnant? Thought about being a mom? Tired of your sister calling you the Rich Auntie?"

She briefly wondered how Kevin knew about the name her sister viciously called her when she'd been overly gracious with the kids and bought things she knew her sister couldn't afford, but the kids wanted. "I raised those kids like my own, and at times I did want to feel... loved like they were my own, but I don't want to be in this situation with three men and become a mother, Kevin."

"Why not? It's perfect. You'll never be ignored for the baby —one of us would always spoil you and help. It'd be perfect, Tori."

Tori shook her head. "No more baby talk, Kevin. Let me give you the kink and you give me the pill in four days." She hoped she would escape or signal for help by then.

He made a dramatic zipping of his lips, kissed her forehead, and then said, "Turn around so I can hold you while you sleep," he said. "I'll hold you until it's time for Shawn to come in."

Without hesitation to his orders, Tori turned over. "Does he have to?"

"He has the night shift, Tori. Unfortunately, I work early in the morning, and Duncan uses the night to work on the house when he's not at work." Kevin slid behind her like he always did and wrapped his arms around her middle section while nuzzling his face in her back. "This will probably be my only day off in a long time. I have you to thank for that."

"What did I do?"

"That damn proposal you wrote up, I was able to take to the bank and get the loan I wanted for my business." He nibbled on her shoulder. "Thank you, Tori. I've been trying for years to get them to support my ideas, and your writing skills blew it out of the park."

She yawned again - this time longer than last time. "I'm… glad." Sleepiness was filling every pore, and she could barely keep her eyes open.

"Tori, it was amazing what you accomplished for me," Kevin said with appreciation.

"It was… nothing. Your idea was solid. It just needed fleshing out, Kevin," she explained, drifting to sleep. "You deserve it."

She wasn't sure if she said the last part. Maybe she shouldn't—he might get the wrong idea.

~

The darkness threw her off; Tori gathered her wits, realizing she was still a hostage. Her shoulders slumped in defeat. She noticed Kevin was gone and sighed, missing the comfort of someone beside her.

Immediately, she looked at the dark part of the room, but her eyes had yet to adjust to see if Shawn was in that chair and if he was awake.

Too pissed off still to check and see if he was there, she looked at the skylight and saw a half moon, which led her to determine it must be two in the morning. It was enough light for her to get out of bed and trudge to the bathroom.

Opening the drawer to look at the birth control pills, Tori shivered, hoping they wouldn't try to shove one down her throat, and she would have to go with the pretense that she took one daily so she wouldn't hurt the baby.

When she came out of the bathroom, remembering Kevin had said she could roam, Tori realized she had barely eaten and was still hungry. The prospect of food pulled her focus away from the weight of her earlier thoughts; she wondered if Duncan had left some of her favorite snacks in the kitchen.

She only wore the loose tank top and decided not to put anything on her feet as she walked to the door. If Shawn were there in the darkness, he would stop her, right?

The door opened, and she smiled, not looking back to where she suspected Shawn was sitting. If he followed her, so what!

The hallway was dark, but she could see a small flint to her left and followed that, where a motion light came on at the top of the steps. She breathed a sigh of relief because she would have fallen down both flights of steps.

The stairs felt sturdy and silent, even a bit cushioned, so no one would notice someone passing. The insulated walls ensured that even if she screamed in this stairwell, others in the house wouldn't hear her.

Just as Kevin had promised, he left the door cracked enough for her to slip through because that door was hefty and wouldn't budge even a little when she pushed on it.

Recalling how Kevin had carried her, she retraced that route to the kitchen. Motion lights along the baseboard guided her path.

There was no need to search for a light switch, as motion lights had also been installed under the cupboards, allowing her to navigate over to the large refrigerator. The refrigerator was extra large, but she assumed that with three men in the house, if they had to stay on the island for an extended period, it would need to have a lot of food in it. Tori figured there was probably a root cellar or a couple of large freezers around somewhere, too.

As soon as she opened the door to the refrigerator, she giggled seeing the snacks she liked in front of the low shelf. Immediately, she pulled it out and started munching on them but then decided to get herself some water.

The cupboards were clear, but everything was made from glass. She took a medium-sized glass and returned to the refrigerator. There wasn't a water dispenser on the front of the door, but there was an eighty-ounce glass water pitcher on the highest shelf, full to the brim. She needed both hands to pick it up and take it over to the counter where she had left the glass.

Carefully pouring so she wouldn't make a mess, Tori then lifted it back and started for the refrigerator, but as she turned around, she caught sight of Shawn standing near her. She tripped, releasing the pitcher and stepping back. She felt the water splash all over her as she screamed when the glass shard went through the middle of her foot, and she would have fallen, but he caught her to lift her onto the counter.

She started to get down, but Shawn said sternly, "Tori, NO! Your damn foot!"

Tori looked down to see that blood was profusely dripping from the sole of her left foot, where it hurt like hell.

"Let me get my bag," he ordered. "Don't get down!"

As he walked away, she noticed he was dressed in silk gray pajamas and wore some house shoes. The bottom of the pajamas had gotten soaked, which meant he'd been close enough to receive her mess, but how long had he been that close that she hadn't noticed?

Raising her foot to her thigh, she screeched, seeing a large piece of glass still there, and it looked deep.

Dammit!

Shawn returned with a satchel, which he opened for her, revealing a multitude of medical tools inside. She lingered at the scapel that had a triple strap over it, and she'd have to fight to get it out.

"Get me to a hospital, Shawn! It's bleeding too badly. I might need a shot or something."

"It's glass, Tori, not metal," he negated coolly. "I just need to make sure there isn't anything in there." He reached into his medical bag to retrieve a headlamp with a magnifier attached to go over his eyes.

"Call Duncan!" she demanded.

The request stopped his movements like she had slapped him. "I'm perfectly capable of fixing your foot, Tori. I'm a foot doctor, dammit," he sneered, going over to wash his hands before returning to her.

She pulled her foot to her. "Then call Kevin. I don't trust you."

"Dammit, Tori. We're not waking them up in the middle of the night because you want to act like a spoiled... child."

"I'm not acting like a child. I hate you! And I don't want you to touch me, Shawn!" Tori winced because she'd moved her foot, sending white-hot pain up her leg.

"Tori, you'll bleed to death just because you hate me?"

Obstinately, she hissed, "Yes!"

Shawn looked down at her foot, and his look softened. "Please, Tori, just let me get the glass out."

It hurt like hell, and by now she was bleeding all over her thigh and her shirt was getting stained.

Reluctantly, Tori gave in and allowed him to treat her foot, and she hated to admit how gentle his touch was. His face was so serious, but not mad like it was whenever he looked at her. He really loved what he did when it came to feet.

"Why podiatry?" she demanded to know as she flinched through the pain when he took several shards out.

By now, he'd put on the head lamp and was holding really small tweezers, inspecting her foot for any more tiny shards of glass.

Tori needed some type of distraction before she started screaming from being in pain for so long.

Shawn answered without hesitation. "It was the only part of the body my mother didn't make me feel was disgusting to touch. It's the only part of the body that leads to healing other places in the body."

"Who's your podiatrist?" she questioned.

"My feet are fine."

"But your body isn't."

Shawn looked as if he realized something new, but quickly looked away from her, concentrating on her feet. "I'm fine, Tori."

She snorted, getting a sharp, heated look, and then she winced, feeling something pinch her arch. "You did that on purpose!" she accused him.

"I'm just making sure there isn't anything else in your foot," he smoothly assured her and applied antiseptic to prevent infections."

"That burns!" she cried, purposely being dramatic.

"I can't stop it from burning, Tori. You took a big step trying to get away from me on a floor full of glass shards."

"Why didn't you get any glass in your foot?" she pouted.

"Looks like your foot swept it all up."

Was he teasing?

She snapped sourly, "Are you done?"

Shawn was wrapping her foot, and from his pocket pulled a pair of socks.

Why did she allow him to put each sock on her feet without stopping him, but just watching him in fascination as he looked like he took great pleasure in treating her?

"I have to carry you out of the room so I can get this

cleaned up, but you can't get up. You need to keep your feet where I set them to stop the bleeding," he ordered. "And you don't need to put any weight on your foot."

Tori allowed him to pick her up and carry her over to the doorway, where a chair he'd set up was waiting. Then, Shawn went to return the satchel before heading back to the kitchen. Yes, she wanted to dart up to her room and hide under her covers, but when she looked down at her bandaged feet, knowing how much effort he'd put into taking them off, she decided not to defy him.

Shawn quickly found a broom and then a mop to clean up the kitchen. He also grabbed her snacks before returning to her to lift her up and take her back up to her room. Did they practice lifting her weight so all of them could do it without straining, she wondered?

"What about my drink?" she complained as he walked up the two flights of stairs without breaking a sweat.

"There's a mini fridge on the outside of the door," he let her know as he lay her on the bed, but immediately went back outside to get water from the refrigerator and came back in. "Duncan keeps it stocked with your snacks and things you drink."

She could hear a bitterness in his voice. "You don't sound too happy about that?"

Shawn moved to the end of the bed, his posture rigid, his gaze burning down at her like a flame threatening to consume everything. "What's there to like, Tori? My brothers are in love with the same woman we once agreed to take down, and now you want me to just forget the misery you caused us?"

"I'm not that girl anymore—"

He cut her off with a sharp edge to his voice, his words laced with years of hurt. "You say that, but how do we really know? How do I know Tori isn't still the same manipulative person who would do anything to get what she wants?"

Her gut twisted painfully at his words, and for a moment, she felt like a stranger looking at herself through Shawn's eyes. He hadn't seen her in years, yet this was how he still viewed her. It hit her like a sucker punch—*why* did he still think that of her? "I don't have to prove anything to you, Shawn," she responded, her voice low but steady. "And if you'd given me a chance back then, maybe you would've seen that your mother was full of shit and that you're *worthy* of being loved."

"Really, Tori?" He scoffed bitterly, ripping off his pajama top as if the very act would expose the rawness beneath. Turning his back on her, as he hurled the pajama top across the room, he hissed through gritted teeth. "Do I look like I'm worthy?"

Tori froze as her gaze locked on his bare back up close for the first time. The raw scars and old burns snaked across his skin—each one a painful reminder of the torment he'd endured. It was like a brutal map of suffering that he had worn alone. Had she been so blind, so selfish, that she never noticed? She felt the weight of regret crushing her chest as she looked at the marks that spoke louder than words.

Her heart raced, and without thinking about her injury, she slid off the bed and moved to him. Her hand reached out, trembling as if touching him would somehow shatter the fragility of the moment. Slowly, she laid her palm against his skin, and the instant she did, he flinched—as though the scars still burned, still had the power to hurt him.

"How could she do this to you?" Tori whispered, her voice thick with disbelief and sorrow. The horror of what she was seeing ripped through her, and all she could do was gasp. "Shawn... I didn't..." She choked on her words as a sob tore through her chest. The grief she felt was suffocating. "Whatever hell I gave her... she deserved every bit of it and more."

Her lips pressed softly against the curve of his spine, a tender apology for all the years they'd lost. Tori didn't know how she could ever make up for this, for what his past had done to him.

Shawn didn't flinch at her kiss, but she heard a sharp breath escape him—like a quiet surrender. Moving around to the front of him, she cupped his face in her hands, her fingers gentle against his stubble as she gazed up into his pain-filled eyes. "You've always been worthy, Shawn," she murmured, her voice a quiet promise. "You can't let her win for the rest of your life. You endured this... You survived. That *says something* about you. It proves you're stronger than anything you've ever been through."

A single tear slipped from the corner of his eye, falling like a tiny fragment of his soul breaking free. Tori's heart ached as she reached up to catch it with her fingers, wiping it away with the gentleness of someone trying to heal a wound they had no right to touch. But she did it anyway—tenderly, lovingly, because for the first time, she wanted him to feel that he was worth every ounce of love she could give.

Slowly, his body sank to his knees, drawing her body to him, pressing his face into her stomach, and squeezing her tightly, muffling the large sob that seemed to come from the bottom of his soul, shaking her to her core.

Holding him with all her strength, Tori cried silently with him, tenderly stroking his head, softly assuring him everything would be alright from now on.

CHAPTER 14
That was it?

Shawn stood up abruptly, frowning, gripping her shoulders. "Hate me, Tori," he demanded.

The unexpected anger caught her off-guard, but she wasn't scared despite the hard, intense look on his face. "I do!" she responded.

"Don't you fucking fall in love with me." He shook her by the shoulders, as if shaking her would stop what he feared.

Tori swore, "I promise."

He kissed her hard, molding her body against his, and dammit, she responded. Her body stiffened at first but then relaxed into him. This was the kiss she wanted so many years ago behind the garage; his lips pressed urgently against hers. As her arms circled his neck, his lips parted, and his tongue slid into her mouth, entwining with hers.

She moaned further, encouraging him to kiss her harder, and he lifted her up and carried her to bed.

The kiss never broke; he moaned as he shifted his weight, his full body pressing gently on top of hers.

Tori was a hot mess inside and out. Her hands trembled

and her breath caught as she realized she wasn't going to resist him.

"Hate me!" he demanded.

"Yes!" she promised.

Shawn dipped back into another kiss, this one even more passionate, and Tori was aflutter all over.

Shawn grabbed a handful of Tori's hair at the back of her head and kissed her with increasing intensity. Tori responded by pressing closer, matching his energy and feeling as if she were merging with him.

Air was an option, and they took breath where they could, rubbing and grinding their bodies together, hands roaming, lips seeking skin, as if they could not get enough. This is what she would have loved if they had come together as teenagers: raging sex drives, a desperate need to be inside each other's arms, and an uncontrollable passion that left them breathless.

Tori felt herself become dizzy. Yes, she hated him, but she wanted him. He looked formidable and angry, yet his hands moved across her skin with a hard yearning, his touch curious, as if he needed to possess her completely.

His unfamiliar but eager kisses roamed her mouth. Shawn's whole body pressed her into the mattress. Tori needed this as she grinded herself against him, matching his roughness and surrendering to him. Damn, she'd never experienced anything like this as a teenager or adult. Long, slow foreplay—Shawn was making all her crush dreams come true. Would she have been a changed woman if she'd gotten him back then?

If he made out like this, she'd probably have!

"Fuck!" Shawn hissed in frustration, tearing his mouth from hers, both of them panting for air. "We fucking can't, Tori."

She got a small orgasm off, but she was so ready for a big one, so his frustration became her own. Grinding her need hard against him, she pouted. "Why do you have to be the voice of reason, Shawn?"

"Because you getting pregnant is not part of the plan, Tori." He cursed again, jumped up, and began pacing along his side of the bed, his steps quick and restless as he tried to shake off his sexual frustration. "We've already ruined your life." He halted abruptly and let himself fall heavily onto the bed.

Tori thought his weight would break the metal frame, but she was distracted by the lost look in his eyes, as if he had murdered her. She looked down, checking to make sure he hadn't stabbed her while she was too caught up to notice. Seeing no blood, she looked back at him.

"We fucked up, didn't we?" he said in the saddest voice.

Taking a deep breath, realizing he was coming to terms with his other two brothers about their decision to ruin her life, Tori said, "Yes, Shawn."

Shawn cursed again, burying his face in his hands.

Tori rubbed his back in consolation. "So, you'll let me go?"

Looking at her with disbelief, he said, "No! We can't. Dammit, we should be punished."

She frowned at his refusal, but responded to his guilt, "You all do."

"Tori, this isn't funny. I can see you're just placating me."

"What do you want me to do?"

"Get mad! Scream! Try to tear my eyes out."

"If I try, I'll only be expending unnecessary energy."

"I mean it when I say I still want you to hate me."

"I'm pissed at all of you. You've destroyed me financially, personally, and mentally."

Shawn jumped up and started pacing again. "You shouldn't go around letting us kiss you or... Why? Why are you being like this? You have to be violently angry on the inside."

Tori lay back and stared at the ceiling, pushing away her sexual frustration and tapping into that part that should be pissed off at all of them.

"Beck will find me. Probably try to break every bone in your bodies, and then I'll be rescued. I'll still leave Detroit. Find somewhere no one will ever find me, start over, and never see any of you ever again."

He stopped pacing and glared at her. "You can't leave us, Tori. We've just started... I just started... Dammit, we can fix this."

"Shawn, I don't know the real you. You were just pretending to like me just to hurt and destroy me."

Moving to his knees in front of her, he lay his head on her lap, just like he would when they all lay down in bed together. Dammit, why did it grip her heart so hard? Lying her hands on his strong shoulders, she slowly started to rub his back. She felt the muscles under her palms were tense, and she knew she wasn't hurting him, but he was forcing himself to become comfortable with her touch.

Remembering how Kevin had massaged her back, Tori began running her hands down his back and loved how Shawn eventually started to relax and speak.

"I was pretending in the beginning," he admitted. "I've never desired to be with any woman, but Duncan said in order for us to get you to believe everything, I'd have to... try."

Tori remembered Duncan admitting how he wanted to convince Shawn to join him and Kevin. She should have been upset that the brothers had used her, but she had so much more to be upset about.

Her fingers continued to knead his back as she also visually took in the horrendous scars and old burns all down his lower back. If his mother had still been alive, Tori felt this woman needed a good barnyard whooping for the hurt she had put on her son. Had her father known? She kept this question to herself as she continued to listen to him.

"That night before the first date alone with you, I felt like a teen going on the first date. I think I had already become enamored from the blue room."

Her breath caught in her throat at the mention of her first night with the brothers. The night she had become enamored by them. Most likely, it was all planned by Duncan to seduce her.

Shawn spoke, seeming to answer what she was thinking. "Duncan said we needed to love bomb you because you were already getting your needs met by Beck."

"Wait, wait?"

He looked up at her. "Duncan explained that most women with alpha males aren't just going to be enamored by flirting. You were also very much in control of your life in all aspects and wouldn't be intimidated by being in control. This was mostly for Kevin. I was still unsure what to expect. I just thought you were self-centered, spoiled, and didn't care about anyone except yourself. Duncan insisted you had to be overwhelmed, and we needed to make sure you understood how much we were in love with you."

"But you weren't. Everything was an act and for show."

"Initially, no, we weren't in love," he admitted. "Tori, we weren't, but the more we got to know the real you, the more we found ourselves..." A glossy, confused look moved over his face. Watching him reveal his conflicting emotions for her in real time made her heart swoon.

Shawn lowered his face in shame. "I couldn't believe myself or my feelings. I swore I couldn't be in love with you, Tori. I tried... I tried to go back."

"Go back?" she pressed.

Looking back at her, he confessed. "I tried to go back to Norman. I was so sure I could just... and it felt so good that he still wanted me, especially knowing I owned all his property. He was grinning like a damn Joker willing to give me everything I'd wanted for us, but all I could do was think of you. all I could do was desire to be with you and my body..." He groaned, pressing his face into her thigh. "I thought if I tried someone else, but my body, my heart, my fucking soul all wanted you. And I hated you more."

Tori was stunned bythe confession and waited for a moment before revealing, "I wasn't trying to fall in love with you all. Duncan used my past crush on you to get to me, and that wasn't fair."

"I'm glad he did. I'm not sorry for that, Tori, because I would have never gotten to this point - to this feeling."

"What feeling?"

"That you not only take away the chaos in my life but the chaos in my soul." Shawn placed several long, juicy kisses on her lower stomach. "You've made me see the horrible person I have been to myself and my brothers." Shawn closed his eyes as if in so much pain, and she couldn't stop herself from running her hands over his head. He took a deep breath and looked up to her in gratefulness. "I can never thank you enough for the peace you brought me." He lay his head back in her lap and hugged her lower body tightly.

Tori bit back the frustration and tears that wanted to explode out of her, and then she almost wanted to laugh as she realized how all of them came to the decision that kidnapping her had become a really bad decision for them, but they were all in flux on how to handle this situation. No amount of loving or spoiling her was going to make her change her mind about leaving, and they knew that.

He'd been watching her closely and was starting to pick up that annoying Duncan skill of reading her too well. "What if I tore up the divorce decree?" he suggested.

His head was still lying in her lap, and since he wasn't

looking at her, she wasn't sure how he was feeling. He didn't sound like he was joking.

With precaution, Tori approached the subject. "It wouldn't matter, Shawn. My rep is ruined. I'm not sure I can even sell my art here anymore, and I pray I can salvage something online so I can at least find a way to make a living elsewhere. At least leaving clear instructions about the group home can help Beck and whoever they find to take over."

The devastation on his face was getting harder and harder for her to look upon. "We'll take care of you, Tori," he implored. "We can work everything out. We swear."

"And what will you tell the public? Your job? What about the Cosgraves who believed in our relationship? And my reputation?" she demanded.

"I'll tell them I was jealous," he hastened. "'ll tell them I accused you wrongly and you've forgiven me."

Quickly, she responded. "I haven't."

Shawn leaned back up on his heels, slumping his shoulders in defeat. "Then I'll still grant you the divorce. If it takes the rest of my life, I will fight to bring you back into my life and be worthy of your heart."

Tori stood up to get away from him, going around the bed and turning her back to him. Her entire chest felt like it had been punched through. Every piece of her soul wanted to give in to him, love him in return, because this was what she always wanted, but after the deceit.

He moved right behind her but didn't touch her. "I will work diligently to remove any body who tries to hurt you - family or foe - and keep you safe so you can love and be happy. I swear this to you, Tori. Please!"

Tears welled in her eyes as she fought giving in to his words.

"Being with you has shown me the man I want to be, Tori. Yes, it was all fake at first, but I started feeling myself. The old

Shawn I used to be when I could smile without it being forced, laugh without crying, and... love without being scared. I love you, Tori. I would do anything for you. We all would. You've done the one thing we've always wanted: to feel connected again, and you put yourself out there. Everything, Tori. We'd do anything for you.

Deep in her soul, she could feel he wasn't lying. This was his true self. Why did seeing them at her beck and call, spoiling her for the rest of her life, give her goosebumps? Slowly, she turned around and looked up at him.

Her direct gaze, full of sorrow, seemed to collapse him to his knees in front of her. "I'm sorry for all the pain you've suffered because of us, Tori - because of me. I beg from the bottom of my heart for your forgiveness."

"And if I give in to you? Into this, Shawn? Forgive you? You'd keep me on this island? Away from the world? So, I won't press charges for what you've done? The three of you are convinced that loving me and fucking me is going to make me forget what you've done? With no consequences for your actions?"

Full of resignation, Shawn sighed, looking up to her. "You're right, Tori. We should all go to jail for what we've done to you."

It was sweet; he and Kevin felt they should serve time, and she knew Duncan would feel the same way about what they had done to her. And she was almost tempted to kiss Shawn for his confession but held herself back from giving a reward.

Shawn promised, "I'm still going to tear up the divorce decree."

"I'll still divorce you, Shawn."

"It's only fair,"he conceded. "On your terms."

Tori took a deep breath and lowered to her knees in front of him. "I'll still allow you to tear the apartment building down," she admitted, loving how his face lit up in excitement.

"But you'll have to build another one in a three-year span and help me find units for the tenants displaced." The apartment building was old, and even Beck had agreed that a newer building would be more effective than trying to repair and update the building. She wasn't going to let Shawn know she had already submitted plans to the city and was waiting on approval.

"And give a partial rent stipend,' he insisted.

Tori was taken aback by his offer. "Do you really think you can afford all that, Shawn, until the new building is complete?"

He only shrugged off her worry. "If I can't, Duncan will cover anything. He's the wealthy one."

"Wait? How is he the wealthier one?"

"He owns an island, Tori," Shawn said, obviously. "And a boat, a whole damn house, and a lot of property. He will most likely have a property that the tenants can move into until the building is completed. We all had our vices to fight through what our mother and your father did to us. Kevin was cars, mine was work, and Duncan was gambling. Lots and lots of gambling with big players that put a lot on the line. You're about the only one outside of us who reads him clearly. No one else can see his tells, so he makes a perfect gambling player, but he's never done shit with his money until now. Until you."

"I thought he just fixed boats."

Frustrated, Shawn asked, "Dammit, Tori, can we fucking get back to kissing?"

Tori couldn't stop herself from giggling, feeling his horniness because she was feeling randy herself. "I guess you enjoy kissing me more than Norman," she teased.

He pulled her to him, and she allowed him to mold her body against him, feeling his hardness against her belly. "You're less hairy and you smell incredible."

Teasing, she nipped at his neck, and he nipped at hers

hungrily, running his hands over her body voraciously as if he wanted to tear the skin off her body. "How do you know you won't want more women now that you find yourself attracted-"

"Tori, my heart, my body, and my soul will belong to you forever. I love you, woman, and I know this," he hissed and kissed her until she felt it all the way down in her toes, but she forced herself to push away from the kiss because she knew what it would lead to.

"Kissing will lead to more, and you know it, Shawn, but you said we couldn't. I'll get too horny."

He groaned in her neck, knowing they needed to stick to his rules since he assumed she took a Plan B. Tori was willing to throw all caution to the wind and jump his bones, but she loved seeing how frustrated he was.

Taking him out of his misery, she suggested, "There is something we can do to satisfy each other, and we can be completely naked without breaking your little rules."

Shawn looked willing and open to anything as he began to quickly strip down all his clothes. In between, as each piece of cloth came off their body, Shawn kissed her ravenously until she was very amorously again. Guiding him to the bed, she pushed him down, fondling his thickened shaft. He gasped, and she could tell he loved the touch of her on his body.

Tori moved around to the other side of the bed, where she stood over his head. Immediately, he understood what she was suggesting, and his arms came up, parted her legs, and pulled her down on his face until she was sitting over him. Shawn didn't care about her weight either as he smoothed her down and immediately began orally giving her pleasure, while she leaned over and engulfed his manhood. Having him down her throat felt so good. Sucking up and down, tasting the precum on the back of her mouth, slobbering all over his shaft, and even being able to reach down and suck on his testicles.

Intermittently, she had to pause as his tongue dug into her and then licked down to her clitoris, up past her perineum, and then back down to circle around her clitoris, while his finger dipped into her. He was loud, not as erotically savage as Kevin, but the sucking, slurping, and humming he was doing between the groans she pulled out of him from the pleasure she was giving him was an erotic turn on for her as well.

She could feel he was close in her mouth because she could barely pull him down her throat. To increase his pleasure, she moved one hand to massage his testicles, while her other hand circled around his taint and then dipped lower.

His hips bucked, and he squeezed her hips tight as he called out her name like a curse over and over again. And she gulped down his hot, thick essence, drinking him like he was blessing her with the fountain of youth, not wasting a drop.

Tori giggled in pleasure, licking up his remnants over her hands and licking by his base to clean up her mess.

"Woman!" Shawn hissed and then dipped back between her legs, occasionally trembling as she playfully suckled on his tip.

Abruptly, Tori had to stop because her body was trembling uncontrollably, and she buried her face into his thigh, grinding her hips into his face in time with the licking of his tongue.

Shawn was taking her there and snatching her soul at the same time. Tori could feel the flood of joy squirting out of her as she cried out, singing his praises. He chuckled proudly as he drank all of her essence and then rolled her on her side so he could languishly lick all her juices and clean her up.

"You taste so good," Shawn whispered, dipping his finger into her again and licking that clean.

Damn! Tori needed to get the fuck out of there before she would let them trap her on this island, letting them all fuck her morning, noon, and night and loving it.

Shawn thought she started crying as an after-sex emotion, so he gathered her into his arms and held her. Tori was crying because she was so close to giving up her freedom for the love they all could give her.

No, you can't! No, you won't! She repeated in her head, but she had to use all her willpower to keep her mouth closed.

CHAPTER 15

Everything should be alright

Tori didn't know when she fell asleep, but being emotionally invested in Shawn all night had taken a toll on both her body and mind. When she awoke, it was to the smell of something delicious, and Duncan was coming into the room with a tray of food.

Morning light came into the ceiling window, and she stretched her whole body out. She was still naked, and her lips were very sore. Shawn had awakened her again in the middle of the night, eating her, and she twisted around and started nibbling on him again. They were like teenagers just enjoying munching on each other until she passed out again.

"You're happy," Duncan noted, setting the tray by her bed, filled with buttermilk pancakes, the fluffiest eggs, freshly rolled ground turkey sausage, fresh-squeezed orange juice, and coffee just the way she liked it.

"Good breakfast doesn't change anything," she said, still stuffing food in her mouth despite her sore lips.

Duncan sat on the edge of the bed after taking the extra coffee off the tray and drank slowly, watching her with his eyes, dancing in pleasure. "I owe you."

"Fuck you, Duncan," she muttered through pancakes, then moaned at the taste. "I hate you. I hate all of you."

Duncan picked up a napkin and tenderly wiped the corners of her mouth.

Tori stuffed all the eggs in her mouth, loving how soft and buttery they were, rolling her eyes on the back of her head. "Gawd, I hate you the most."

"Because my plan is working?"

By this time, she was chomping down the three sausages, almost crying at how perfectly seasoned they were. "Kick fucking rocks, Duncan," she muttered.

"Your anger is understandable."

His calmness made her angrier. "You manipulated everything just to get your way," she snapped.

“I didn't count the kidnapping."

"Fuck you, Duncan."

"You know what I mean."

He coolly put his cup down on her tray and cleared his throat. "You want to know that I desired you the moment I laid eyes on you. When I saw what drew Shawn in the middle of the night, I knew I had to be with you. *We* had to be with you, Tori." He leaned over the tray until his face was centimeters from her syrup-covered lips." And if I have to serve the rest of my life in jail knowing I had these moments with you and my brothers, it was worth every damn law I broke and every moral code I crossed."

"I hate you for that," she pouted.

He softly kissed her sticky lips and licked his lips. "I fucking love you, Tori. And I will love you forever, even behind bars."

She clenched her fists, fighting the urge to forgive him. I should be furious, she thought. Am I justifying their actions? They kidnapped me. They disrupted my entire life—and yet, why does it feel complicated now that I'm here?

Burying her hands in her face, she moaned. "You're all driving me crazy!"

"Welcome to our world. You drive us insane, and I like it," Duncan teased.

Jumping off the bed, stomping in a pout to the bathroom to relieve herself, freshen up, and brush her teeth. In her peripheral vision, Tori watched as he took the tray and placed it outside the room, then stood at the doorway of the bathroom, wearing a pair of pink jogging pants, a sweatshirt, pink socks, underwear, and shoes. She almost screamed, knowing she could get dressed, and jumped up in his arms.

"You're going to help me in the solarium," he said. "I thought it'd be a good way for us to talk about last night and my promise to you."

She eyed him. "What's to talk about? Don't go back on your word, Duncan."

Duncan gave her a soft, longing kiss. "Meet me there. We'll talk."

Tori wanted to talk about it now, but Duncan had that commanding tone, and she knew she wouldn't get her way no matter what she did. He wanted her to join him out of the room, and probably not half naked, where she would have the advantage.

You should be pissed and upset! she reprimanded herself, but not having clothes for the past couple of days and now having them in her favorite color brought her so much joy.

Washing up quickly, Tori pulled her two strands into a high ponytail and then finished dressing.

The choker was almost hidden as she pulled the shirt over her head, making her forget briefly that she was a prisoner to three brothers who had ruined her life.

You will fake your way to freedom, Tori vowed. Just keep your mind clear—don't let yourself get lost in this trap.

Yet deep down, she didn't feel like she was faking her

acquiescence to them. She wanted to be there. She needed to be around them.

Placing her hand on her stomach, she reminded herself again of her agenda - Freedom.

Going to the closed door, Tori braced herself as she pulled the handle, ready for the lock to stop her. Yet not this time. The door opened easily, and she found herself out in the hallway. The house was so big she couldn't hear anything, and this part of the house was even more enclosed.

Going down the several flights of steps, Tori was relieved that the heavier door was open wide, and she could enter the main part of the house. Just like last night, she remembered how to get to the solarium where they had tried to have dinner the night before. It was past the kitchen, and she listened to figure out where Duncan was located. There were some pink Timberlands at the doorway, and she giggled to herself, putting them on, knowing these were for her.

Past the tropical plants, there were several rows of dirt with fruit trees growing around them. She gasped, moving over to an apple tree and plucking one of the fruits. It was the first week of November, but the temperature in the solarium was a nice seventy-five degrees, and the sheen over the glass sucked in more sun, giving all the plants ample light.

"You like apples now?" Duncan inquired just as she bit into the sweet, delicious fruit.

"It's your fault," she said, annoyed, but took another bite because the apple was so sweet. "You said we're talking. Are you reneging on the deal you made with me?"

Duncan motioned her to follow him as he spoke, "No, Tori." Stopping in front of a large, raised planter with small holes all over, each area carefully labeled, he handed her several packets of seeds. "One per hole."

She frowned because she had never gardened before in her life and wondered why Duncan needed her when he could have done this himself. Yet she found herself opening each packet of beans, chard, basil, tomatoes, and squash to drop in the assigned holes. He was working on some larger plants at another raised bed right by her.

"Shawn came downstairs this morning, smiling brighter than sunshine, and said he had to do some things before he came home tonight, but he didn't want to go into a discussion."

She asked, "Is that bad?"

"Shawn's not been happy most of his life unless we were doing the plan against you, and now I don't know. He's changed. I can feel it, but every warning light in my body is lighting up, or maybe I'm just waiting for something terrible to happen when I'm so used to it. Nothing ever goes right for all of us. What happened?"

"A lot," she responded with a shrug. "He fixed my foot, and we got to talking about his mother. I really wish I had done more to make her life miserable after I realized what she had done to him, Duncan. Honestly. For the first time in my life, I don't regret being the bitch back then. Maybe if I had opened my mouth in front of Keir and you guys, it would have brought a lot of things to light. And then... well, he wanted me to hate him and I wouldn't. And well..." She blushed. "All in all, Shawn realized just like you and Kevin that you guys fucked up, and then he was sorry. Really sorry."

Duncan frowned harder. "He said sorry?"

"Yes, why do you act like that's hard to believe?"

"Tori, can you stay one more day-"

"No, Duncan, you promised."

Running a frustrated hand over his face, he quibbled, "I know what I promised, Tori, but this Shawn is so unpredictable. I followed him the other day. He went over to Norman's house." He stopped speaking, biting his lip as if he were trying to decide if he should continue.

Tori pretended she didn't know what he was going to say. "What?"

"He went over there, I guess to prove he didn't feel changed, but I watched Norman go down on him for two fucking hours, and Shawn couldn't get it up."

Biting back a wicked smile, remembering how Shawn couldn't stop standing at attention when she even looked in his direction, she said, "What do you think?"

"I think Shawn's head over heels in love with you, and if you go away-"

She cut him off. "I don't care! I need to leave! Shawn's feelings have nothing to do with the deal we made. You said if I helped him heal, and I think I've done more than enough."

Duncan huffed in more frustration, but Tori was sticking to her guns. If this were the only way she could get off the island, then she would be adamant about it.

"Fine Woman!" he hissed.

Tori had finished what he had told her to do.

Duncan took the seed packets from her, handed her gloves, and then motioned her to follow him over to a staging area. He took a deep breath, calming himself down, and Tori had to wonder if Duncan would have tolerated her pout if he weren't in love with her.

He picked up two heavy bags of compost and perlite and poured them into a large metal bowl in the staging area.

His tone was soothing as he instructed her to mix the compound together, while he added the peat moss.

"How are you a gardener?" she asked. "You don't look like you would enjoy this?"

"If I didn't want to end up in jail like Kevin, I had to find something. I started small at the other house, but once I received this island, I decided to add this addition so I could do this all year long. I need an outlet for all my energy, and sometimes I dream of being holed up here for months, not associating with anyone if I don't have to."

"The perfect place to be alone," she said, feeling uneasy as he started helping her mix everything up.

With his large hands, like all the brothers', he was able to get down in the dirt, and Duncan didn't use gloves. Why was it so erotic to see his hands get so dirty and wish he'd put them on her, knead her skin like that?

"Tori, I know you're not being unreasonable," Duncan said, slowing his words down considerably despite his agitation with her.

She was glad to hear his voice to draw her away from her illicit thoughts.

Duncan continued, "But I need to be sure that this new Shawn can handle you not being there."

Forcing her to stay away from the forbidden thoughts, she asked, "Why do you think his new behavior is sketchy?"

"He came downstairs whistling. Something Amos used to do in the morning when he was happy. It chilled me to the bone. For Amos, it always meant he was thinking of something diabolical." Duncan shrugged. "Maybe it was a trigger for me, and I'm overthinking. I was already exhausted from fighting with Kevin all night. "

"Fighting about what?"

"Kevin wanted to join the frey. He said he was wasting time waiting for our little brother to reconcile with the past when we all could be having fun with you. I knew the two of you needed that time alone together to get through to Shawn. Kevin would be a distraction. And fuck, I'd have joined in too. So I had to wrestle Kevin most of the night to keep his ass from breaking down your fucking door."

"I should thank you?" she asked sarcastically.

"I'm never looking for thanks, Tori. I know Shawn needed the time, and I was willing to do everything in my power to give you the time you needed so I could fulfil my promise. And I will, but when I asked him about tonight, Shawn said he will be back a little late because he had to do something important. Afterwards, he told me about the apartments and said he would give me whatever money he could after he returned the money to you that he took." He shrugged. "I don't give a damn about the money. I just want my little brother back, and that's why I'm asking you for twenty-four hours. I need to observe him with all of us together. Something just feels a little off."

"So you expect me to wait around for this surety, while you guys figure out your feelings and what to do about me? Are you going to bury me under another shed?"

Duncan flinched at the reminder. "Tori, we're not going to hurt you. I love you."

"You guys have a funny way of showing it. You kidnapped me, and you destroyed my life, so what am I supposed to believe? How can you ask this of me, Duncan?"

"One more day," Duncan begged, holding onto her hands in the dirt. "Please, Tori, just one more day, and I will give you anything you ask for and never ask you for another thing ever."

Tori hated herself because she felt the need to give in to him, but she knew that staying any longer with them could reveal her condition. "This isn't fair to me. I've lost everything, and you're still asking for more. How can you even ask anything of me after what you have done to me?"

"I know all the apologizing in the world will not repair what we have done. But what if, financially, we can at least repair a little of what we have destroyed? And once I release you, you can take what I give you and start a new life somewhere else or stay here. I can replace the apartment building as needed. I can help with that."

Squinting her eye suspiciously from his monotonous tone when it came to money, she asked, "You can cover the entire cost of rebuilding a brand-new apartment building, plus helping the displaced tenants that are there while this apartment building is being built?"

Duncan shrugged as if it were no big deal as they began mixing the dirt together again. "If it's going to help Sean to demolish that place and then give you a brand spanking new apartment building, then yes, I'll cover the entire cost."

"Duncan, you don't have that kind of money," she refuted, not believing one word he said. "You're just saying anything to make me want to stay and dangling money in front of me, thinking that I'm just going to forget everything that you've done."

Snatching his hands out of the dirt and washing them off, before retrieving his phone from his pocket. "Tori, give me your bank and account number, then state your price for everything you need right now," he demanded in a very firm and forceful voice.

Tori knew Duncan could not possibly have any amount of money that could even come close to helping her recover what she mentally and emotionally lost. After reciting her bank information with a roll of her eyes, she challenged him and threw out a ridiculous amount, "Twenty million."

He typed quickly into his phone and then turned the screen to her to show her a bank transfer into her account. Tori immediately stepped back as if he'd hit her in the back. She'd even held both her cheeks with her mouth wide open.

"Twenty-four hours, Tori. That's all I ask," Duncan said, getting down on one knee. "I don't want to break a promise to you, but I need to ensure Shawn doesn't regress after all you've done for him." He took a deep breath, gripping his chest. "It hurts fucking hard to give you this promise because I can't imagine you not in our lives, but a promise is a promise, and I fucking love you so much, I will do whatever it takes to make you happy. One more day and then I will take you where you want to go, please."

Damn the yearning in his voice; it tore at her heart, and she found herself throwing her gloves to the floor and moving to him, wrapping her arms around his neck. He pressed his face into her stomach and moved his arms around her waist.

Tori gasped, feeling a slight wetness near her navel, and she knew it wasn't from her. This meant more to Duncan than he was saying.

Twenty million dollars more!

That can't be. How could he have that type of money?

'Duncan is the wealthier one,' Shawn had said.

"How do you have that type of money, Duncan?" she asked, still holding him.

"I don't spend shit and I gamble very well, but this is the first time I've ever wanted something to pay off." He looked up at her, still holding her close. "Out of everything I've ever won, Tori, you would be the best prize of all."

Dammit! Dammit! Dammit!

She couldn't stop herself from getting on her knees and kissing him. Duncan immediately responded, pressing his tongue inside her mouth to wrap around hers. Their bodies fell back to the ground as they rolled around until their clothes started coming off.

Gardening was forgotten, except when Duncan was plowing her fields, bringing her unbelievable pleasure. When she was naked and nicely turned on, she straddled him on the floor of that solarium, riding him to glory and beyond.

He cried out her name, worshipfully over and over, exclaiming all his vulnerabilities in his voice, letting her know his need for her would never go away.

Don't you give in! Tori screamed in her head as she collapsed on his chest after her third orgasm.

She'd take his money and run away. Far away from this

crazy addiction, she called the Carter Boys. That would be the only way to escape the need to want them in her life.

By this time, he was drawing circles on her back. He'd come as well, but he was still semi-hard inside of her and made no attempt to remove himself afterwards.

It was a nice full after play sensation, while listening to his heart calming down.

"I want to give the journals to the detective on the Amos case," she announced.

He didn't stop the circling, but she could hear his heart rate increase slightly because she still had her head on his chest.

"It'll expose everyone, even your mother. People will see that she wasn't just this wealthy, sweet daughter, but an evil, vindictive bitch."

"And it'll expose your mother as well."

"We don't care about that, Tori. This is all about you."

She had a feeling he meant that in all contexts and not just about the diary. "I think everyone needs to know, and we need to bury the past forever. Giving those journals away will put to rest the devils that have plagued us. And I can live in peace knowing that at least I'm not dictated by the people and actions of my past. We all need to heal, and I think doing this will help us."

"I agree." He kissed the top of her head.

"And I don't want you all to go to jail," she said. "I won't press charges against any of you for kidnapping me."

Duncan stopped making circles on her back, and his heart rate increased further.

Tori continued. "You'll release me at the bus station in Detroit with all my stuff, and I'll be done with you all and get as far as I can away from this city."

"Where will you go when this is over?" he asked softly.

Tori took a deep breath and said, "If I told you, you'd come find me and kidnap me again."

"I would," he admitted. "But why can't we give you the desire to stay, Tori?"

Raising up slightly so she could look at him, she said, "Because if I stay even one more day, I may never want to leave."

He gathered her in his arms and rolled her over, dislodging himself , but staying above her while she now lay on his clothes, so her back wouldn't be on the hard floor.

Duncan's hard brown eyes turned soft as he stared down at her for a long minute before he started kissing her again. The ones that pulled at her heart and soul, bringing tears to her eyes.

"Can you trust us, Tori, for tonight?" he asked.

Tori was panting from the deep, long, heart wrenching kiss he had just given her, barely able to think straight. "For what?"

"Just say you trust us. Give us this night together with you."

Why did it feel like her permission would seal her fate? She shouldn't do this.

"Yes," her defiant, lusty side agreed.

He kissed her again, long and beautiful.

CHAPTER 16
One Last Night

After showering, Tori continued gardening with Duncan. He showed her all the winter plants he was focused on to make fresh dinners, and he also experimented with the spring appetizer that would always debut at the restaurant.

"If you're wealthy, why are you a lowly sous chef and a boat mechanic?" she inquired.

"Millionaires can have hobbies. The chef needed ideas, and he and I met on a boat trip, and we hit it off. I've put my efforts into other hobbies instead of doing things I might do if my hands are idle," Duncan explained. "I love boats. I love water. It's soothing. Makes the bad things I think about go away when I'm in the water."

"What would you be doing?" She stopped and saw a terrifying look in Duncan's eyes. "Idle hands are the devil's workshop?"

Duncan chuckled, tapping on the large water can she held like he wanted to throw it down on the ground and take her again. "Definitely true, now let me make you lunch while you finish distributing the nutrients."

Tori was really enjoying herself too much helping him, and she loved seeing how much he enjoyed doing his hobbies.

He'd be such a good father, she said. *Teaching their children everything he knew. And Duncan knew a lot.*

Biting her tongue to reprimand herself for having such heinous thoughts, Tori concentrated on the task at hand while she wondered what they had up for tonight. Duncan wouldn't give her any details but only told her Kevin would deliver something to wear this afternoon.

After lunch, Duncan led her back up the two flights of stairs, but they didn't go into her regular room. He took her to the room beyond her door, and she gasped when he opened it for her.

The room was built like her tufting room at home.

"You broke into my storage?" she asked suspiciously.

"No, I remembered everything that was there and recreated here - for you, Tori. I thought you'd like to spend the rest of your afternoon doing something that relaxed you."

Obstinately, she pouted, "This won't change my mind about leaving."

"I know, but I had to show you before you decide to go," he explained, but she could tell he was still bothered by her not changing her mind. "You're free to walk back and forth between the rooms. That device you're wearing unlocks both those doors."

Tori hugged and kissed his cheek. "Thank you," she said.

Duncan gave her several of his beautiful, soft kisses and tapped her backside. "I have some work to do, and I will see you for dinner."

"You really aren't going to tell me what's planned?" she persisted.

"No, but you must trust us," he reiterated, kissing her one last time before he left.

She watched the door for a moment, wondering what they

were up to. Turning to the room, she ran her hand over the various tufting machines and then the three canvases that were already set up.

Immediately, she started a simple design, realizing she missed doing this more than she thought.

Tori had lost track of time until she heard someone open the door and had to take a moment to finish her line before turning to see who had come into the room. Kevin was standing at the doorway, still in his work coveralls, holding a large red box. She could tell he had washed his face and hands, but he'd come straight to her afterward, smelling like work, sweat, and outside.

Why did this get her going, seeing him all grimy?

"I can't come in. I don't want to mess up your room," he said.

She came out of the room and went into her bedroom as he followed her, getting an even bigger whiff of him. The smell was making her delirious. "It smells like it's going to rain."

"Late-night thunderstorms are predicted," he said casually, but that look in his eyes as he raked over her body brought a swell to her center.

At the same time Tori jumped into his arms, Kevin dropped the box to the floor and caught her. He lifted her, walked into the bathroom, and pressed her body into the shower. All the while, their mouths had met, and they were trying to suck each other's tongues out. The animalistic lust enveloping her was infectious, and Kevin didn't miss a beat.

Somehow the shower was turned on, and the water soaked their clothes. Between hot deep kisses and hard feels, they stripped down to nothing and titillated on the feel of their naked bodies rubbing together. Kevin even teased his tip around her womanly entrance before plunging up into her.

"Gawd, the fuck I've been thinking about your pussy all fucking day, Tori!" he cried in need.

"Fuck me then," she ordered before silencing him with kisses, sure that Kevin chose the bathroom to give her permission to refuse him.

Kevin did as he was told, giving her long, hard strokes, rocking her hips against the wall of the shower so hard she was sure anyone on another floor could hear them bumping and grinding like their life depended on it.

Tori was also screaming her sexual pleasure to the heavens and above, not caring if anyone heard.

It felt so damn hot and good.

Knowing he was loving the baby-making kink and feeling her orgasm coming along, she demanded, "Cum in me, baby. Cum-"

"Arrrrggghghhhh," Kevin bellowed, vibrating her body to her core as he bucked hard up in her, but held her shoulders so she had to take everything!

His hot cum filled her to the brim, even dripping out of her as she went off the deep end, loving how his shaft quivered and jerked, mixing with her juices.

Breathlessly, Kevin hissed, "Baby fucking making sex is the best!"

Tori chuckled as he slowly lowered her legs. Grabbing the soap and washcloth, she lathered him all over, rubbing the grease and grim from his body. Kevin relaxed and let her. As she was soaping his legs, she looked up at him.

His gaze was soft and loving. "I've never had a woman attend to me like you do, Tori," he said sadly.

Pushing him under the water to rinse, she stood on the tips of her toes to wrap her arms around his neck and kiss him. Kevin plunged his tongue deep into hers. This time, it was slower, but Kevin was still his rough self. She could tell he was enraptured, and she loved the feeling of how he craved her so much. Somehow, they made it out of the shower and on her bed, wet from not drying off, but not caring. Kevin scrambled down between her legs, and his delicious mouth took great care in giving her multiple orgasms. Each one he slurped down loudly and then started on the next one, until she had to push him away, or she thought she'd die.

"Fuck," she hissed. "You're not fair."

"Duncan said to show up and show out," he admitted. "It's fucking fun making you come, Tori, and you taste fucking delicious."

"Fuck!" she screamed louder, kicking her legs in his direction. Her hair was still damp, and she wondered how she was going to get it dry by tonight without taking out all her braids. "I have nothing to do with my hair for tonight."

"Your hair is perfect," he complimented with a chuckle, getting up to retrieve the box he'd dropped earlier. Tossing it on the bed beside her, Kevin went out the door slightly to pick up a pile of clothes for him on the table he must've left when he came up.

Tori sat up to open the box. There was a pink silk dress with spaghetti straps, but it was barely mid-thigh length, paired with matching open-toe Jimmy Choo pink heels, and it didn't have underwear. Instead, there was a two-piece pink swimsuit.

"We're going to the Bahamas? It's fricking November? I'm not going anywhere with this outside on the island. And I'm definitely not getting in that damn pool."

"The pool is heated, and I thought Duncan said to trust us," Kevin reminded her.

She growled. "Even you can agree with me and say this is sketchy, Kevin. And how do I know you're not going to film this for blackmail?"

He pulled her up into his arms and gave her an adoring kiss, even ending it by rubbing the tip of his nose against hers. "No filming, we promise. Trust us, Tori. Take an hour, get dressed, and I'll meet you at the entrance to the steps." And then he smacked her rear before exiting.

Tori huffed, looking down at the contents of the box. They'd even included some waterproof makeup.

Were they going to drown her? What had she agreed to? Her demise? She paced for several minutes but then looked up at the sky. Clouds were rolling in, and she remembered Kevin's smell from outside. Not the arousal sweat and funk, but the smell of rain.

And he said late-night thunderstorms are coming.

By the look of the oncoming evening sky, she could surmise rain would be there by the end of the night. She couldn't hold them off on dinner, though. Duncan had mentioned something about rain and the power grid. Would this be her chance to escape? There had to be a boat dock somewhere. She still had her gardening clothes and Timberlands, which she put by the door so when she came back to her room tonight, she could throw them on and get the hell out of there.

You'll have to do whatever they are planning. If Tori was apprehensive or fearful, and not the fun-loving, go-with-the-flow type, it could disrupt the night.

What about the brothers? One was always watching her, unless they were all together. She could be insatiable tonight.

You will be. It'll be your last night with them. They would give her everything. She'd tire them out and use the adrenaline to stay awake to get the hell off this island and away from The Carter Brothers forever.

Pinning her hair up and letting only ringlets of natural curls on the side fall, along with taking out two of the braids in the front to make a puffy curly bang, was genius on her part.

She knew her hairstylist could do better, but given the limitations she was working with, she felt she did an excellent job of making her look so cute. With the dress and shoes, she was fabulous. The choker complemented the outfit, not making the area around her collarbone look bare.

Along with the makeup she wore, her look tonight was the epitome of fun-loving, and she knew the boys would fall head over heels more in love with her.

On the outside, she was carefree, but inside, she was conflicted, scared, and wary. Taking a deep breath, Tori took one last look at herself before heading down the two flights of stairs. Kevin was standing there in dark purple sweatpants and a shirt, but holding a pink rose and a black mink fur hat.

Tori remembered reading that a pink rose signified admiration, joy, affection, and gratitude.

She shivered, remembering the last night each man had a rose. That night had been delicious and dangerous.

What was tonight?

"You look adorable," he said, kissing her cheek.

She noticed he'd shaved and was wearing cologne that made her feel deliriously excited.

Keep your head and heart together, whore! she reprimanded herself.

After he handed her the items in his hand, he took her left hand and led her to the first floor, all the way to the kitchen, where Shawn was standing with a pink rose and a thick, black, floor-length fur. As he handed his rose to Tori, he gave Kevin a fuck off nod, but Kevin crossed his arms across his chest.

"A moment," Shawn growled to his brother.

Kevin snorted and walked out the patio door, closing it behind him.

Shawn was wearing the same thing as Kevin, but his was a royal deep purple sweater and a pair of sweatpants. From his pocket, he took out the divorce papers and tore them up into little pieces. "I know we can't undo what we did to you, Tori, but we can do better by you." He nodded toward the table by the door, and she gasped, seeing her messenger bag. "Dunc asked me to bring it out because you had to know we're not going to keep you like you're a prisoner anymore. You deserve to be free, and we need to accept the consequences. I know your computer and phone are in there, and you want to communicate with everyone, but if you could wait until morning, I'd appreciate that."

Tori nodded and smiled gratefully. "Thank you, Shawn." Sadly, there was no family she wished to contact right away to let them know she was safe. There was really only one Beck, and only because she didn't want him to be worried about her. Nothing more. The only people who really cared about her were the Carter Brothers.

You are with the only people who really love you, she reminded herself.

Shawn continued, "And I want you to know it wasn't all sex that changed my mind about you, Tori. When Malea..." He paused, as if in pain. "I was drunk a couple of nights ago, and I went to Norman's to try to be who I used to be with him, but I couldn't. All I could think about was you, and I knew nothing could satisfy me other than you. I was so fucking frustrated I left, but Malea..." He paused again, and Tori felt as if he were leaving something out. "She was there when I left and started rattling off things in this insane way, and she revealed *you* paid off our mom's debt."

Not expecting him to bring this up, Tori admitted, "I did because I felt a little bad for my past behavior, Shawn."

"But you did that, selflessly. We could have paid for it. We would have paid it, but you took your own money and did it," Shawn stated.

Tori didn't know how to respond. "It was nothing," she said with a shrug of her shoulder.

"No, Tori. It was something because Malea had us all believing that she had done it before that other night. And that's why she was broke, but she wanted to make up for the past and what *you* had done."

"Why would Malea do that?" Tori wondered out loud but then shrugged. "I guess she's trying to make you feel sorry for her. I know she needs money. She was never good with it. I never told you guys, but she's hiding her spending from even her husband. That's why I set up the trust for her children to make sure they were taken care of despite their mother's foolishness and greed."

"But Malea made you look like shit, and I came back needing you to hate me because I hated myself for hating you when all you have ever done, even when you were a bitch in the past, was help me. You were the only one who challenged my mother, and you were the only one that she was ever scared of. I needed you in my life so long ago, and I hate myself for not seeing that until now."

"Shawn, it's fine."

He shook his head. "It'll never be fine. Our sorries will never be enough. I know this. I've accepted this. Duncan told me he's going to pay for everything and anything extra that you need, but I know we still owe you a lot more. Nothing can ever amount to the hardships we put you through because of the past and our misunderstanding - well, fuck, me. Because of me, but I'm going to do whatever I can-"

Tori kissed him tenderly. "Let's just take moment by moment. Tonight, we'll enjoy, and tomorrow, you guys can do something else to make me forgive you," she said because she saw how upset he was becoming. She hoped that when he saw that she was gone tomorrow, it was just something they had to sacrifice to make up for what they had done to her. "The past is the past, even for shit that happened yesterday. All we can do is forgive and live in the future."

He drowned her in kisses, holding her close. "You're amazing, Tori. You know that."

"I know," she giggled. "But I love when you all say it."

Shawn chortled as he helped her on with the coat, only clasping it at the top. "This should warm you up to get to the pool house."

"Pool house?"

He nodded out the glass doors to the pool area, where an enclosure had now been built over it. "They were working on it partially last night. It usually goes up by Thanksgiving because we like to spend the whole weekend out here, but Duncan decided we could put it up early for date night. We drained the chlorine out to produce filtered water. For you, Tori."

The walls were partially see-through, like greenhouse glass, but she could see that there were heaters inside the enclosure, which meant that once she was inside, she wouldn't be cold. Shawn opened the glass door and took her hand to lead her off the patio and down the solar-lit pathway to the pool enclosure.

It was after sunset, but the sky was a cool orange, and the November winds off the lake whipped about. She could still see dark, heavy clouds coming up and thought briefly about the upcoming thunderstorm. The enclosure was built strong enough to withstand it, and she had a feeling that by the time the rain started, she would barely hear it, too engrossed with the boys.

The mink coat was very necessary and kept her warm. If she stayed, they'd probably spoil her death.

You're not staying! She told herself as she pulled her arm around her waist to hug the fur tight on her.

Don't you dare fall in love, Tori! Don't you dare lose your mind and promise to stay no matter what they do!

When she entered the pool enclosure, Duncan was there at the doorway, handing her another pink rose—the heat from the propane heaters rosied her cheeks, making her flush.

"Kevin was right, you do look adorable," he said, dressed in a dark lavender sweatshirt and sweater.

It was now that she noticed they all wore black swim shoes, but now she knew why. The pool was filled in and looked beautiful - right out of a magazine, with glowing waterproof candles around the edge. However, seeing all that water so close made her slightly terrified.

Duncan pulled her into his arms so all she could see was him. "Breath, my love. And close your eyes."

"I'm not comfortable," she whispered, trying not to shake at the proximity of water.

His body had begun to sway, and somewhere soft R&B music played.

"You're going to trust us, Tori," he said determinedly. "You are going to be free of this fear of water."

"You say it like it's just that easy," she said, almost with a sob.

"It will be because we love you, and water is the last thing in this world to fear when you have our love."

Gawd, why did he have to sound so sweet?

CHAPTER 17

Tori's Floating

By this time, Duncan was moving their bodies sensually to the music, and Shawn moved behind her. With her chest pressed to Duncan, his slow, steady breathing calmed her anxiety and fear, as she let the heat from his body envelope her like his arms were doing, removing apprehension. She didn't have to open her eyes to know Shawn was there, helping her off with her coat and hat. Shawn then pulled her back to the front of his body, wrapping his arms around her waist, not missing a beat as he sensuously swayed her to the music, planting small, luscious kisses on her shoulder and neck.

Tori let the music fill her consciousness, while Shawn relaxed her with dancing and kisses in a very highly erogenous zone on her chest, shoulders, neck, and face. His calm breathing became hers, and she was lost with time, but soon felt Kevin mold himself perfectly to the front of her body, swaying a three-way perfectly with her and Shawn as if they'd done this since they were born. She noted he didn't have his sweater on. The fabric of the dress was thin, and she could feel Kevin's heat emanating from him.

It felt wonderful to feel their bodies on hers, and Tori was getting aroused quicker until... she gasped, feeling water on her toes. Her legs started to give out on her, but Kevin's firm hand moved up her dress as he began planting kisses on the other side of her neck.

Tori became engrossed in feeling Kevin's fingers move between her legs, and she lolled her head back against Shawn, who kissed her, while she felt Kevin's fingers glide through her slippery lower lips, titillating her.

"Sweet pussy," Kevin whispered, while she moaned in Shawn's mouth, feeling Kevin's thick finger press inside of her.

Shawn eased their sway to pull her thigh up, and Kevin took the weight of her, holding her leg, while sliding his hand deeper, using her essence coating his fingers to ease also into her rear access. Tori whimpered, grinding her need into his hands, feeling her eyeballs roll to the back of her head.

With only three short presses to her back, Shawn made her knead her clit against Kevin's wet palm, and she was orgasming, convulsing, and whining while kissing Shawn as Kevin's fingers continued to twitch inside of her, increasing the strength of the pulses inside of her.

Tori was out of it for several minutes before she realized the water was at her knees. By this time, Shawn had moved away, and Kevin pulled her closer to him to kiss her deeply. She gripped her arms around his neck tightly, shuddering.

"You're safe, Princess," he said, hoisting her higher so her other leg could easily come around his body. "You're loved and safe."

She wasn't cold, but she was shaking, unsure whether to be aroused or scared, because now the warm water was up to her waist. "No, I'm scared," she admitted. "Please. I can't. I thought I could."

Softly, he kissed her and pulled her to him, holding her close and rubbing her back.

Duncan was on the edge of the pool, in only black swimming trunks, watching them. Then, he dove in, coming to her, and moved to the side of her. He gripped her nape and directed her lips to his. Soft, comforting, and passionate.

Tori could almost hear his voice in her head saying, *'Breath with me, Tori.'* And as she kissed him, she did. Deep until she felt her lungs fill and then slowly out, all while they kissed in so many ways. Her body easily slipped around him, locking her legs on his back and her arms around his neck.

Duncan distracted her so much that she didn't realize the water was at her chest until Shawn pressed behind her, pulling her dress up, and she had to stop kissing Duncan to allow her dress to come off.

"You're there," Shawn said proudly, kissing her nape and the back of her shoulders as a reward. "Now relax, Tori."

Duncan continued kissing and breathing with her - even deeper this time, and she found herself holding her breath. The third time, he dipped her underwater slightly and brought her quickly up. She didn't panic. Feeling comforted that all of them were there kept her calmer.

Kevin, without his sweat suit, was behind Duncan, smiling just as proudly when she came up the second time, and she could feel him taking off her shoes before he moved to the side of Duncan and took one of her arms when she came up for the third time. Kevin carefully moved her into her older brother's arms, but Duncan didn't let her lock her legs around Kevin.

Duncan leaned toward her and softly kissed her some more. "You know we love you." He kissed her more, and then Kevin turned her face so he could kiss her, and then Shawn, who was still behind her, leaned her face back so he could kiss her.

Tori knew the tears that came from her eyes were real and flowing heavily because she could feel their love.

Kevin assured her, "I'm holding you securely, Princess."

"Release and relax, Tori," Duncan ordered, massaging her thigh, which was close to her side, and then her arms, relaxing her.

Looking up into Duncan's eyes, she could feel the trust. Shawn was slightly behind her, now gently massaging her rear muscles and down her other thigh. Duncan's assertive tone calmed her tension, and she saw Kevin nod, taking a deep breath.

She blushed, knowing she had been almost wringing his neck in her grip.

"Now, we're going to teach you how to float," Duncan announced as Shawn's arm came around her waist to replace Kevin's. By this time, the water was at her neck, but she knew she was being hoisted to their height, so if she tried to touch the bottom, she would be underwater. "Don't tense now."

Kevin guided her head back on Shawn's bare shoulder, with a wicked smile on his lips as he began to kiss down her body, moving her thighs on his shoulders, but his mouth moved between her legs while Duncan's mouth took in her breast. Tori was very distracted, yet remarkably relaxed, as her body began to float. Shawn placed adoring kisses on her face and lips repeatedly.

"Such a good girl," Shawn commended between kisses, and also massaged her other breast. "So beautiful. So amazing."

Kevin's tongue beautifully fluttered up and down between her clit and perineum, as his fingers dipped into her and behind her. Duncan switched to the other breast by going under her.

"You're floating," Shawn whispered.

Tori drew her mouth away and realized the boys weren't helping her stay afloat, and she giggled, but then gasped as Kevin pressed his finger deeper in her. She tightened as her body went underwater, but he followed her, while Duncan took her arm and held her by her side so her face wouldn't go underwater. That didn't stop Kevin, and she was too aroused to feel scared as she culminated, shaking, so grateful Duncan never stopped holding her.

Kevin released her lower body, and Duncan moved between her legs. He was naked, and somehow, she was too, not remembering when they had removed her swimsuit. His mouth consumed her as he took her to the edge of the pool, slightly lifting her higher so her arms could hold herself up on the edge. Shawn lay down so her head could rest on his thigh, while Duncan dipped his face to her breasts. She could easily grip Shawn's beautiful phallus while Duncan was tantalizing her breasts with his mouth. The middle brother lifted his thigh between her legs, but also to steady them on the side of the pool, and she promptly used him to rub herself.

Tori selfishly took control of the orgasm, loving how she could elogate her pleasure, and they allowed her to. They wanted her to use them, and she did.

"Ahhh," she cried out, feeling the explosion shake her to her core, shooting all over.

Duncan raised her so that she could sit on the edge, and she immediately dipped down to engulf Shawn into her mouth. She loved going down on him so far back in her throat she'd make herself choke. He'd gasped, loving how the tip of him smashed into her mouth. She could see it in his eyes and how they couldn't stop watching her, as if perplexed as to how she could draw such pleasure out of him.

"Fuck, Tori, please don't make me come yet. I want your ass so bad."

She let him fall out with a popping noise as she giggled. "What about what I want?"

Duncan came over with a really thick pink towel and helped her to her feet. She let him dry her off before leading her over to a waterproof love seat. After thoroughly kissing her, he sat down and spread his legs.

Gawd, she loved that about them. If she wanted something right away, another brother could quench her thirst, and they didn't care about sharing her among them. This turned her on so much. Tori immediately dropped to her knees and proceeded to fill her mouth with Duncan's gorgeous shaft, slobbing on the base, side, and tip until she returned to go up and down on him, loving how thick he was getting.

Usually quiet, Duncan gasped, moaned, and threw his head back, enjoying every lick and suck she delivered until he bucked his hips, at the same time holding her by her nape so when he came, his hot liquid shot down her throat.

"Arrrgghhh...ummmmm," he raged, holding her head tightly.

Tori held her breath and swallowed what felt like a gallon of him. Tears welled in her eyes, but she loved every second of what he gave.

When he finally released her, Tori had to fall back and gasp for air and saw Kevin and Shawn watching them in concern, both wearing a towel around their waist. She smiled as Kevin helped her to her feet.

"I thought he twisted your fucking neck off," Kevin said. "What the fuck, Dunc? You said show out, not take her out."

"Hey, that's my job," Shawn teased, pulling Tori into his arms, but she could see he was checking her neck before he gave her a short kiss. "You're beautiful, you know that."

Duncan was still dazed and panting, trying to gather himself, but shot Kevin a finger.

Kevin smacked her butt. "Let's eat before we enjoy the night. It looks like you're going to need more energy."

Tori was shocked that they could just so easily forget about formerly thinking about killing her, and how easy she allowed them to do so without getting pissed off and mad. She was still partially dazed and aroused from going down on Duncan. That had been intense, and maybe because she hadn't pulled all her oral tricks out of her pocket until now with Duncan. He had a lust demon hiding behind that cool and smoothness, and she knew if she really took it any further, he could damn well lose control. Why did that thought arouse her even more?

'*That would mean you'd have to stay longer, and you aren't doing that, remember*,' she told herself.

"I fucking told you her mouth is delicious," Kevin warned his middle brother, helping him to his feet.

Duncan wrapped his towel back around him, while Shawn presented her with a thick, terry-cloth pink robe and some pink pool shoes.

"You guys aren't going to spoil me enough to want to stop hating you," she warned.

"We can fucking try though," Kevin said.

Shawn chuckled and led her over to where they'd had a small dinner setup. Grilled chicken with pineapple, fettuccini with heaps of carrots, and snow peas in a buttery sauce. Her stomach growled as Shawn helped her sit down, and she noticed how they still acted like gentlemen, not sitting down until she did.

Tori dived into the meal while Shawn spoke.

"I went to see Malea today," he announced.

Kevin and Duncan stiffened, looked at Tori, who was stuffing her face, acting nonchalant, and then back at their younger brother.

"Why? She has nothing to do with what we've done to her," Duncan said.

"I already told Tori I spoke to her because I wanted Tori to know Malea told us information about her that was untrue."

Kevin hissed, "I don't think we need to spoil the night talking about Malea. Don't you agree, Tori?"

Knowing her sister could give two fucks about her, she nodded. "I don't think we need to. Malea is clearly out to manipulate you guys for money. If she knew you had money, most likely she was trying to find a way to get some for herself and pay off her gambling debts before Scott found out about it."

"Wait," Duncan said, shifting uneasily. "Scott doesn't know?"

"As far as I can ascertain," Tori answered. "And she wants him to stay in the dark, which is why she's been blocking him from even talking to you, Duncan. She had to sell the boat, they had to cover expenses, and she's drained all their accounts."

Kevin gripped the table, showing he was becoming upset. Since he was right beside her, she placed her buttery fingers over his.

"But like Kevin said, we aren't going to disrupt the evening by speaking about my sister. I've maintained a level of offishness with her on purpose because I know she's mismanaged her life so much it could destroy everyone around her. And the sad part is, she doesn't care." She stuffed some more chicken in her mouth, delighting in the fact that the food tasted so good. "I'd suggest you open your own restaurant, Duncan, but then you won't have time to spoil me with this food. Gawd, I could eat this forever and a day."

He smiled proudly. "If it makes you happy, Tori, you know we'd do it all the time."

She gritted her teeth because it did make her happy, and the food made her want to stay. Their love, their food, and their actions just made her want to say fuck it, forgive them, and stay.

Shawn looked at Tori's left finger. "Where's the ring we gave you?"

She blushed. "I took it off and put it in my bag. I didn't want a reminder of you'all."

"That's understandable," Duncan said.

"Is it?" Kevin questioned. "You didn't destroy it, though."

"It was too beautiful to destroy, and it was significant." She wasn't going to admit she was going to give it to the baby as some nice, sweet sixteen gift. "I still wanted to treasure the good times."

Duncan pushed a ring box across the table. "It's from all of us, and it was to complement your ring."

Tori looked at all of them. "But I was leaving. When did you plan to give me this?"

"The day after we kidnapped you," Kevin explained. "I thought of it. I thought if we gave you something to help you understand you needed to stay, but Duncan noticed you'd taken the other ring off and said you'd toss this one across the room if we gave it to you too soon."

Shawn sighed in a grave tone. "Tori, we need you to understand we know-"

"Shawn, wait-" Duncan cut him off and looked over her head with a deep frown just as the rain started to fall. "Kevin, take her to her room now."

Kevin snatched the ring from the table and then gently took Tori's hand to lead her to the door, while Duncan and Shawn started to put on their clothes.

"What's going on?" she asked as Kevin helped her put on her hat and coat.

A worried expression was on his face as he gathered his clothes before leading her out of the pool enclosure and returning her to the house.

"Tori, you said you'd trust us, right?" he reminded her.

"Yes, but what is going on?"

He was taking her to the second floor, where she knew the big door was. "I don't know, but Duncan felt danger, and we want to make sure you're safe."

"What danger? The weather? That's ridiculous."

He pulled the big door open. "Let me go help them out,

and then I'll come back to tell you everything. I promise. But for now, we need you safe."

Tori looked at the door; she knew he'd closed it behind her, and worried how she could get it back open. "Fine."

Kevin roughly pulled her in for a delirious long kiss before shutting her through the door, stuffing the ring box in her hand, and closing it behind her. Tori rushed up to her room, changed into her garden clothes and Timerlands, and then put on the mink and hat again. By this time, the rain was coming down like a river over the one window she had. Just as she was putting the ring box in her pocket, the electricity in the house went out.

Tori could only hear silence for a moment before she heard bumping somewhere in the house. There was a lot of bumping and a lot of things breaking. It sounded like a herd of elephants bumping a floor below her.

She went to her door, and it opened easily. Despite the darkness, she went into the crafting room, remembered where the industrial heavy-duty rug tufter was, and carried it down the two flights of stairs. The needle point was able to be jammed into the door slot enough, and even though she knew it would cause damage to the gun, she was sure it could give her the leverage she needed to open the heavy door.

Pressing with all her might, she could hear the wood cracking, and then the gun gave way, breaking from the stress, but at least she was able to make a dent. Using the other side of the gun, she began to knock at the small crease she had made.

Suddenly she heard a loud gun explode, scaring her so bad she dropped the rug tool and the broken needle dragged down her leg, going through her clothes and puncturing the side of her calf. Fuck!

But that wasn't what was making her heart race as another shot bellowed out, shaking the whole house.

What the hell?!

"Kevin!" she screamed, using her fist to hit the wall again, but there was no answer, just silence. "Duncan!"

Still no answer.

"Shawn! Please!"

Nothing.

She picked up the tufter again despite her leg hurting and started hitting the door, praying one of them had to be alive to save her.

"Tori!" a deep growl on the other side of the wall.

Her head swooned back in shock. "Beck? Beck, is that you?! I'm here! Yes! It's Tori!"

"Fucking hell!" he sneered. "Get the fuck back away from the wall."

As soon as she stepped away, something jammed in the crease, and the door inched open. Emergency red lights illuminated around the massive frame of the ball-headed red beard construction manager dressed like he'd just gotten off work. There were bruises on his face, but other than the sheen of sweat, he looked like he'd just run a mile and was fine. Did he swim to her?

Beck was holding a large, sharp-ended tool, but she still flew in his arms, and he looked grateful to see her.

"We gotta go," he declared and started to pull her away from the door toward the second-floor steps.

"Wait! Did you kill them?"

"Tori, there's no time."

"Beck! Did you-"

A third blast shook the house.

Beck swore viciously. "That's your Duncan realizing they're just blanks and that means we really got to go or they're going to make sure-"

An African American teenager wearing all black from head to toe ran up the steps, with Tori's bag on their shoulder.

"Beck, we have to go," they ordered frantically, running back down the stairs.

Tori couldn't tell if the teenager was a boy or a girl because they were wearing a black hoodie that covered their head, and their body was clad in jeans and black shoes.

The teenager hurriedly explained, "I put the small charges by the door and once they figure out how to get out of the enclosure-"

A more minor explosion sounded as Beck was practically dragging Tori down the stairs to the first floor. Tori didn't have time to think, but she ran toward the front of the house, which was unfamiliar to her; however, the teenager seemed to know exactly where to go.

A substantial front door was in front of them, but just as the teenager reached to open it, two kitchen knives shot straight over their heads, embedding in the wood.

Tori looked back to see Duncan holding three more knives, looking pissed.

Beck snatched Tori behind him toward the teenager. "Get Tori out of here," he said, not taking his eyes off Duncan as he pulled out the large, sharp tool again and snatched one of the knives from the wall.

"You're not taking her, Beck," Duncan hissed. "And what the fuck did you do to my brother?"

"I was trying to punch that smart ass mouth of his off his fucking face!" Beck snarled, raising his hands ready to defend himself.

"Duncan, don't do this!" Tori cried.

"Stay out of this, Tori. Let the grown men talk - with their fists," Beck ordered, and she was positive she saw a smile on her construction manager's face. "Now get!"

That was the last thing she saw before Duncan charged at Beck, slamming him almost through the wall by the door as the teenager dragged Tori out of the house down a walkway and darted into the woods.

CHAPTER 18

The Destruction by Shadow

It was almost pitch black with a quarter moon, but the teenager seemed to know where they were going.

"What... about... Beck?" Tori huffed as she followed the teenager.

"Beck can take care of himself-"

Another boom, this one not as loud, came from the house, and Tori gasped, seeing part of the side of the house on fire.

"Oh Gawd! Someone could be hurt."

"Good," the teenager snarled as they made it to a lot of large rocks and fallen trees where an inflatable boat was tied up. "That big one tried to take Beck's head off. I locked the two in the pool enclosure, but that middle one is smart, it's fuck. How the fuck did he realize I was shooting blanks?"

Tori could hear sirens in the distance as another explosion came from the house, but this sounded more like a gas explosion. "What did you do?"

"Get in the boat, woman," the teenager ordered. "I don't break my promises, and I promised to get you to safety."

Why did that feel like a threat, and if Tori didn't get in the boat, this teenager could do something terrible to her?

This is your escape! Her conscience screamed. But Tori wanted to go back and save her men.

"Look, they don't give two shits about you. This was all some sick joke to destroy you," the teenager said. "You don't see the big picture because you're clouded by lust, but if I had three men eating my body all the time, I'd think twice about trying to be rescued, too."

"You're a girl?" Tori asked, shocked.

The teenager rolled her eyes. "Get in the fucking boat," she ordered, tossing Tori a life jacket and putting the messenger bag in the boat.

Tori got into the inflatable, squeezed a life jacket over her fur coat, and then gathered her bag on her shoulder, hugging it slightly because she had missed not having her personal items near her. What amazed her was that she wasn't scared of water as much anymore, and she grimaced a smile, knowing why. Looking back at the island, Tori saw that the fire was consuming the back part of the house. Police and fire boats were getting closer, but she knew most of the house would be destroyed by the time anything could be done.

"What did you do?" Tori demanded to know, but she was feeling wretched about all the hard work Duncan had put in.

"I was just a distraction. We'd been sitting on the island's back edge most of the day, trying to see if you were really there. I was waiting on the roof and signaled Beck when I saw you come out of the house with the mink." The girl chuckled. "Man, they really slobbered your ass-"

"You shouldn't have been watching."

"I mean, the glass was frosted, but I saw a lot of clumps of bodies, and I knew what y'all were doing. There was very little to the imagination."

Tori blushed. "You don't understand. You're too young."

"I do, but Beck found out a lot of shit about them. And when you didn't show up at his brother's, Beck had me tail them."

"You're just a child."

"Yeah, well, you're a whore, but I'm not pointing that out all the time." The teenager laughed, and Tori wanted to shove the little girl off the boat, but she wasn't sure how to maneuver it.

"I knew what they did, and I was fine with it. I was going to save myself."

"How? That's a pretty fancy state-of-the-art security motion system. I had to use all my tricks to get through undetected, and Beck couldn't infiltrate it until the storm came. And then there was getting off the island. This boat barely made it across the current, and Beck said you couldn't swim."

"I was going to steal their boat."

The teenager snorted. "Yeah, well, you couldn't if you didn't have the key fob, which they have on their wrist in an invisible tattoo. It unlocks everything on their stupid island, which is why I couldn't get into the house."

"How do you know all this? You're a child."

The girl rolled her eyes again. "Stop calling me a child. My name is Shadow."

It was the most ridiculous name for a girl, and Tori was too pissed off to get into a verbal fight with the teenager after being called a whore.

But you are!

Tori forced that thought away, seeing they were still nowhere near the shore. "How far are we going?"

"Near the riverfront, right by a private marina. It was the only place we could launch without being seen."

"Seen by who? All the brothers were on the island."

Shadow responded, "Beck said someone had been

following him for a couple of days, but he didn't mention who."

"How does Beck know you? And how do you know so much?"

"I'm resourceful," the girl said proudly and pulled off the hood to reveal thick hair slicked back in one low ponytail. Her phone chirped and she pulled out an old flip phone, which Tori was shocked to see someone her age have. "Beck's good," she confirmed. "He said to tell you no one's dead."

Tori sighed in relief.

"You really care?" the girl asked.

"Yes. I care about them."

"You sure it's not some Stockholm syndrome? Cause I've seen that big mouth and the middle one in the underground fights, and they're pretty wild. Untamed, if you ask me."

"I didn't ask," Tori snipped. "You still didn't tell me how Beck knows you. Where'd he find you?"

"People don't find me, I find them. I need something from him. He asked me to find him a girl."

"You find people for a living?"

Shadow smirked. "I find what people desire."

"Beck and I don't have that kind of relationship."

"You misunderstood me. He wanted me to find a particular girl for him, not you. And then he came back the same day and told me about you. I knew I could find you faster than he desired because Beck is not a nice guy, and any girl I find for him is likely to find a headache and a cracked pelvis. There's nothing gentle about that man."

Tori grimaced at the young woman's vulgarity, although she should be used to it from Kevin. It was odd to think of her construction manager having a desire, knowing what she knew about him, but then realistically, every man had needs. Beck's were just difficult to fill, and unfortunately, what the young woman said would be true when it came to dealing with Beck.

"Why would Beck come to you with such a strange request? You're too young to be some madam."

Shadow snorted. "I'm not a madam. I'm resourceful." She immediately changed the subject. "Did you know they were named after their father?"

"Who?"

"Your brothers."

Taking offense at the relational connection, Tori quickly said, "They aren't my blood brothers."

"Really? Because it's your father, they're named after. Isn't your father, Keir Dawson Snow?"

A chill swelled in Tori even though she was wearing the mink and fur hat. "How'd you know?"

"I'm resourceful," Shadow reminded with a wicked smirk. "I'm shocked you didn't get it too. Your father's initials are K-D-S. Kevin - Duncan - Shawn." She chuckled. "I thought it poetic, and I bet their moms did too. Probably how your mother figured he was sleeping with their mother." She ticked her tongue. "I know your sister figured shit out. Well, at least a little."

"What makes you think that?"

"Well, she got a letter about three months ago from your mom's estate lawyer. Seems there's some money left somewhere, and whatever the letter said, your sister went to the brothers to help her get it."

"What did the letter say?"

Shadow shrugged. "I was paid to look into the boys. Not your sister. I just got a little curious and went through some of her messages to a greaser named Norman. That man gives me the icks. He don't know what he wants to be - gay, straight, bi. But to each his own, and he damn well hates you for taking his Shawn away. Once his parents stopped funding his life, he realized he needed Shawn more than he thought, but you snatched up not one but all three brothers, and Norman can't do shit to get him back."

Tori frowned, thinking about what her mother's estate could say that Malea didn't tell Tori about. Tori was positive there was no money because when her father got word that their mother had passed, he spent years making sure there was no money out there for him. True, it was greedy of him to do so, but her father wanted every penny, and now she knew why - for his suffering and sacrifice. Was that why her sister was pressing her about their father's things?

"So, you're okay, fucking your brothers?" Shadow asked all of a sudden.

"They aren't my brothers."

"I know by blood they aren't, but it's like a brother relationship, since they are your sister's brothers."

"Stop trying to stir up shit," Tori snipped.

Shadow chuckled again. "That's my middle name, according to Beck. Shit starter."

To draw attention from herself, Tori asked, "Why do you need Beck?"

"I got an uncle who needs some things, and Beck knows how to build some devices. Very unique devices. One very unique device that we need for an enemy of my uncle, and the only way I can get Beck to do this is if I help him out, because I know he won't help my uncle if I ask him outright." She reached behind her and pulled out some binoculars. "You think your brothers are going to jail for a long time for kidnapping? Are you going to visit?"

"I'm not pressing charges," Tori said. "And none of that is your business anymore."

"But I'm nosey and a shit starter, so it'll stay my business until I say so," Shadow quipped, looking back at the island, then forward in the direction they were going. "We have half an hour."

Tori was going to die mentally if she didn't get away from this juvenile. She could jump in the river and float to shore. There weren't any dangerous creatures in the Detroit River.

"I wouldn't do that if I were you, even if you know how to float," Shadow warned, reading Tori's mind. "That water is freezing cold. You'd die of hyperthermia before you get to shore. You and the baby."

Gasping, Tori covered her stomach protectively. "Beck told you?!"

"Nah! I can smell your pregnancy a mile away. That's one of my talents. A family blessing and curse. A month? Almost two, right?"

Tori was feeling nauseous all of a sudden. "Please stop."

"The boat? Or you want me to stop, brother fucker?"

The meal she had just had barely made it off the boat as Tori turned to throw up in the water.

"I don't see why you're upset," Shadow said. "You got all that money from Duncan. You can do anything you damn well want to now."

Tori threw up again. She really hated this juvenile.

The small engine on the boat suddenly turned off, along with the small light that illuminated their path. Shadow shoved a bottle of water in Tori's hand as her phone chirped again.

"Beck is asking me where I am," Shadow informed Tori, but there was a disturbed tone.

Tori took a swig of the water to rinse her mouth out. "Tell him," she ordered. "He's probably with the coast guard, and they can get us to the mainland faster than this little boat could."

Shadow whispered a curse. "We lost signal." She raised the phone in the air. "Nothing can go out or in."

Tori dug in her bag to find her phone, but it was dead, and

so was the rechargeable battery she had in there. "Get the boat back running and let's get to shore in a hurry."

"Something doesn't feel right," Shadow expressed, but she still turned the boat and the light on to head to shore. Occasionally, the teen would look back at her phone to see if anything had changed, but there was nothing but darkness.

Tori didn't realize how big the Detroit River was and how really far they were from the mainland. Duncan's island was a perfect getaway, but she had ruined it with her rescue, and she felt awful about destroying his property.

"He's filthy rich, you know," Shadow said, doing that mind-reading thing again.

"You don't know who I was thinking about," Tori grumbled.

"You were looking back on the island, and that middle brother owns the island, but he's fucking filthy rich. Like mega million rich. That ten million he sent to your bank account is chump change. He can make that at any casino he walks into on a nightly basis if he wants."

Tori was feeling sick again. The more truth this child threw at her, the more nauseous she became. What the hell was wrong with her?

"That's the only bottle of water until we get to land, so use it sparingly," the teenager warned.

Putting her face in her hands, Tori really wanted the girl just to shut up.

Shadow's phone chirped, but that only got another curse from Shadow. "Beck's message sent blank. We must be hitting Canadian towers."

Looking up from her palms, Tori could see the land. "Let's just get to land and a working phone. Do you have a car?"

"Who doesn't?" Shadow snapped, rolling her eyes. "That's a stupid question. Just because you think I'm a child doesn't mean I don't have a car. I can rig explosives, but I can't operate a vehicle."

Tori bit her tongue because the child was getting on her nerves. When she spoke to Beck again, she'd make sure to tell him not to do shit for this little cunt.

You sound like Kevin.

Almost there. Almost at the land.

She stayed quiet. By now, Tori couldn't see anything of the island, but at least the land was coming up. Shadow still looked at her phone, behind them, and then in front of them, constantly.

Tori assumed, like any person this young girl's age, that she needed to be in constant communication or connected, but that was with a flip phone, which was unusual for someone her age. "Don't you have a newer phone?"

"What's the point? So, people can track you? No, thank you. I prefer burners," Shadow answered.

"How do you stay in contact with people? How does anyone call you?"

"They don't. I contact or call them."

"How do you-" Tori stopped talking when Shadow gave her this dark look, and she could hear the little girl's voice saying, '*I'm resourceful.*' Changing the subject, Tori asked, "Why doesn't Beck like this uncle?"

"No one likes my uncle. I don't like him, but I need to use him to keep him away from my best friend."

"So you use people to get what you want."

"Don't we all use people? If not, you should. That's what human beings were put on this planet for. To use each other."

A very mature outlook for a very young woman, Tori noted. "And this contraption you need Beck to build. Will it hurt him?"

"No. It won't, but it'll definitely trap the person we need to catch in it. And Beck might even get a kick out of." Shadow smiled wickedly. "Paybacks a bitch, as Beck would say." She rechecked her phone in disappointment. "Even if Beck were coming with the coast guard, they could probably get to the mainland faster, but it'll take them about ten minutes before they can get over to us. Where we are, larger boats couldn't get near."

That was nice of the young woman to assure Tori of anything, and the feeling of nausea was slowly starting to go away. Maybe it wasn't the girl. Perhaps it was being out on the water that was irritating her. She'd never been in a boat like this before, or any vessel for that matter, except her first night with the brothers.

"You're thinking about them again," Shadow sang knowingly. "Did you really do it with all three? Weren't you overwhelmed?"

Tori wiped the secret smile off her lips. "You're too young to know about that."

"You'd be surprised how much I know, but fine. If you don't want to talk about it, I completely understand. That life should be kept private because a lot of people wouldn't understand you, and that relationship they have where they are fine with sharing one woman." Shadow huffed. "Do you, boo." She turned the engine off.

Tori became alarmed. "What's going on?"

"I don't want to damage the blade on the rocks. We can coast to shore," Shadow explained.

From what Tori could see, there were all rocks along the shore, so it was completely understandable, but it just felt like it was even longer to get there.

Soon, the boat came to a stop, and they both stepped out into ankle-high water to pull it up onto some rocks so it wouldn't drift back out to sea. They had to climb over the rocky cliff up to the land carefully. It was dark, but there was still some light from the road, allowing Tori to follow Shadow toward what looked to be a small, gray SUV parked under a streetlight.

Shadow continued walking on ahead in a hurry to get to the vehicle. Tori was still woozy from the boat ride and had to pause to collect her equilibrium now that they were on land. Although it was dark all around her, Tori knew that now, being away from the island, she was semi-safe from being kidnapped again, and Beck would be there soon.

Shadow's phone chirped, but by this time, the teenager had reached the SUV and stopped to check it. Tori was about fifty feet behind Shadow and still trying to center herself from the boat ride and be grateful she was back on the mainland.

"Come on!" Shadow called impatiently.

Just as Tori was about to walk to the vehicle, she heard a noise to the left and looked that way to see a familiar form in the darkness and then stopped because she couldn't believe it. Only when the form was arm's reach in front of her, she called out, "Malea?"

Her sister raised her arm and swung something that hit Tori in the head hard, sending her to the ground. If she hadn't been roughhousing with the boys, this probably would have shaken her harder, but she landed fine, just a little dizzier.

"Stop right there, little girl, or I swear I'll put a hole right in her head!!" Malea screamed hysterically and kicked Tori in the leg. "Get the fuck up, Tori!"

Tori had to shake off the fuzziness and stumble to her feet.

Shadow was about ten feet away, holding up her hands in surrender, and Malea was aiming a very familiar .22 at Tori.

"Is that Daddy's old gun?" Tori asked, shocked. "You broke into storage."

"Where's the fucking journals, Tori?!" Malea demanded, shaking the gun at her. "I was in that fucking storage all day looking for them! I know they were in Momma's chest!"

Tori was confused. "Why are you using a gun for some silly diaries Dad kept?"

"I've been trying to get those damn diaries from you forever! I don't know what the fuck you did to Shawn, but he was supposed to get them and give them to me along with all the rest of the money you stole from me."

Holding her head to fight the fuzziness, her eyesight cleared up enough to see Malea in jeans, a sweater, and a long trench coat, but she looked spastic and gaunt, almost pale and sickly.

"What's wrong with you?" Tori asked in concern.

"Look at you! All my life, I've had to watch you get everything you wanted. The life I wanted. The men I've wanted. Everything always works out for you, no matter how awful you were. It's not fair. And you didn't even fucking care about the level of hatred I have for you, Tori. Cause you so-fucking-happy! It's not fair!" Malea snarled. "They gave you that mink. Shawn said he was giving the money back to you. But it's mine! It's all mine, and you stole it just like you stole my daddy. He wasn't even your father! He was mine, and I couldn't have him. All my life, I had to watch you get everything! EVERYTHING! And I got nothing!"

Tori looked at Shadow and nodded to assure her that things were fine. That gun was so old, and the bullets were probably even older. Yes, her sister was trying to prove a point, and maybe she was financially destitute; she needed to go this far. Tori had seen the signs but ignored them—the vague way of mentioning money woes and the attempt to steal from the safe. If the boys had not been in Tori's life, she would have paid more attention to things, but what was done was done. "Malea, it was all a game our mother played on him, you and me. I read the diaries. I read what our mother did to Keir because of his infidelity and greed. And I know who my real father is."

"I DON'T FUCKING CARE!" Malea screamed. "Now you'll come with me, take me to the diaries, or I'll fucking shoot you and still get all your shit."

Tori was going to say she didn't have Malea as her beneficiary.

"Put the gun down and I'll come with you, Malea," Tori said calmly. If she could calm Malea down, Tori was sure she could overpower her sister and retrieve the gun, so this could finally be over. The gun hadn't been fired in decades, and Tori was doubtful her sister even knew how to aim correctly.

Malea started to lower the gun, but then Shadow said, "She don't even have you as a beneficiary. If you kill your sister, Malea, everything goes to the group home project."

It was Tori's turn to roll her eyes at Shadow, and now she really understood why Beck called her the shit starter.

"You fucking bitch!" Malea screamed, raising the gun back at Tori. "You manipulating fucking whore!"

Tori was very tired of being called a whore. "Malea, I didn't manipulate anything. Daddy left me everything, and I split it all down the line for you. I even gave a portion of what I had left to help your kids."

"All that money was mine. It came from Momma. Not him. Daddy had run all his businesses into the ground, and when Momma died, she left that money in a trust. She dangled it for him to continue his ruse of loving you over me and then forced him to leave it all to you."

"Was that what was in the letter?" Tori questioned.

Malea shifted and then coughed - no, it was more like a hack, and Tori was sure something had come up because Malea spat at the ground a darker substance than spit.

"You're dying," Shadow said. "You've got cancer."

Tori frowned, wondering how the young girl knew that.

As usual, Shadow read her mind. "I can smell it from here. When she coughed, it was evident. She's stage four."

The hand holding the gun shook, and Malea's eyes welled up in tears. "It's not fair," she hissed. "I tried everything to make Keir love me... but he never even looked at me." She threw off the trench coat, and Tori gasped, seeing her sister's emasculated form. "LOOK AT ME!"

The sweater and jeans barely clung to her gaunt body, and Tori could even see the port in her sister's chest.

"I deserve something good from her! Not this! Not her cancer!" Malea cried through sobs.

"Tori!" Shawn cried out, running up behind Shadow, followed by Duncan, Kevin - still nursing his jaw, and Beck.

The distraction made Malea grab Tori and hold the gun by Tori's side. It was already cocked and could fire at any time. Tori forced herself to stay calm as Malea's scrawny arm came around her neck to drag her back towards the rocks.

Tori thought about the baby and trembled. "Please, Malea. I'm pregnant."

"You're fucking what?!" Shawn exclaimed.

"By who?!" Malea demanded. "Which son of bitch is the father? So, I can watch him die when I shoot this fucking bastard out of you?"

CHAPTER 19

Time After

Shawn approached slowly with his hands up. "Malea, this is no one's fault but mine, but we didn't expect to fall in love with her. You didn't tell us Tori had changed. She's not the evil bitch we all assumed her *still* to be." He looked at Tori. "And she's kind, selfless, and the most giving person I have ever met. She's shown me how to love even the ugly parts of my life and myself, and I can never say thank you enough to her for what she's done for me." He looked back at Malea. "Yes, I hated her with everything holy, but that was before my soul was touched by the angel she is now. We all love her, and that baby is all of ours, no matter who's the biological father."

Malea's scream pierced the air, a raw expression of her shattered trust and love. "You all lied to me," her voice cracked with anguish. "You all promised we'd hurt her. I'm your sister! Your only sister! You're supposed to love me over her! You all promised we'd destroy Tori, and then you all fell in love with her?! She took you away from me, just like she took Keir. It's not fair!"

Tori felt the hard butt of the gun jam against her side, sending an earth-shattering wave of pain, and she doubled over, refusing to fall to her knees. Immediately, Duncan and Kevin started toward them, but Tori quickly held her hand up to stop them. Malea was still close, and the gun was still cocked. Whether her sister could use it right or not, it could still be possible to hit Tori in a vital organ and hurt the life growing inside of her.

"You get everything!" Malea's voice was a mix of rage and betrayal. "Just tell me where the journals are before I kill you, so I can get what's left of Momma's estate. You owe me that, Tori. You owe me your life for taking my life away."

"What the fuck does the journals have to do with anything?!" Kevin snarled.

"It's the letter," Tori explained calmly. "Something in a letter she received a couple of weeks ago that she didn't tell anyone about."

"Momma needed me to destroy the journals, so her name wouldn't be ruined. If I destroy them and send the video to her lawyers in Europe, I can get the money."

"It's just another game," Tori implored. "It's just games she played to destroy people's lives, Malea. There is no more money. Keir made sure of that. This is just a game our mother is playing against us, even in death. Can't you see?"

"Shut up! Shut up!" Malea said, shaking.

Forcing herself to stand straight, she addressed her sister. In Maela's weakened condition, Tori surmised she could get to her sister and wrestle the gun away.

"Tori, don't!" Duncan growled.

Dammit! All these mind readers were getting on her damn nerves.

"Malea, you think after I tell you about the journals and you kill me, they're going to let you walk away from here? Sister or not, they love me, and they are going to make you pay for hurting me. I know the police are on their way, and you'll die in jail and never see a dime of that money or your husband or children. Did Momma know you would get the cancer, too?"

Malea sobbed. "When she got it, she told me to get tested, and it said I was a high risk."

Tori asked, "Why didn't you tell me to get tested?"

"Because I didn't want you to know," Malea snarled as if it should be obvious. "You should die too with this pain. Not me. That's why I used all the money. It wasn't for gambling, you stupid bitch. It was to pay off all the medical care that I needed. And still need to keep myself alive. Now stop fucking around and tell me where the journals are!"

Tori gritted her teeth and eased a little forward. "Momma knew what she was doing sending that letter now. She knew by that time some of the cancer symptoms would have surfaced, and she probably put so much hatred for me and Keir in your heart, it would drive you to do this. I know there isn't any money."

Malea looked weakly at the brothers and then back at Tori. "Do you love them?"

Tori looked at Shawn, Duncan, and Kevin and then back at her sister. "With all my heart."

"Even though you know they were planning with me to hurt you?"

"It doesn't matter. I still love them. I've done some awful things in the past, and I definitely don't deserve their love, but they love me. I can understand their hurt, pain, and anger, but I still love them with all my heart. And I'll love them for the rest of my life because no man will ever make me feel like they have made me feel. I know this without any doubt in my heart, Malea." By this time, Tori was arms' length with the gun pointed at her chest. All she had to do was knock Malea's hand to the left, but if Tori threw herself at her sister, they could fall into the water.

The water.

Shadow said the water's temperature could be fatal to anyone.

"And I love you, Malea. You're my sister. You've always been my sister, and I'm sorry for what I did, who I was, and what was done to you in the past. You're right. It wasn't fair, and it's still not fair, but we can find peace and be a family. I *love you*, Malea."

Malea let out a sorrowful sob, her grip on the gun tightening. Tori lunged to knock the gun in another direction, the air thick with tension. The gun exploded, a deafening sound that echoed through the air, and a piercing, sharp pain shot through Tori's body. At the same time, they both lost their balance and tumbled over the rocky cliff into the water.

The water!

Her consciousness struggled to break through to the surface of reality. Water was all around her.

Don't panic, she told herself.

It was so cold, and there was a lot of pain on one side of her body. The grip her sister had on her was released. Seconds turned into minutes, and it only got colder and darker.

Tori felt air being forced out of her, and no matter how hard she tried, she couldn't draw any in. Was she choking? So much pain. Her body wanted to give up and give in.

But what about the baby? What about her men?

A burn seared her lungs and chest, and then she could suddenly hear a lot of bellowing.

"I got you, Tori," Duncan said.

Yes, of course, he would have dove into the water after her. That's why she wasn't afraid. Her Duncan loved water, and he told her never to be scared.

"Where is she fucking bleeding from?" Kevin raged.

"Calm down, asshole, it's just a flesh wound," Shadow snarled.

"Beck, come get this little girl before I forget my manners and punch this bitch in the mouth."

"Like he punched you?" Shadow shot back.

By this time, Tori was able to open her eyes slowly and saw a commotion, or at least Beck shoving Kevin for trying to choke the younger woman.

There were flashing lights, which meant the police and EMS were on the scene.

Shawn was holding onto her arm while Duncan was over her, checking her vitals.

"Let us take over," a female paramedic implored.

"She's pregnant!" Kevin yelled as if that meant everyone should expedite the matter.

Tori gasped, feeling excruciating pain on the left side of her body as she was moved to a gurney. The boys all had to step aside and let the paramedics do their job.

"Shut up!' Duncan ordered. "She's awake."

"We're going with her," Shawn demanded as the paramedics were loading Tori into the gurney.

"We can only have one," the other female EMT said. "Which one?" This question was directed at Tori.

Feeling very weak and in a lot of pain, Tori could barely keep her eyes open, let alone speak. Tori looked at the deeply concerned faces of Shawn, Duncan, and Kevin. Kevin and Duncan looked like they had fought with a Sasquatch. They were bruised all over, while Shawn just looked very stressed, although his clothes were scorched and burnt on the edges. Any one of them would be fine going with her, though, but for her... There was so much to process.

On the side, Beck and Shadow stood, and she nodded to Beck.

He happily jumped in, looking like a whole building had fallen on him, but he smirked at the boys.

"You look like you need medical attention, too, sir," the EMT noted. "Pretty much all of you do. Do you want us to call another -"

"No," all the men said in sync.

Shadow chuckled and started skipping to the SUV. The ambulance doors closed, and Tori turned away so she wouldn't have to watch the brothers' sorrowful faces anymore.

When they arrived at the hospital, Beck stayed by her side. Once the medical staff had Tori situated in her room, all patched up, unable to get the choker off, and only wearing a gown, while she still had the garden pants and socks on. They'd gotten distracted by trying to take the choker off and said they'd need to call an exceptional locksmith because nothing was working. Even Beck tried, but he said the metal was so strong that his tools would break.

Through all this, Tori found out her sister had died.

"Was it because I fell in the water?"

By this time, the detective who had been investigating Amos's death had arrived to deliver the news about her sister.

"No. When you fell in the water, she actually fell in the boat that was left there, so that we were able to recover her body immediately. The old bullet ricocheted off your Ulna bone and went all the way through Malea's chest, killing her instantly."

'You get everything!' Malea had yelled.

Tori couldn't believe how everything had worked out for her, and nothing worked out for Malea.

"According to her oncologist, she only had a couple of months to live. Her husband has been contacted. And the DA is not going to charge you. We've taken witness statements and understand she was holding you hostage and had shot the gun before you hit the water."

This still didn't assuage the guilt Tori felt for what she had driven her sister to.

"Now I was told those boys kidnapped you. Is that true? Are you pressing charges?" the detective asked.

Tori looked over at Beck, who had a wicked smirk on his lips. He would very much enjoy seeing all three brothers in jail.

"No, everything is fine between the brothers and me," she stated, softly touching the choker that was still on her neck. "But please speak to Duncan Carter about the Amos case. He has some journals that could help your investigation."

"Thanks, I hope things get better for you, ma'am."

When the detective left, Beck said, "You can't feel bad about the good things that happened to you, Tori. Hell, I didn't deserve my wife. I used to think so much about how lucky I was that I didn't appreciate her enough while she was alive, because I was so deep in guilt about not deserving her. Don't do that. You're trying to be a better person - even if it's with three men - but you're doing what you can, and you should focus on you. And living your life."

Tori's hand went over her stomach, and she wondered when the medical staff was going to return with the results from the ultrasound she had to endure painfully, plus the gallon of blood they had taken to make sure the baby was fine.

"You can go, Beck," Tori assured him. "I just made you come because I knew it would hurt them the most. I had to get them back somehow for kidnapping me and working with Malea."

"And I think despite the ass whooping I gave them, seeing you choose me over them hurt the most," Beck stated. "That gave me so much joy, Tori, but you know that's not going to keep them away."

Shadow sauntered into the room, dressed in a light blue hoodie with matching jeans and shoes. Her hair was still in a low ponytail. In the light, she looked at least eighteen or nineteen with the blackest eyes. "I love walking past those big lugs standing miserably around in the hallway, scaring anyone who walks by."

"Why are you here?" Tori asked, disturbed by the young woman's presence and by the fact that Shawn, Duncan, and Kevin were standing in the hallway, not leaving her side. "You aren't welcome either. Isn't there security outside my door?"

"He didn't even see me slip in," Shadow said. "I'm resourceful."

Tori was about to demand the little girl get out, but then Shadow said, "Don't you want to know if the baby's okay?

"How would you know faster than the medical staff?" Tori doubtfully snipped. "I'm waiting for the test results."

"But I could tell you faster," Shadow teased. "If you let me touch you."

Tori was desperate to find out if her baby was fine and didn't know how long the staff would take. Could Shadow really do what she said she could do? Moving the covers away to give Shadow access, the young woman approached the bed and reached under Tori's medical garb to press her full palm on Tori's lower stomach.

After a moment, Shadow said, "The baby's okay."

Tori rolled her eyes. "You could have made that up? Is this some parlor trick to stay around me to annoy me more?" Suddenly, Tori felt a glimmer all through her lower stomach, and she gasped.

"The baby's heartbeat is faster than yours. It's nice and snug and..." Shadow stopped suddenly as if she were hiding something.

"What?" Tori asked.

"It misses their voices."

"How would you know that?"

Shadow took out a small kit from her back pocket with some odd tools. "Lean forward and I'll get that choker off."

"No one can get that off," Beck growled. "We all tried. The hospital is going to see if they can get the fire department in here with the jaws of life."

"That's a bit extreme," Shadow said with a chuckle as Tori sat up so the young woman could get to the clasp on the choker. Picking up a small electrical instrument from the tool kit and another sharp tool, Shadow went to work like she was trying to break down a DNA sequence. With her being so close, Tori could feel the room get a little chillier for some reason.

In two seconds, something clicked, and a beeping noise died, and the choker fell in Tori's lap.

"Why can't you work that fast to look for the young lady I requested?" Beck growled.

"I found her. I'm going to meet her at a bar tomorrow. Don't you worry." Shadow scooped up the choker. "I'm going to borrow this for a day or so. If the lugheads ask, the detective took it." She gave Tori a playful wink and slipped out of the room.

Tori suddenly realized they were at Shawn's hospital. "You really should go, Beck," Tori insisted. "I'll just sleep like the dead tonight and get released by tomorrow once I'm assured the baby really is fine. My arm hurts like hell, but I should be good and can take care of myself."

"Do you want to come back to my house until you get things sorted with the new divorce?"

"How'd you know?"

"They explained everything to me when I finally stopped choking Duncan. It was Shawn who had a feeling you weren't safe on the mainland, and Duncan agreed. He said he'd told Malea they weren't going with her plan right before he came back to the island for that pool excursion with you and your sister, and she didn't take it too well. Called him all kinds of names and tried to scratch his whole face off. On the way there, Shawn let me know he canceled the original fucked up agreement with Malea and was giving you back everything. That's when I realized it had been Malea following me all day, and we took their boat back to the mainland and found you. I hate that they were right."

"I won't trouble you by going to your house. I still might go up to your brothers, though, if he'll have me, but this time I'll fly up to Marquette."

"Of course. He'd love your business input on his endeavors, but I should warn you he's a bigger asshole than I am, and he won't beat anyone up like I would. He'd shoot them."

She knew Beck was referring to whether the brothers decided to follow her to the Upper Peninsula. "I need to be done with them, Beck," she said desperately. "I'm sure if I go up there, they won't follow."

"After you told them you love them? Do you really think they're going to let you go so easily, Tori?"

"They have to. I can't be around them, not after everything. And whose side are you on? Or did Duncan beat something into your head to make you change your mind about them?"

"I just know no man fights even when he knows he's going to lose for nothing. Kevin and Duncan were fighting for love. For you. They knew I could kill them, but I didn't because I love knowing they are suffering. But damn, Tori, they are pretty keen on you. Shadow said they share you like you're all theirs. That's special-*strange*, but special."

"She also called me a whore."

"Shadow's a shit starter. If she's not getting under your skin, it doesn't matter to her. That could mean she likes you, but I haven't figured her out yet either."

Tori really wanted to be vindictive and tell Beck not to do shit for the little cunt, but when Shadow put her hand on

Tori's stomach, a glimmer passed through her, and she knew that wasn't some parlor trick of Shadow's.

"Be careful with her, Beck. Whatever she's after, just be careful. Okay?"

Beck kissed her forehead. It was the first affection he had ever really shown her. "You can't kill me here, boys," Beck said without turning around. "The hospital is neutral territory, but I can meet your asses in the parking lot and rip you all a new asshole."

She looked past Beck to see Shawn, Duncan, and Kevin standing by the door inside the room. Despite her request, they'd come in anyway.

Kevin started toward Beck, but Shawn placed a hand on his brother's chest to stop him, yet he was staring at Beck, like the other two brothers, with a look of pure hatred.

"Just keep your hands and those crusty red lips off her, Beck," Shawn sneered.

Rolling her eyes at their rule-breaking, Tori huffed. "I don't care how much you paid security to look the other way, I don't want to see any of you."

"She should," Beck said, gathering his coat and giving her a wink. "You should at least until the test results come back about the baby. It's only fair."

Tori gritted her teeth and shot Beck and *I'll get you back* look.

Beck walked past them, although they reluctantly moved out of the way.

Kevin snarled. "Don't fucking touch her ever again, son of a bitch."

Beck snorted but kept walking.

Now that they were alone and she could see them up close, Kevin and Duncan looked even worse than Beck.

"He Molly whopped your asses," she gasped out.

Kevin had two black eyes, and it looked like his jaw was

broken. Duncan had a minor cut under his eye, but it left the area swollen. He was wearing only his jacket, which matched his purple sweatpants, with the zipper a little down, and she could see bruises on his body because of his lighter skin.

"The man hits like a fucking Mack truck," Kevin grumbled. "Like fucking titanium for bones, I fucking swear. Duncan's blade broke when he tried to stab that son of a bitch."

Tori cried, "You stabbed him?"

"The man only looks like he had a tussel with kindergartens," Shawn said. "Not these two lugs. I found Kevin passed out and had to drag his ass out of the house before it burned down."

Going back into her guilt, Tori said, "I'm so sorry, Duncan."

"It was just the back of the house. That punk ass little girl put explosives on the propane tanks under the patio," Kevin explained.

She noticed Duncan hadn't said much. He was just staring at her.

Lowering her eyes, but then raising them back up, Tori looked back at the middle brother. He was waiting for her to beckon one of them or all of them. He wanted answers. He wanted to know if what she said to her sister was true. He wanted to know about the baby. And he wanted to know if she was going to stay or go.

CHAPTER 20

If She's Not Broken

"I don't know, Duncan," Tori said, responding to Duncan's look. "You all worked behind my back with my sister. Why didn't you tell me that?"

"We were," Shawn said, coming to the end of the bed. "At dinner before everything we were going to tell you before we were rudely interrupted."

Kevin moved to her left side apprehensively as he spoke. "She came to us about a month ago, pressing about how she was our sister. We were already looking for a way to get to you, and we just felt this was fate. She cried about how you'd stolen everything from her and felt no regret for anything. She even rubbed it in that you'd only paid our mother's expenses to show off how rich you were."

Tori looked at Duncan, who still stood away from the bed.

"I realized that was all shit when I saw the truth," Shawn admitted, massaging her feet, but she felt this was more for him than her, even though it felt good. "Kevin and Duncan realized it way before, but I was the holdout." He looked ashamed.

Kevin explained, "It's why we were presenting you with

the ring. It was to let you know there would be no more lies, no more secrets, and no more deceptions or manipulations. By any of us."

Even though she had the hospital top on, she still had the bottom that had dried before she got to the hospital. The nurse had said she would come back and change her into something more comfortable once the fire department arrived with the jaws of life to remove the choker.

Tori had to use her non-dominant hand to get the ring box out of her pocket.

Duncan moved to the other side of the bed and helped her open it because she was struggling. To feel his tender touch against her affected her, but she forced herself not to show it.

He held the box while she removed the ring.

It was a silver band with a deep-pink rose-shaped sapphire and diamonds all around it.

Duncan nodded to Shawn.

"I gave you the divorce papers with no expectations. I even sent a copy over to your lawyer already. You get back everything, and you can choose to demolish the apartment or not. Or take the ten million and live your life, Tori. With or without us," Shawn stated, pulling papers from his jacket and setting them down on the table by her. "You can sign them and have your lawyer take them to the court. I've already signed them."

"You can even take back the offices," Kevin said begrudgingly. "If you so choose. It's whatever you want, Tori. We had no right to conspire with Malea, but that was before we knew who you were. Before we fell deep in love with you."

Shawn said, "You have every right to hate us. And to keep the baby away from us. We're awful people, and we can understand if you don't want us in your life. Or even in the baby's life."

Tori again looked at Duncan, who only stared intensely at

her. The look was so deep she could feel him reach into her body and hold her heart.

She was barely able to speak, but she forced out, "I need time. It's too much pain... hurt, and betrayal." Tears burst from her eyes and ran down her cheek.

Duncan reached over and caught several tears, and it looked like he wanted to fight those, too. He was mad by her tears as if they had hurt her by running down her face.

The door opened, and a large, black, mid-thirties-year-old doctor entered. "Ms. Snow, I'm Dr. Chance Jefferson, your gynecologist."

"I know the fuck you aint," Kevin growled.

Shawn put a hand on his brother's chest as the very gorgeous doctor looked Kevin up and down. "She's still Mrs. Carter until she signs the divorce papers, Dr. Jefferson."

The doctor's cool brown eyes swept over the room. He had a chiseled jaw and looked like what God would have designed the first man to look like. He was way too attractive to be a doctor, and Tori could clearly understand why Kevin took offense. "Looks like you boys have been put through the ringer," the doctor said and looked at Tori, who was quickly trying to use the back of her good hand to wipe her face. He went to a supply cabinet and took several boxes of tissues to put on Tori's table. "Are you upsetting my patient?"

Duncan handed several tissues from the box so she wouldn't have to reach for them.

Shawn introduced himself to the doctor. "I'm Dr. Carter, and these are my brothers. We were visiting my wife."

"Oh yes, the new admin podiatrist. I've... I've heard about... this is your wife?" He looked around the room at each man. "And these are your brothers. Are you okay, Mrs... Snow? Carter?"

Tori blushed because she knew the rumors were probably all over the hospital by now. "Dr. Jefferson, I'm fine," Tori assured him. "And you may refer to me as Mrs. Carter. "You have the results about the baby?" she said.

"Yes," he said, starting to come to bed, but Kevin moved in front of him.

Shawn pushed his big brother out of the way, and they looked like they were about to fight, but Duncan snapped his fingers, and they stopped whatever they were about to do to each other.

"Are you sure you want them here? It looks like you're upset, and in your condition, you shouldn't be."

"I just need them to know about the baby, and they will leave," she assured the doctor.

"Well, you're fine. The bullet ricocheted from your bone, but it didn't break. There's going to be pain, but you've been stitched up just fine, and it's more or less helping you heal faster, so you don't break the stitches, which is why we have you in the sling. The baby seems fine, although it's too early to tell. I will run some more tests in the morning, but for now, you need to rest. A lot. And alone." He shot a look at each brother before looking back at her. "Unfortunately, there's going to be pain, and we can't give you anything other than OTCs due to the baby."

Duncan looked at her, and she nodded, clearly telling him they needed to go.

Reluctantly, each brother filed out of the room.

"Do you want me to put restrictions and an extra guard on the floor?" the doctor asked. "You don't look comfortable."

Tori looked down at the ring. "No. They won't come back until I need them."

"Will you need them soon?" the doctor asked worriedly.

Tears started to well up in her eyes again because she was really confused about her decisions and choices. "Not too soon. I need to rest."

Her arm hurt really badly, and she had a horrible headache, but nothing hurt as much as her heart.

She wanted to reach in and tear it out so it could stop pounding with hurt on every beat. "Does the baby's heart beat faster than mine?"

"Yes, but it's hardly detectable now. I'd say you're about a month and a half."

She estimated that it was about the first night all of them had been together on the boat.

"I want to keep you overnight just to make sure you and the baby are good," Dr. Jefferson said. "I want you to get as much rest as possible."

"I'll try, but my sister-

"I know," he cut her off. "I know what happened to your sister, but I know you didn't pull the trigger.

"Her insanity started way before tonight, and I know I had a part of it."

"Whatever you had a part in, people who blame others for their unhappiness never loved themselves in the first place. That's something you can't control, no matter how you treated them. You shouldn't feel the weight of the world for what your sister chose to do, no matter how she was treated. If you've forgiven yourself and tried to do better than what you have done, her death can be gotten over. Your mental health during your pregnancy is even more important than your physical health."

Tori understood what he was saying and nodded.

"If you need anything, please call the nurse or security no matter the hour," the doctor insisted. "I'll be doing the rounds for the next couple of hours if you have any questions." He set her chart at the end of the bed. "I do have one more question to ask. And it has to do with the brothers and your involvement."

Bracing for what he wanted to know, Tori said, "Anything," she offered. "Ask away."

"Are you curious about who's the father?"

Without hesitation, she answered, "I didn't think that far, honestly."

"But would you know who you were with-" He stopped because maybe her facial expressions with her brows rising high and the wicked smirk on her lips that she couldn't stop from happening. "I could run a test in a couple of months."

"I don't think that's necessary," Tori responded, pressing her hand on her stomach. "I know they'll all be great fathers if I stay. I have no doubt."

"If? Are you indecisive because of your sister's death?"

"It's more complicated than that. I'm still mentally processing that along with everything else." She couldn't tell the doctor about being kidnapped for almost a week. "I just know I need to decide on what I'm going to do in the upcoming days."

"Well, keep me informed. This situation is interesting but also concerning. I wouldn't want the stress to hurt you or the baby. You're a fortunate girl. I'm sorry about your sister, but please get some rest. It's been a long night for you."

Tori watched as the doctor left, and she took a deep breath, looking down at the ring she still clutched. Staring at the pink rose, she thought about their night in the pool and how much she trusted them despite her captivity. She thought about all the times they had made her happy and spoiled her.

And then she thought about her confession to her sister about the Carter Brothers. Every word had been the truth. She did love each one of them with all her heart.

Tori thought about every moment she had shared with the Carter brothers - the good and the bad- and she started crying, because she wanted more to happen with them.

Despite the incredible pain she was in from her arm to her heart, Tori was able to go to sleep.

The sound of the gun going off and then seeing Malea's face, contorted in agony.

'Everything goes right for you, Tori. You took everything! EVERYTHING!'

Tori screamed, "I'm sorry, Malea! I'm sorry!"

Tearing out of the dream in mid scream, she somehow wrenched her shoulder around, and the pain from moving her stitched-up arm tore through her sleep. She felt too weak to move. With her other arm, she searched for the nurse's button, but it must've fallen to the ground in her sleep, and she couldn't reach it.

Tori sobbed, frustrated by her dream and the current pain she was experiencing, but suddenly she felt a dark presence in the room. The only light was above her head, and she couldn't see anything else in the room, but in the darkest part, she could feel a heat emanating from there. The nurse button was suddenly near her hand.

"W-Who's there?" she demanded.

Duncan stepped into the light, looking concerned.

She pushed the nurse's button, and in seconds, a young black nurse rushed into the room.

"I'm so glad that mean ass man finally left the hallway. Gave me chills. I thought- Oh Jezz-" The nurse screeched, seeing Duncan in the far corner of the room. "You can't be in here! It's only family! I'll call security."

"No," Tori said. "He's, my brother-in-law."

The nurse looked at Tori to be sure she wanted this.

"It's okay. Please help me," Tori insisted. "I can't move, and I need something to elevate my arm."

In her dream, she had squirmed around so that the pillow her arm had rested on had fallen to the floor.

The nurse was able to adjust the pillow, but even she struggled trying to help Tori turn her lower body, and Tori felt horribly weakened trying to do it herself.

Duncan came over to bed and gently lifted her lower body. The nurse positioned the pillow correctly, then Duncan slowly lay Tori back down in a comfortable position.

Immediately, he stepped back into the dark corner, leaning against the wall, because there was nowhere else to sit.

Had he been standing there all night?

For her?

Tori tore her eyes away from him to see the nurse taking her blood pressure and checking her arm. The movement hadn't ripped the stitches, but it had caused fresh bleeding. The nurse changed the area, and Tori gasped at the half-dollar-sized stitched area.

She *had* been lucky. The old bullet hadn't caused much damage, and Tori knew that in a couple of days she would be as good as new. Instead of looking back at Duncan, she looked around the rest of the room and was happy to see her phone was lying on the table by her bedside, charging up. He'd most likely gone in her bag looking for the choker.

Keeping her eyes lowered so he wouldn't read her thoughts, she pretended to pay a lot of attention to the nurse.

"I'll get you fresh water... oh, never mind. There's ice and water already in your cup," the nurse said and nervously looked at the dark corner. "Do you think by the morning you'll have enough strength to get to the bathroom? Do you want me to take out the catheter?"

It was uncomfortable, and Tori nodded.

The nurse pulled the curtain around the bed more for her comfort than Tori's and removed the catheter.

Tori took a deep breath, feeling a little relief and glad she was on the road to recovery.

Once you are good, will you stay or go? she asked herself.

She didn't want to try to come up with an answer. Not in the middle of the night. The doctor was right. She needed more rest.

Tomorrow, she would try to figure out something.

When Tori awoke in the morning, it was to see Kevin leaning against the wall, arms crossed, wearing some jeans, cleaned tan Carhartt work boots, and a green long-sleeve waffle tee. His Carhartt jacket was lying on the windowsill.

They'd changed, most likely, so Duncan could get to work.

"Shouldn't you be at work?" Tori snipped.

He looked shocked when she addressed him, then smiled. "I should, but I took off. Shawn's working, and Duncan needed to meet with the insurance claims adjuster, but he said to tell you it's not your fault. We're going to sue the fuck out of Beck."

"No, you're not!" she protested, but then felt her bladder kick in hard, and she tried to scramble out of the bed, but could barely move.

Kevin immediately came over and helped her out of bed and over to the bathroom. As a courtesy, he stepped out and started to close the door, but Tori cried, "I can't get my underwear down!"

Without hesitation, Kevin helped her, pulling the pants and her underwear down so she could relieve her bladder.

He didn't look the least bit embarrassed as he helped her clean up. A pack similar to what they had provided in her room of captivity was in the hospital bathroom, and Kevin helped her wash her hands.

"Want to get out of those clothes?" he asked.

Tori would love that, but she had nothing to replace them. The bathroom was like a wetbath, and the shower looked so inviting.

He seemed to hear her thoughts and left the bathroom to pick up his coat. Underneath was a pile of clothing that he brought to her.

Some pink pajama bottoms, more underwear, and socks.

Kevin wrapped her arm in a plastic cover and then scrubbed her from head to toe. His heavy breathing indicated he was aroused, but he stayed focused on getting her cleaned up and dressed.

His big frame filled up the small bathroom, but she didn't mind him being there, especially when he seemed to be eager to help her.

When she was back sitting on the edge of the bed, Kevin unwrapped the plastic from her arm and then helped her into the bed, making sure to puff up the pillow on her side so her arm was elevated correctly.

She started to say thank you, but he pressed his finger to her lips.

"Don't you dare thank us for shit, Tori," he growled. "We don't deserve you after what we did. The grace and mercy you are giving us is close to god-like." Kevin tucked the covers around her. "Now rest like the doctor said. Your breakfast will be here in a couple of hours."

Dammit! She hated that she wanted to kiss the fuck out of him! She hated feeling all warm and squishy inside!

She hated that she loved them.

As Kevin said, breakfast arrived, and although it was hospital food, it was enough for her. Kevin helped her through a nice pancake, eggs, and bacon breakfast, and then Tori slept some more.

When she awoke again, Shawn was there leaning against the wall in his doctor's coat, looking concerned.

Tori didn't know whether she wanted to speak to him. Talking with Kevin seemed easier. Shawn was very complicated.

Getting up to use the bathroom seemed more straightforward, but she kept the bathroom door open in case her body lied to her and she actually did need help.

Tori wasn't a prideful little girl anymore, and she understood her body had gone through a lot and would need help.

The door to her room opened, and Shawn immediately came to the bathroom door and stood in front of it to protect her privacy.

"I'm here to see Tori," Sinclaire said stiffly.

"She'll be out in a moment," Shawn countered.

Tori smiled, loving how protective he was, but she had to hide her emotions as she flushed the toilet and washed her hands. By this time, Shawn had moved away from the door and was giving the lawyer his meanest mug.

Sinclaire was holding her on, annoyingly tapping her foot and holding a brief while she waited for Tori to come out of the bathroom.

"I came as soon as visiting hours were open, but that annoying prick of an ex-older brother-in-law wouldn't let me in because he said the doctor demanded you rest. Until the papers are officially filed, I can't kick them out of your life, Tori."

"I know," Tori said, feeling her strength leaving her slightly.

Shawn seemed to sense this and immediately came to her side to help her get back in bed.

"Is this marriage over or not?" Sinclaire demanded.

Tori waited until Shawn was back across the room, shooting daggers at the lawyer, before she said, "Can you give us a moment, Shawn?"

He looked surprised she had addressed him directly, but after that moment, he walked out of the room.

"What the fuck is going on here?" the lawyer demanded.

CHAPTER 21
What's Next?

Sinclaire, her lawyer, was dressed in her finest sharp suit, hair flying, and looking like with a stroke of her pen she could tear a new asshole to anyone that took her on.

"I've been trying to contact you for the past week because his lawyers weren't giving me any information. Shawn never turned in his divorce papers, and I was half a mind to call on my husband for help."

Tori chuckled. "I thought your husband was an accountant? What was he going to do? Count me?"

Proudly, Sincalire said, "He knows certain people underground that could find a needle in a haystack."

Remembering Shadow, Tori was sure Sinclaire wasn't talking about that annoying teenager. Instead of going further down that rabbit hole discussion, Tori nodded at the paper Shawn had left on the table that was still there, untouched.

Sinclaire opened it and gasped. "Yes, just like I was sent, and why I needed to speak to you. This isn't the same divorce as the original or the one you proposed. Tori, what did you do to make him change his mind? He's giving everything back and more! Tori! How?!"

"You get more bees with honey than you do vinegar," Tori said sweetly, but the phrase left a bad taste in her mouth. "Let's just get the papers filed and go from there. I still want someone over the project other than myself, so I'll keep looking for a candidate. Until then, I know Beck won't mind handling things while everything is still under construction, but at least now I can be included in decisions again."

"And the offices?"

"It's still theirs. I'm not going to take back a gift."

"And them? I know they did something to you, Tori. You can lie all you want to the police, but in my bones, I knew they were a part of you missing this past week."

"Nothing is to be done to them. This is what I want, Sinclaire." Tori changed the subject. "I need to hire an assistant. If you have someone in mind, please send them my way. I'm going to take a hotel room out at the St. Royal Hotel. I'll send that information to you, in case you need to see me before everything is finalized." Tori signed the papers. "And I don't know what I'm going to do. I still need a lot of rest."

Sinclaire nodded, took the papers, and left.

As soon as the lawyer was gone, Shawn came back in.

"Is it done?" he asked. "Are we divorced?"

Tori nodded and put the ring on the table, pushing it in his direction, not making eye contact with him. "I'll find the other ring and choker and return them to you as soon as I get out of this hospital and get things together."

"Don't bother," he growled. "Keep them."

She heard the door to her room open and close. Once she realized she was alone, she looked up to see the ring still on the table.

The pink rose sapphire glared right back at her.

Admiration, joy, affection, and gratitude.

Closing her eyes, Tori whispered over and over to herself, "Don't you dare forgive them."

But she couldn't ignore her heart, or that they had never left her side, despite her pretending she didn't care.

The following afternoon, Scott came with her niece and nephew to visit her. Unfortunately, the police had not updated them on precisely what happened.

"I didn't know she was so sick," he said miserably. "She kept everything a secret. Our savings, our assets, are all gone. I had to quit my job because I'm so damn embarrassed."

"I'm so sorry," Tori said quietly.

"No, don't be, Tori. If you hadn't given my business a boost and been helping the kids, we would be shit out of luck. We came to thank you."

Tori was grateful for their appreciation, but she was still quite upset over losing her sister and leaving this family without a mother.

When they were getting ready to leave, Scott asked, "I thought you were staying away from those brothers since they were working with Malea?"

"I'm divorcing the family, yes."

"Then why is one of them outside your door as if waiting for your permission to come in?"

Tori frowned. "Can you tell him to come in on your way out?"

"Are you sure?"

She nodded.

A moment later, Duncan entered the room. He'd change into khakis and a dark green dress shirt with matching green dress shoes.

"You all have no intentions of leaving me alone. I know you know I signed the divorce papers."

He tensed. "Tori, you're carrying our child—marriage or

not. We will take care of you. Kevin even wanted to know how to invite you to the family group chat and calendar."

Shifting her weight uncomfortably because hearing that shouldn't have made her so giddy, Tori patted the bed next to her.

For the first time, Duncan looked uncomfortable, but after dropping his coat on the windowsill, he sat where she wanted him.

"Were you all really going to tell me the truth about your collaboration with Malea that night at dinner, when you were giving me that new ring?" she demanded.

Duncan flinched as if someone had harshly pinched him, and he cleared his throat. "What does it matter? You've made your decision."

"Divorcing Shawn meant nothing about my decision to involve you all in my life."

His eyes drifted down to her stomach, excitedly, and back up to her face. "Malea was adamant about joining forces in taking you down. We thought, at the time, we could still incorporate the seduction -"

Tori cut him off and corrected him. "*You* thought."

Nodding with guilt all over his face, Duncan said, "I convinced them we could still do the seduction, while still going along with her plan. When Shawn told Kevin and me how you were going to sign the papers to get married, which would complete Malea's plan to get everything from you, I should have pushed the stop button, but I wanted you, Tori. I wanted to taste you, touch you, and feel you so bad, I didn't care, until I cared."

The sentence was confusing to hear, but she understood him.

"By then, I knew it was too late, and I had to tear myself away from what I was feeling for you for the loyalty to my brother.

And when Shawn realized Malea's plan to hurt you wasn't for him, by this time, we knew we had destroyed any chance of having you forever. So, kidnapping you at least helped Shawn, and to let you know our true feelings was the only way. At least while we were in jail, you would know our truth. Our feelings. Our true intentions, even though we fucked up." He took a deep breath. "I know you're tired of hearing it, but we are sorry. After the dinner date, I was going to drop you off on the mainland that following morning, and then we were going straight to the precinct to turn ourselves in, whether you wanted us to or not."

Even if that had happened, Tori knew she still wouldn't have pressed charges, but she didn't dare say this out loud and continued to listen as he spoke.

"It was true, though, what we said at dinner. No more lies. No more manipulation. No more hurt for you, Tori. We will spend the rest of our days making you happy. Being the men you need, whether you want us there or not."

She reached over and touched his hand. Duncan gasped and closed his eyes as if he were trying to contain himself. He trembled so hard the bed shook slightly.

Tori softly expressed, "I didn't sign those divorce papers just to protect myself and the group home project. I signed those divorce papers because if I can't be married to all three of you, I will have to be fine with not marrying any of you. It's not fair-"

Duncan shot his hand behind her head and dragged her lips to his.

Tori didn't realize how much she missed his sweet kisses until she felt his mouth on hers again. She lost herself in his pleasurable mind, losing kisses that left her breathless.

"I fucking love you, Tori. With everything in me, I fucking love you."

"I know," she said.

The nurse entered the room, and Duncan shot to his feet as if he'd been caught stealing something.

"I've come to check your vitals, and your lawyer has told me they aren't your relatives anymore," the nurse stated.

Tori looked at Duncan.

He picked up his coat and started out of the room.

"I'll be checking in the St. Royals," Tori informed him. "Can we all meet in a week? For dinner? Next Thursday? I should be well rested by then."

Duncan nodded and left.

"Does he ever speak?" the nurse inquired.

"In more ways than one," Tori teased and then let the nurse finish her afternoon check-up. "I'm shocked you've been so kind to me. I know you've heard the rumors."

The nurse admonished, "I'm not a person who believes in rumors. Good news for you, the doctor has your release papers available for the morning. He has scheduled an outpatient visit in two weeks for the baby. I know you're excited about that. Boy, the St. Royal Hotel is so fancy. I can only dream of getting a room there. I know we have some after-care rooms reserved there."

"No, I should be fine booking my own accommodations, but that's nice to know," Tori said.

"Do you need any pain management?"

Tori was feeling better and shook her head, not wanting any over-the-counter medication that would only make her foggy. "I should be fine."

Picking up her phone, as soon as Tori turned it on, she saw all the missed calls from Beck and Sinclaire.

Sinclaire had sent her a couple of references for assistance, which would be helpful to Tori in running her apartment complex project and ensuring each tenant's needs were adequately met.

Tori contacted Beck to update him on her plan to get out

of the hospital tomorrow, but she refused his request to pick her up. The St. Royal had an ambulatory vehicle service that could take her from the hospital to the hotel.

There were several calls from an unknown number, but no message was left. She didn't think too much of it, because she was sleepy and decided to get more rest until the morning, when she would be leaving the hospital.

Knowing that the brothers were aware of the baby and her feelings for them made sleep easy. And legally divorcing Shawn made sense because it protected her and them.

~

An hour before visitor hours ended, Paulette Cosgrove appeared in her room, carrying a beautiful get-well basket with lilies, fruit, and a spa package that smelled delicious.

"You don't look a bit sick, or do you always look so beautiful, all the time?" Paulette questioned.

Tori flushed. "You were the last person I thought I would see come into my room, Mrs. Cosgrove. I'm so sorry-"

The older woman interrupted her. "Oh, don't be, and it's still Paulette for you, young lady. You don't know how much having that ceremony rejuvenated my husband and me. I've increased my charitable work tenfold, and your whole situation really made me see how complicated life is for others. Shawn has let us know you're making better friends than husband and wife."

"But the situation with his brothers?" Tori felt that her reputation and the gossip could hurt the older woman. "It could be so embarrassing for you to associate with me."

"Pa-shaw!" Paulette said, waving her hand as if flicking away a fly. "Shawn said it's water under the bridge."

"Thank you for understanding, Paulette."

"I had to show my appreciation for you, because the

auction for your donated rugs has tremendously helped my charitable contribution this year, especially with so many other organizations being hard hit by the economy. At this point, you couldn't do anything to raise my ire, Tori." Suddenly, she became serious. "My condolences on your sister, and I've pressed my husband to offer Scott his job back. We've also arranged a scholarship for her children to help with their college costs and any funds they need. My husband's business partners have made a large contribution to African American cancer research, and I've offered to arrange the funeral for him."

"Really?" Tori asked, surprised. "Oh, thank you, Paulette. Thank you."

"It's my pleasure. I'll keep you abreast of everything, and I'll arrange the burial in two weeks. Scott said that's fine. Their children have gotten leave from school, but I wanted to check in with you personally."

Reaching out and hugging the woman for her thoughtfulness, Tori said, "Paulette, your kindness is touching."

They spoke more of Paulette's other charitable efforts before the older woman had to get ready for another event.

Left alone, Tori went to the bathroom, glad she could go by herself without feeling too weak. Yet, when she stepped out into her room, she was only slightly startled to see Shadow sitting on the windowsill as if she had always been in the room, but Tori was just noticing.

Today, the young woman wore a dark green hoodie, black jeans, and green sneakers. As usual, her hair was pulled back in a low ponytail, but immediately Tori noticed the bruised knuckles, and there was a bruise on her neck.

"Someone finally tried to choke you for your smart mouth?" Tori inquired, only slightly concerned.

"Unfortunately, Unc feels I need more ways to protect myself. I'm learning Jodo."

"You never told me about this uncle no one likes, but you seem to respect him."

Shadow snorted. "Respect is loose. As I've said, I need him."

"Oh yes," Tori remembered, returning to bed. "You like to use people. What is the pleasure of this visit, Shadow?"

Getting down from the sill and coming over to help Tori get tucked in, she said, "I thought I'd return this." Shadow presented the choker. "I thought you should know, it's a key to everything of theirs."

"What do you mean?"

"It unlocks things and turns off alarms. I tested it myself. I walked into their home in Detroit like I owned the place. Aside from avoiding the inside security cameras, it triggered nothing."

Tori gasped, receiving the choker. "Did they catch you?!"

Another snort. "I'm resourceful. No one saw me, but I didn't stay like Goldilocks, so those three bears could try to beat my ass. I just thought you should know and keep it safe, or return it since you aren't married to them anymore. I think they left it like that to let you know you will always have access to them."

"You think so?"

Shadow disgustedly rolled her dark eyes."I know so. They are obsessed with spoiling you. It's almost sickening."

Tori smiled and fondly caressed the choker, which had been a bane to her during her captivity, but to them, it meant more. Much more. "For a little girl, you know a lot more than what you look like you know."

"I know that," Shadow said confidently, sitting on the edge of the bed. "And in truth, I admire you and your ability to handle yourself with them. That's pretty cool, you're so confident and make them better when they're around you."

"How would you know?"

"You'd be surprised what I see, Tori." Shadow stood up. "Beck said I should apologize for calling you a whore." She paused and went to the door. "But I won't. I mean, good lawd, woman, you're having twins from having sex by three brothers."

"What? Wait!" Tori looked down at her stomach as if she could see what Shadow had announced. "How would you know-" When she looked up, Shadow was gone.

She had a feeling that even if she ran out into the hallway, the younger woman would not be around. Pressing her hand against her stomach, Tori wondered if she should let the brothers know of her condition.

No, they can wait until she was sure with the doctor. Her first appointment was in a few weeks.

Which brother should she choose to come with her?

It sounds like you might be staying, she determined to herself.

Clasping the choker, she lay down and went to sleep with a smile on her lips.

Three dozen red roses were delivered to her room an hour after she arrived at the St. Royal with a card from each brother and a personal note.

Hurry up and get well. xoxo Kevin

Miss you. Feel better, and let me know if you need anything. Shawn

Thank you. Love, Duncan

Tori felt like a teenager getting the crush response she'd only ever dreamed of. There was a special menu for her, and she had a feeling Duncan had a hand in it, since there was a special delivery of roasted chickpeas.

The suite was filled with drinks she liked, and the most

comfortable king-size bed that she knew she would love sleeping in.

As the concierge showed her around the suite, she noticed amenities in the hotel room that she'd never seen before.

"There's a special menu just for you, and anything you order is already included in the room," the concierge informed her.

Before she could comment on that, Tori noticed something as they went into the bedroom. "Wait, there are clothes in the closet," she noticed. "And they are my size!"

"Yes. They were sent up this morning, and the staff made sure the wardrobe was ready for your use."

"Whose clothes are these? she asked.

"Yours, Ms. Carter," he said, obviously.

Tori didn't have to wonder who did this; she knew, as Beck said, the boys were going to take care of her whether she wanted to or not.

Spending the rest of the day working through all her emails, she saw she had received another call from that unknown number and, since she had nothing else going on, answered it.

"Hello?"

The line was quiet, but she was sure someone was there.

"Who's calling?" she asked.

No answer, and then the line disconnected.

Tori received another call from a tenant and didn't think twice about it, as more work surfaced. Afterwards, she caught up on the construction logs. Beck was good about daily updates, and she could facilitate anything he needed from those instead of weekly or daily meetings. He was very thorough about keeping in communication, and she was glad to be almost back into the swing of things again.

With her niece and nephews in town, they came to the hotel for lunch with her. Her niece was eager to take on some assignments an assistant would typically handle for the next couple of weeks, while her nephew helped her with the new apartment and the demolition of the older apartment building. Tori taught him how to read the logs, get the supplies Beck would need, and keep tabs on the budget.

"In case you disappear again?" her nephew teased.

Tori only chuckled but wondered why in the back of her thoughts she almost wished she could get kidnapped by the brothers again. The small vacation had been needed more than she knew - without the tie downs and choker, of course.

Scott was taking them out to dinner at his new investment business, so they left Tori by midafternoon to get ready for it, while Tori finished up her workday.

Beck called soon after she signed off on the logs showing she had caught up.

"How's it going?" he inquired.

In the background, she could tell he was still out in the field.

"Oddly comforting, getting back to my norm but with some extras." She looked down at her stomach.

"I know you don't plan on spending the whole time in that hotel room. What have you decided?"

"I don't know. There's so much to think about personally, and I've been avoiding it."

"I went over to the storage space that was rented, and yes, according to the security, there was a break-in. I was on the contact list, but you'll have to go over to see if there was anything other than your chest that was taken. I wasn't sure. I had it put into another storage container, and you even got a whole year for free after I showed my displeasure with their security."

"Thank you, Beck. I really don't deserve you."

"You don't. Were you looking for a permanent residence?"

Somehow, she had wandered over to where the choker was

sitting on the television stand in her bedroom. Her fingers lightly felt over the cold metal, bringing back very erotic memories of being with the brothers during her captivity. "I don't know yet. I still need time."

"What about transportation? Were you able to get your car back?"

"No, Sinclaire had already arranged a seller, and the money was split, but all that money Shawn took was put back in my account, but I haven't had time to get another vehicle."

"I'll have some free time in a couple of days. We could go around to some car lots."

"Beck, you've done more than enough. Plus, they're taking care of me behind the scenes without me even asking."

"Yeah, but if I help you out, it'll piss them off more."

Tori didn't have to guess who he meant, but Tori wasn't about to help Beck make them jealous. Hurting them more wasn't what she wanted from them.

Her silence on the phone was evident, and Beck said, "They are going to drive you crazy if you don't decide between them soon. You can't go the whole pregnancy letting them do these behind-the-scenes arrangements while trying to ignore how you feel about them, Tori. You said it yourself. You love them."

She had said it, and she had meant it. "Let me think about it," she implored.

"I'll contact you in a few days. I'm going to pull the security tapes from the storage and see if your sister only bothered the chest. If I suspect anything else, I'll bring the tapes over."

Glad Beck changed the subject, Tori questioned, "I'm sure you put a solid lock on there. Malea was able to break through that?"

"I was thinking about that too. I know it's the past, and you're going through some healing, but when I get a chance, I'll check into it," he promised.

"Thanks, Beck." She got off the phone with him but decided to run things over with Duncan; she didn't have his direct number. That could be the unknown number. Knowing Shawn could still be at work, she decided to text him to ask him for Duncan's number.

Would Shawn be jealous if she were requesting the middle brother's number?

Only a few minutes after texting, her phone rang, but no number appeared on the screen.

"Hello?" she answered warily.

"You need me?" Duncan asked.

Well, damn! She thought. "Yes, would you like to have dinner-"

He cut her off. "Yes! What time tonight?"

Tori flushed because she felt rushed and could almost feel his hands on her body through the phone. *You're not fucking him! You only want to talk!* She reminded herself. "I can be ready about six, but I was thinking of the restaurant in the hotel. I really don't want to go out in my condition. My stitches are still healing, and I'm just catching up on sleep. My hair needs doing, but I thought I'd roll something around in your head because you could probably think it out better."

"I'll be at your suite at that time tonight, Tori," he confirmed. "Thank you for thinking about me."

Tori hung up before she said something more, feeling a blush throughout her body. Of course, Duncan would already know which suite she was in. She had no doubt they were keeping tabs on her somehow, but that didn't bother her in the least bit. Being spoiled by three men who she had literally wrapped around her finger kept her on a forbidden high she knew no other woman could ever experience.

Squealing, Tori ran to the bathroom to get dressed, all the while saying over and over in her head, *You aren't going to have sex! You aren't going to have sex.*

Yet as she felt the time draw closer and closer to Duncan's arrival, Tori finally picked out a light blue cocktail dress with no arms, a flair that perfectly showcased her small waist and thick curves, paired with matching sandals. Since they weren't going any farther than inside the hotel, she didn't need a coat, but she did have a large white shawl she could use to cover her shoulders in case it was cool in the lobby.

You aren't going to have sex. You aren't going to have sex!

CHAPTER 22

Love Love Love with a Side of Punishment

At precisely six, there was a knock on her door, and she opened it to reveal a freshly cut Duncan wearing white linen pants and a light gray casual buttoned down textured shirt with horizontal lines showing his brawniness and power, but throwing her off her game to be alarmed by his roughness. Tori was all butterflies and tingles on the inside and was barely containing herself on the outside.

"You look delicious, Tori," Duncan drawled, running his eyes up and down her. "Are you ready?" he asked, offering his arm for her.

She grabbed her shawl and a small purse that held only her wallet, phone, and hotel key. "Yes," she said, coming out of her room and taking his arm.

Duncan led her to the elevators, and once they were on, he said, "You know I love it when you use the mango body butter. And what is that added? Black seed oil?"

His scent detection was too good.

"I started moisturizing my stomach area so I wouldn't get that many lines once my skin started stretching," she responded, feeling strange having this conversation with him, but also feeling so normal. "I want to start now, so I can make it a habit."

"Kevin can make sure that's done every night, if you want."

Tori smirked, knowing Kevin would definitely love rubbing oils all over her body after they'd had a shower and giving her a deep tissue massage.

"After all this, I still find it odd that you all are so comfortable with sharing me."

"Tori, it's what we desire, and we understand that finding someone who loves to be shared is a once-in-a-lifetime experience. Now that we have a second chance, we aren't going to fuck it up." Duncan moved very close to her, and she could feel his sexual arousal pulsating from him, but just as she was about to press herself against him, the doors on the second floor opened, and a couple walked in.

Duncan took her hand and led her out.

Correcting him, Tori said, "The restaurant is on the first floor."

"But the private booths are on this floor. I've reserved one for us."

She remembered the blue room that had been reserved, but they weren't going in that direction. He really was taking her toward the restaurant, but on the second floor. A hostess greeted them and, without Duncan saying anything, they were led to a private booth with dark black curtains all around, soft candlelight on the table, fresh roses in the middle, and appetizers already set out for them. The table was set for two, not booth-style seating. Still, there was a lot of privacy behind the curtains for business meetings or other things wealthy people wouldn't want the regular crowd to see or hear, because she couldn't determine if anyone was around them or not, and behind the curtains, the volume was lowered from around the rest of the restaurant.

"I know these are hard to get," Tori commented as they were seated across from each other.

"You'd be surprised what people will throw in a pile when they think they're going to win a hand of cards," he commented. "A reservation like this was bought years in advance. I won it, and I was holding on to it for someone special." He took her hand in his and kissed her palm. "Honestly, I never thought I'd use it, but you've got me doing things I never thought I'd do for anyone, Tori."

She contained her excitement. "I should get to the matter at hand," she said as a waiter filled their glasses with a creamy seafood soup and set out vegetables. Slices of fresh baguette complemented the meal.

"Of course," he said, leaning forward, ready to listen.

As she explained to Duncan what Beck had said about the storage container, she felt increasingly comfortable. If someone told her a year ago that she'd feel like a queen sitting at dinner with Duncan Carter as if they were the best of friends, she wouldn't have believed them.

"I can check out what's going on if you'd like," he offered.

"Well, Beck was going to try-"

Duncan cut her off. "Tori, you aren't going to remind us constantly of what Rebecca does for you? Otherwise, I will drop you off after dinner, go find him, and try my best to break his titanium fingers so he can't work for at least two months."

"No!" she gasped. "That's not what I was trying to do, Duncan. And you don't have to call him by his government name."

Duncan snorted, but didn't take her correction. "We allow Rebecca so much because we know you need him for your project, but with personal things like this, we'd like you to come to us. We're here for you, and you don't have to think you're alone. All we need is your permission."

"Then yes, you have my permission to find out what you can," Tori responded, biting her lip on the inside so she wouldn't smile because she loved how he showed her they were still going to be there for her.

Before they finished their soup, the main course was served, and, as always, good food made Tori happy.

"I still don't have your phone number," she noted.

"May I have your phone?"

She didn't think twice and handed him her device.

Duncan typed his phone number in and said, "I'm also giving you permission to the group chat and calendar. We've agreed that you need to put your doctor's appointments on there so one of us can be there for you. And I don't want to hear a protest, Tori."

When he returned the phone to her, Tori only nodded.

"How long will you plan to stay in the hotel?"

"I don't know," she responded. "I need to get my work together, and then I'm going to focus on my personal life. I don't have a doctor's appointment for another two weeks, so I can get myself situated, possibly find a car, and then look for-"

He pushed a valet ticket across the table. "There's your car. I bought it from the person who purchased it from your lawyer. It's parked in the valet parking of the hotel, and Kevin carries the extra in case you need him to work on it."

She loved and hated that Duncan had already come up with solutions to her problems. Wasn't this what she wanted?

Dammit! Tori was almost too flushed to eat, wanting to rip the clothes off of Duncan.

The waiter appeared again to see if they needed their drinks refilled, and Tori asked, "Can we wrap this meal up and have it delivered to my room?"

The waiter looked at Duncan, who only nodded. "Yes, ma'am."

Duncan stood up and offered his hand to Tori.

She took it and let him lead her back to the elevator. The sexual intensity she could feel between her legs almost dripped down her inner thigh.

People were on the elevator as they went on, but by the sixth floor, everyone had piled out, leaving them alone.

Tori didn't wait until the doors fully closed before she turned to Duncan, who immediately lifted her in his arms and tore into her mouth like she was going to be his last supper.

She didn't know how they made it to her hotel door. Duncan only moved her purse in front of the locking mechanism to open it, and then, after kicking off his shoes and kicking the door closed, he carried her into the bedroom.

Clothes off, kissing, lying on the bed, touching, and then so much tasting. Gawd, Tori didn't know whether to go down on him or kiss him, but he was the same, and Tori loved how erratic but in sync their passion was.

"Fahhhhh-uuuuuuuhhhhhckkk," he snarled as only the tip pressed into her.

Tori was so tight, she joined his snarl with a whimper, but feeling him inside of her only aroused her more, and with more kissing and Duncan dipping down to give her breasts all the attention her nipples cried out for, he sank into her easily.

"Uuughhh, Tori," he praised. "Fuck, you feel so good."

She would have complimented him as well, but he'd already started repeatedly plowing into her in deep, long strokes, tugging her core and blowing her consciousness to another level. All she could do was pleasurably whimper as his body took her. "Don't stop," she knew she was trying to say, but it took so long to form the words, by the time she finished, she was exploding from the inside out.

"Yeaaaaahhhh!" he moaned.

And he came, joining her orgasms, his hot essence over-filling her, making her pulse and tremble. Tori knew she wanted more, but would give him time to recover. Until then,

Tori planned to use her mouth to clean him up so they could start again.

~

When she awoke the next morning, there were several roses on her pillow and the smell of Duncan all around her. She gloated to the bathroom to clean up before she went back to work.

For some reason, all day long, she was trying to figure out an excuse to get Kevin to come over.

"Oh, that's cool, you have a car now," her niece said during a video meeting. "I input all the invoices for each project last night."

"You didn't have to spend your whole night doing that. I'm sure you wanted to catch up with friends now that you'll be in town for a moment."

"It's fine, Aunt Tori. It's nice keeping myself occupied, and I'm going into Forensic Accounting anyway."

"Really? I should get in touch with my lawyer's husband, Dwight Bowman. He has a firm."

"Oh my gawd! I've heard of him. He's incredible with numbers. Could you do that for me, Aunt Tori?"

"Of course." Tori loved knowing she could help her niece, and the reminder about the car gave her an excuse to get Kevin over.

She had his work number, and when he got on the phone, he immediately said, "You don't have to find an excuse to invite me to see you, Tori."

He sounded very perturbed, but she knew it wasn't out of jealousy that she had seen Duncan initially. Kevin just expressed his desire for her through irritation.

"Duncan told me the car is in the valet parking, and I wanted to ask if you could look at it, and we could have dinner after?"

"I can come after work. I'll check it and then come up and shower?"

"Yes," she confirmed.

"Tori, I'm coming to fuck you, *you* know that."

She giggled because his outright honesty titillated her. "And I'm going to fuck you back."

"Damn woman! I'm fucking getting off right now." He hung up on her, and Tori knew he was dead serious.

She took another shower and only dressed in a flowing silk robe.

An hour and a half after they'd spoken, Kevin was knocking on her door. He was still in his work coveralls, with the grim, sweat smell permeating her nose, instantly turning her on. The only thing he'd changed was his shoes, and he was carrying a thick gym bag.

Before she said anything, Kevin pulled her in his arms and ravaged her mouth. She knew the oil would ruin her robe on the front of his work coveralls, but Tori didn't care as he came into the hotel room, kicking off his shoes and dropping his bag before carrying her into the bedroom's large shower.

Scrubbing him down from head to toe was like his foreplay, and then she dropped to her knees and took his shaft down her throat. Slobbering all over him from base to tip, loving Kevin's vocal adoration and curses he doled out to her.

She wanted to drink him dry, and he gave her what she wanted. He pulled her to her feet almost before she could swallow him all to kiss her again and then lie their wet bodies on the bed. He dropped between her legs immediately, and Tori loved how voracious Kevin was, using his whole mouth and tongue and not missing any nook or cranny, licking her down from her clit to her rear. With his fingers and tongue, he had her speaking in tongues, flowing like a river, and the enjoyment was all over his face as he drowned in her.

And when she was out of her mind on her third orgasm,

Kevin raised her waist as he stood on the edge of the bed, and sank his thickened shaft deep in her. They both pleasurably hummed together, trembling into each other. She loved the raw sex Kevin gave, deep, demanding, and powerful, controlling her body like a F1 driver who knew how to cross the finish line.

But since he came earlier, he wasn't done with her body and with all her wetness, he saturated her rear so he could slip right in, just as she was coming down from her fifth orgasm, taking her back up, as he came pulsing hard and fast.

"Arrrrgggg!" he bellowed, trembling all over and shaking her to a climax with him.

It took them a moment to catch their breath, but he recovered first and went to grab a warm washcloth. Flipping her on her stomach, he cleaned her thoroughly and then himself. Aftwards, Kevin kept her that way to massage her backside from her nape to her feet.

Tori was about to get lulled to sleep when her stomach rumbled.

Kevin chuckled. "Get properly clean and meet me in the front room," he ordered.

Even though she was very relaxed, she dragged herself out of bed and bounded for the bathroom.

Since her robe was ruined, she donned a tank top and went to the front room. Dinner had been delivered to the suite, and he lit the fireplace and laid out the feast on the thick rug in front of the fire. He ordered sparkling non alcoholic apple wine, as well as an upside-down pineapple cake.

It was like having a sleepover. Of course, Tori was over the moon, enjoying herself.

"I love having baby-making sex even more with a baby inside of you," Kevin noted as he was changing her bandage on her arm. By this time, he was wearing a nice pair of underwear. She was sure he had more clothes to wear when he left, but she liked knowing he was in no hurry to get dressed. Kevin's body delighted her visual senses, and she knew if they could, she'd want to go to the next round before the end of the night.

Kevin continued, "Shawn's feeling guilty about getting you pregnant. And he says we should feel awful for putting you in this position." He raised on his elbow to look at her directly. "Can I tell him you brought it on yourself?"

She almost spat out the water she was drinking. "How so?"

"You asked for a breeding fantasy with me."

Tori realized she hadn't told any of them that she'd known about the pregnancy before they impregnated her. "I will not agree with that statement, Kevin, so that you can sleep well at night," she refuted. "I will say I don't regret getting pregnant."

Kevin pulled her under him and began his luscious kisses, and she was glad she had gotten something in her stomach because he was ready for round two, according to his shaft pressing hard against her belly. She was also happy the suite had a microwave because she had a feeling Kevin planned to wear her ass out before they could eat again.

Tori was game and matched his passion touch for touch.

She wished she had asked Kevin for another back massage before he left early in the morning. All she remembered of his departure from their front room sleepover was him sweeping her up in his arms and kissing her like he was never going to see her again.

"I love you, Tori," he said.

Getting a late start to her workday about ten o'clock, she apologized to her niece for missing their video appointment at nine.

"That's alright. Mrs. Cosgrove had us consumed this morning with funeral arrangements."

Tori saw the item added to her calendar. "How are you and your brother feeling?"

Her niece shrugged. "We're okay. Momma was wrong to keep her illness from us. I don't think she'd have done the things she did to hurt you if she'd communicated with us. I hope you don't feel bad about what happened, Aunt Tori. It wasn't your fault."

"I needed to hear that."

They proceeded with the updates, and Tori was happy that her niece had checked the outreach email and found some potential assistants.

"I've set them up for interviews next week. I'll be busy packing to get back to school, so I won't be able to attend them with you, but I can at least get them situated once you decide on which one."

"Oh, that's fine. Thank you so much," Tori said with appreciation, checking the time. "Let me catch someone before the end of the day."

"Bye, Auntie," her niece said and disconnected the video call.

Tori called Mrs. Cosgrove. "Thank you again for helping with the arrangements for the funeral. I really appreciate this for our family."

"It's really no problem. My husband is ecstatic that I'm keeping so busy, and he thanks you because I was driving him crazy. How are you, m'dear?"

Extremely happy but craving more of the Carter Brothers! Tori wanted to say, but that would need a lot of explanation. "I'm good, but I wanted to get a moment of Shawn's time at the end of his day without him knowing it was me," she said.

"Oh, really?" the older woman asked, intrigued. "Sounds like something wicked."

"No. I wanted to show a little appreciation for some things he and his brother set up for me when I moved into the St.

Royal suite." Tori had rehearsed what the truth was, but that wasn't the only reason she wanted to see Shawn.

He was a conundrum. As angry as he was about her and then so forgiving, he didn't act like the other two, and she needed to know whether he wanted to be with her, as she wanted to be with him.

"I'm very intrigued. What do you need me to do, Tori?" Mrs. Cosgrove asked.

Tori had never outright seduced a man, but she felt Shawn would need a little coaxing to understand he didn't have to be so damn polite. Picking up the choker, Tori knew what the final step would be to get the life she wanted.

There was the fear of what people would think, but the desire to be with The Carter Brothers was too strong, and Tori knew she needed to walk the path to her happiness and damn everyone else.

CHAPTER 23

She Gets Everything

The nervousness set in as Tori pulled into the hospital parking lot. Without the brace and her past couple of days' activity, she wasn't sore. Her stitches had started to itch, but she coated them with petroleum jelly before wrapping up again. In a lavender Boho ankle-length dress with matching lavender ankle boots and a wide rim velvet hat with a dark purple bow, the short sleeves showed off her bandaged area, but she wasn't feeling self-conscious about her injury.

It was Shawn.

True, Tori knew he loved her, but this new Shawn perplexed her. He wasn't so easy to read. Yet, Tori knew she wanted him even more than when she wanted him in the beginning. He was a part of her, whether known or unknown, and she had to feel comfortable connecting with him, just like she was with his brothers.

Pressing one hand to her butterfly-fluttering stomach and the other on her palpating heart, Tori took several deep breaths.

Mrs. Cosgrove made a late-day special member appointment, which probably pissed Shawn off because these were rarely used by board members when a "friend" wanted to get an appointment to see a physician privately. Once the doctor assessed the situation, the visit could be recorded or not.

The administrative podiatrist was hardly ever used. And rightly so, because who would ever have an emergency foot visit that they shouldn't go to the ER for?

Yet, Mrs. Cosgrove, who always got her way, finagled an end-of-the-day appointment with Dr. Shawn Carter and sent Tori the confirmation under Mrs. Carter's name.

She chuckled at the reference and knew Shawn would assume it was an alias to cover who it really was.

Tori entered the offices and was greeted by the receptionist, who checked her in. The young lady knew this was a VIP and didn't ask questions about the insurance or see ID, but gave Tori a clipboard.

"Since it was last minute, it might be about thirty minutes if you dont mind waiting," the receptionist said apologetically.

"No, it's fine," Tori said kindly.

"Then have a seat, and as soon as he's finished with this patient, he'll be seeing you."

The patient from the lobby was hobbling in with the nurse in the back, and Tori almost wanted to walk out, feeling bad that she was taking away from other patients who might really need service.

Yet she wanted something, and this selfish act should work out unless Shawn didn't like it.

Her nervousness escalated, but she again took deep breaths and focused on what would happen if things went well. About forty-five minutes later, that same patient came out walking much better. By this time, the receptionist had packed up and closed the receptionist area.

Tori didn't mind the wait because she understood this was a last-minute thing, and if it had been a semi-emergency, they would have gone as fast as they could with an end-of-the-day staff.

"Mrs. Carter," the nurse came out.

Standing up and handing the clipboard to the nurse, Tori acknowledged, "Yes."

"Please follow me."

She was led to a room and ordered to sit on a high medical gurney. Of course, everything was cleaned down, ready for a new day, and Tori felt that guilt for imposing on the staff.

The nurse took her vitals and asked, "Would you like to discuss anything with me so that I can prep the doctor?"

A secret smirk broke on Tori's lips, and she liked how the staff respected the VIP status. "No, I'd rather talk with the doctor."

"That's fine. He's finishing up his notes, and he should be here soon. Give him another five minutes. Have a good night, ma'am," The nurse said, taking the clipboard on her exit.

Tori hung up her purse, washed her hands, checked her face, took off her coat, and sat on the gurney, hiking up her dress in the back so it would be convenient if things went the way she wanted them to.

Why did Shawn have to be the most difficult one? One would think Duncan and Kevin would be harder, but Shawn was the conundrum, and this was a challenge Tori liked more as she got involved.

Seducing Shawn sent her arousal levels off the roof, and she wasn't going to deny it.

'You're their whore,' she heard Shadow's voice say.

Tori was accepting this about herself, but loved that none of the brothers called her one.

The door opened, and Shawn walked in, staring down at the clipboard, while he closed the door. Tori had filled in the information as "Mrs. Carter," but had entered all the measurements correctly. She had been evasive in answering the questions on the clipboard, and she knew Shawn would come in confused, with many questions. In the note, where it asked for the problem, she only wrote, "I'll let the doctor know when I see him."

She knew this was somewhat dubious because she also wrote she'd never had any foot problems, so he was probably wondering what kind of emergency this could be.

Shawn was wearing his doctor's coat, a nice dark blue dress shirt, and dark blue dress pants, looking darkly delicious as always.

"Mrs. Carter, what seems to be the prob-" He stopped speaking as he looked up from the clipboard. "Tori? What the hell? Are you okay? Is the baby okay? What's wrong?" He rushed to her, dropping the clipboard to the floor.

The confidence in what she planned immediately went out of her mind, and she felt like this was the dumbest idea ever. "I'm fine, I just wanted to see you."

"Tori, you just scared the shit out of me!" he reprimanded her.

Even though she knew he wasn't seriously mad, Tori was starting to feel less confident by the second. "I'm sorry. This was stupid." She began to get down off the gurney, but he pressed forward, blocking her way.

Shawn immediately pulled her into a deep hug, molding her against him. "I'm sorry. I let my anger override everything."

Tori wanted to cry because she felt his act of holding her meant more to her than anything. "I shouldn't have manipulated to see you like this, but I didn't know how to go about just asking to see you."

Shawn pulled her slightly away and said, "You had no problem asking about Duncan."

"Well, that's different," she said, playing with a button on his shirt so she wouldn't have to look up at him and those impenetrable eyes. "And it's been so long."

"Less than a week. Are you sure nothing else is physically wrong?" He moved those big hands down to her calves, pulling the chair over so he could sit down in front of her.

Tori knew he was still in professional mode, and she needed to activate Shawn's unprofessional side when he was away from the doctor's office. The one she needed and wanted to come out so they could get to the good part. "I'm fine, and just because it was less than a week ago, that doesn't mean it wasn't a long time ago," she pouted.

Shawn smirked and took off her shoes.

"What are you doing?" she questioned.

"You came for a visit with a podiatrist, so that's what I'm going to give you." He inspected the previous cut on her foot carefully and massaged her toes to her ankle.

Tori wanted to kick him in the face, but then, just watching him caress her feet, check for anything wrong, and even inspect the spaces between her toes was quite fascinating.

"You really do have lovely feet, Tori," he commented as he began a deep tissue massage to her calves and then back again.

"That's the first compliment I've ever gotten about my feet." Tori leaned back slightly, enjoying the foot massaging, remembering their first date, when he...

His hand moved up to her calf this time, very slowly, behind her knee, then back down again, plowing the muscles to build an electrical tingle all the way to her toes. Those large hands, similar to his brothers, could get the blood circulating, easing the tension in so many other places in her body, and Tori was really feeling even more arousal.

She couldn't stop her legs from parting, and with Shawn sitting where he was, he could easily see she had worn no underwear.

"Tori!" he hissed, but it wasn't in anger. His hands moved up to push her dress up her thighs. "Where are your panties, young lady?"

Giggling with wickedness, she said, "I didn't think I'd need-" She'd stopped speaking to gasp and groan because Shawn dipped his face between her thighs. Her actions had turned Shawn into a man instead of a doctor. He knew what she had come for, and he was going to give it to her.

His tongue swirled over her clit and then suckled her labia before plunging into her.

Tori splayed her thighs wider, trying to stay quiet, unsure whether the staff was still around.

Yet, Shawn didn't seem to care because the loud slurping and moaning he was doing could undoubtedly have been heard outside of the room. The man was acting as if he were eating the best dinner of his life.

Tori loved how he'd picked up techniques from Kevin, but also added a lot of his own, darting his tongue around both sides of her skene area, fluttering down to her perineum, sending waves of arousal all through her. And the finger plunges, *lawd,* they were driving her crazy. While his tongue had her in a steady lave, one finger would plunge inside of her, and then two and then three, curling just right until Tori couldn't stop her body from giving him what he wanted.

His satisfied moan and even louder slurping while she was coming was even more satisfying.

She was gasping as if her body was going into cardiac arrest, and it was comforting to know she was at the hospital because if she needed resuscitation, she would at least be able to be revived so she could do this all over again.

When Shawn was sated after having licked her clean, he rose, used the back of his hand to wipe her remnants off his chin, and even licked that as well with a satisfied smack on his lips.

Tori was still trying to pull enough air in her body, having to work to stay quiet while he massacred her snatch with his beautiful tongue.

His hand came up to touch her chin and tilt her head up. "Tori Song, you are the most beautiful woman in the world. You make my mind, body, and soul sing with joy that no one has ever done to me. You could ask me for the universe, and I would find a way to bring it to you on a silver platter."

Her breath caught in her throat, and she bit softly on her bottom lip.

Shawn leaned in and sweetly kissed her slowly, softly, but then pressed more, demanding her response until her lips parted and he delved his tongue into an intertwining with hers. His kisses were already delicious, and even more as she could taste herself all in his mouth, and she wanted to suckle every drop out so he could get some more.

Tori wrapped one of her arms around his neck after pushing his doctor's coat to the floor. Her other hand went down to his pants to open his belt. At the same time, Shawn's hands were trying to touch all over her body, and somehow they wrangled her dress over her head and threw it down on his doctor's coat.

His pants moved down as he came up on the gurney with her, and her lack of underwear helped them get to the goal faster. Shawn kissed her hard, soft, passionate, wild, and a million different other ways, but she knew he needed to join with her as his life depended on it.

She reached down, wrapped her hand around the base of his shaft, and guided him into her. Simultaneously, Shawn lifted her waist to elevate the direction he entered, so he slid right on her internal clitoris, sending Tori instantly cumming yet again with a river of her essence shooting from her, soaking the front of his clothes.

Too far gone to feel apologetic, Tori squirmed wildly as Shawn began deep, long strokes into her, lowering and lifting her hips in a strategic move to give her out-of-this-world delirium pleasure. The more she came, the more he worked to bring one after another.

Had this man taken a doctorate in making a woman come in this past week? Because his knowledge of the female body surpassed even what his brothers could do to her.

Tori didn't care if the staff was there; she cried to the stars, the heavens, and all the gods above and below, in thankfulness to the sweet Lord for this man.

Locking her legs behind his back to pull him down on her, Tori could maneuver her hands to cup his well-muscled ass and slip her finger into his rear just as she was building to an orgasm that broke her.

"F-Fuuuuuuuuuuuuhhhhh." Shawn groaned in her mouth as his body started pumping his hot come deep into her. "Tori! Fuck!"

It was like he was filling her entire stomach cavity up, and she was over the moon loving that he took them back. Damn! Damn! Damn! Hot sex in a doctor's office was definitely on her list to do again.

Shawn collapsed on her, and she didn't mind the weight. As a matter of fact, she loved it knowing he was too spent to move immediately off.

Tori sighed, running her hands up and down his body, just enjoying his rapid breathing on her chest. Her lavender-laced bra was still on, but that didn't bother her.

"I knew you'd look nice in this bra," he noted.

"I thought Duncan bought the clothes."

"No, I thought of it at the last minute, knowing most of your items were in the storage or in the Upper Peninsula since we kidnapped you with only your bag."

She kissed his forehead. "Thank you."

"What the fuck!" The door to the doctor's office burst open, and Norman stood there looking pissed as hell. "What the fuck, Shawn?"

Shawn jumped up and stood in front of Tori to shield her, while taking off his shirt. "What are you doing here?"

"I heard you were staying late, and I thought it'd be time for us to talk," Norman said and then pointed at Tori accusingly. "You're still going to fuck around with *her*?! After what *she* did to Malea, your sister?! How could you?!"

Shawn handed the shirt to her calmly as he got off the medical gurney, closing his pants. While Tori put on the shirt, Shawn said, "You're not welcome here, Norman, and just like I told you the last time I saw you, whatever we had is over. It's gone. There will never be you and me ever. I love Tori, and I want to be with her forever."

"You're choosing over me *for this*?" Norman said disgustedly. "She slept with your brothers. Why would you want their disgusting sloppy seconds?"

"I'm asking you to leave Norman," Shawn gritted through his teeth

Tori could see from behind that, even though Shawn spoke calmly, every muscle in his body had tightened.

"You think I don't know you? You think we can't be together, Shawn? You haven't given us a chance. I've changed. I'm different than before. I will never hurt you again."

Shawn moved forward to put more distance between Tori and to block Norman from her view. She didn't know if this was calculated or not, but whatever he was doing, she had a feeling not to move from where she was. Norman was blocking the only exit from the room, and clearly, they were now the only people in the office, so if things went off the rails, no one would be around to witness or help them.

"The only reason you're here is that you found out your mother sold your properties, and now we have possession," Shawn stated. "Norman, you're trying to get back to a time when I didn't know myself, but that's all over, Norman. Now I'm only going to ask you one more time to leave and never-"

Norman pulled out a Desert Eagle .357, pointing it directly at Shawn. Tori gasped in horror. The man was resorting to violence over a lost lover. "Tell her you're using her. Malea told me *that's* what you're doing. Your sister told me the whole plan! You don't love this manipulating, conniving, selfish bitch!"

"Malea and I spoke after you met with her. Norman and I told her, as I'm telling you, Tori isn't the person we were told she was. She's changed, and she changed us. She changed me, and I love her for helping me see I didn't like who I was, but for the first time in my life, I love the man I'm going to be. I won't allow you to take that away, Norman. Now put that gun down and get the fuck out of here before I resort to the man I used to be and beat your ass." Shawn took a slow breath in as if he were trying to control himself and spoke even slower. "And I'd like you not to call my wife names-"

"Your wife?!" Norman cackled. "She divorced your ass! I get the gossip! I know her lawyer filed the paperwork yesterday. Why are you letting her get between us?"

"There is no us, Norman. You're deluded. Put the gun down, you fucking idiot. You won't shoot me, and you certainly won't hurt her."

"Then you don't know how dangerous and crazy I really am, Shawn," Norman sneered. "If I can't have you-"

Shawn moved so quickly that Tori only had time to blink before he knocked Norman's hand to the side, raised his wrist, and punched him square in the face. She heard a resounding crack, and both men stumbled back to the floor, blood spraying from somewhere.

CHAPTER 24

Convincing Herself She's Not the Whore

Tori cried out Shawn's name as she jumped off the gurney. At the same time, the gun dropped out of Norman's hand, falling to the floor by her feet. Kicking the gun away from them and running to Shawn, she gasped more, seeing all the blood on Shawn's face and shirt. Norman was knocked out cold.

Shawn stood up and pulled her into him. "Are you okay?" he demanded while checking her whole body.

"I should be asking you that," she said, doing the same for him.

"Go over to the phone and hit the security button," he ordered as he went over to the sink to wash off his face, collarbone, and hands, where Norman's blood had gushed.

Security answered immediately on the phone's speaker once she hit the button, and Shawn told them the code, who he was, and to send help immediately. Tori couldn't take her eyes off of Norman, still knocked out with blood oozing from his face, with most likely a broken nose and some front teeth missing. The cracking of his face still reverberated in her ears.

As soon as they hung up, Shawn came over and pulled her into his arms, kissing her passionately.

"You didn't let me know if you were alright," she asked, concerned, trembling, still in shock.

"Yes, love. I'm fine," he assured her. "Are you?"

Lightly hitting his chest, Tori demanded, "Where did you learn to hit like that, Shawn? You nearly cracked his face in half."

"With two brothers like Duncan and Kevin, how do I not know how to hit?"

Tori fussed, "And what made you think you could redirect the gun? You could have been killed!"

Shawn smirked. "You're not really mad. You're doing this thing where you look mad, but you care."

"Shawn!" she cried. "You could have been killed. That's a real gun."

Shawn looked at the gun she had kicked across the room and then at Norman, who was still knocked out, before returning his intense eyes to her. "I remember your poor attempt to deflect the gun from your sister. You should have gone up instead of over. I learned from that. Plus, he still had the safety on. Duncan's taught me enough about them to know that about a firearm. Norman's knowledge about guns goes as far as a box office movie."

She hit her fist against his chest, ready to fuss at him some more.

"Damn!" Duncan exclaimed, looking down at Norman as he sheathed his eight-inch serrated knife.

Kevin came from behind Duncan, holstering his gun behind him, and Norman's arm. "Your fist finally landed properly."

"You're late," Shawn growled. "You missed the party."

"You knew they were coming?" Tori asked and then turned

to the older brothers. "You could have stopped him before he surprised the shit out of us."

"Shawn was being sarcastic, Tori," Kevin explained. "He didn't know we were coming. I tagged along with Duncan to the storage, and we got a copy of the security tape. You were right to be suspicious. Malea couldn't have broken into that storage container on her own in her weakened condition. Norman was helping her out all along. We went straight to Norman's after that, kicked his fucking door in to demand answers, and saw he left a suicide note."

Duncan handed her his phone with the note so she and Shawn could read it as Kevin finished explaining.

"Norman was planning on killing Shawn, then you, and then going over to shoot Scott and the kids before taking his life for Malea."

"Fuck!" Shawn hissed as he helped Tori put on his doctor's coat. "I want to fucking punch his face in some more."

Everyone heard security coming.

"Kevin, take Tori to the next room," Duncan ordered, as Shawn tossed Tori's dress to Kevin.

"I can stay and wait," Tori demanded.

"You're wearing his shirt and no underwear, Tori, and you're standing around all three of us half naked," Shawn pointed out. "Go with Duncan to get decent."

Kevin also picked up her purse before leading her into the next room, just as the security arrived in the offices. She snatched her dress from Kevin, put it on, and fixed her face and hair. She really did look indecent, and more rumors would abound in the hospital, but at least the brothers let her be presented as a lady.

"Are you really okay, Tori?" Kevin asked softly.

His concern touched her, and she moved into his body, loving his arms moving around her and holding her tight. "No. I just saw Shawn knock the fuck out of Norman, almost breaking his face because Norman called me a manipulating, conniving, selfish bitch."

"Well, shit, I should go fuck him up again," Kevin growled.

"That's not funny."

"I wasn't trying to be funny, Tori. I hope they fuck him up when he gets behind bars."

Gasping, Tori suddenly remembered the phone call, "It could have been Norman playing on my phone."

"What do you mean?"

She showed him her phone and pointed to the calls. They never leave a message, and when I answered, nobody would speak. I thought it was a prank and didn't think anything about it."

He scrolled through her phone log with a deep frown on his face. "We'll look into it, Tori," Kevin assured her, returning her phone.

Tori huffed and relaxed in his arms until a knock came on the door, and the detective entered, not surprised to see Tori again involved in a mess.

Kevin started for the detective, but she moved in front of him.

"Give us a moment, Mr. Carter," the detective ordered.

Looking at Tori, Kevin didn't move until she gave him a nod.

"Your brother-in-law is overly protective of you," the detective nodded. "Even though you're divorcing his brother. I'm starting to believe you attract a lot of trouble, Ms. Song."

"I'm not trying," she grumbled.

"I appreciate those journals you had your other ex-brother-in-law deliver. It cleared up a lot of what happened to Amos, and I'm sorry you had to learn about your past like that. It can explain a lot of Malea's anger toward you and what drove her, which had nothing to do with you. But I see it also affected Norman as well."

Tori wasn't sure if the detective knew how deep everything went, but she wasn't going to tell Shawn's business either. "I may have been the monster they created, but I wish I had discovered I wanted better for myself way before I decided to change." She huffed, but took a deep, resounding breath. "And I know I can't change the past, and I won't feel guilt about it anymore either."

"I'm going to take your statement as to what happened tonight. I saw the suicide note, and they told me about the security tape and how Norman was helping your sister. I know you came to get your foot checked with Shawn. How are you feeling?"

Tori bit her bottom lip to stop her wicked smile. "Much better," she answered.

Half an hour later, the detective finally let her out of the room where all three brothers were standing. Shawn was holding her shoes and immediately knelt to put them on.

"Thank you," she said sweetly, wishing all the police weren't around so she could kiss all of them.

Shawn took his shirt and doctor's coat from her when he stood up, and Duncan put on her coat while Kevin handed her purse.

"You all can leave, and if we have any questions, I'll let you know," the detective said. "Norman's going away for a very long time, and the Amos case will be shut."

Norman's body was gone from the ground as Shawn took her hand and led her out to the lobby.

"You're coming home with us," Duncan demanded.

Tori stopped letting Shawn lead her out, and she stopped immediately. She had yct to tell them about the babies, and to go home with them would mean everything was fine, and it wasn't. "I said I need time."

Kevin refuted, "You're not safe at the hotel."

"I'll be fine," she insisted. "The detective said Norman's going away."

"She needs time," Shawn defended her stance, coming beside her and tossing his keys to Kevin. "I'll take her back to the hotel. You guys get home."

Duncan and Kevin looked reluctant, but after another couple of seconds, they kissed her cheek and walked away.

"Why are you siding with me?" Tori asked suspiciously.

"As much as we want to insert ourselves into your life and want to protect you, I know you do need your space, Tori," he said. "Most likely, Duncan will have dinner delivered by the time we get to your suite, and Kevin will have some extra clothes for me delivered."

Moving into his arms, she asked, "Then we can finish what we started?"

Shawn smiled wickedly. "You damn right."

As they drove to the hotel, Shawn reached over and took her hand. "Tori, I know why you didn't want to come home with us tonight. You don't think all the secrets we've kept from you are out, right?"

Tori's stomach churned because she was keeping a secret about her pregnancy, never knowing a good time to tell them.

Shawn must've taken her silence as admission to his question. "I think I should talk with you about what happened with Malea the last time we talked."

Tori immediately saw the troubled look on his face and was going to speak, but felt Shawn squeeze her thigh as if he needed her to hear him.

"I left that morning from being with you at the island with the resolve that I was going to fix everything. Not only get you the divorce you should have gotten for our deceit, but also to let Malea know the original plan to hurt you was over. After meeting with my lawyer, she was waiting outside the building, accusing me of breaking my promise to hurt you. I told her I didn't care about the promise I made to her because now my heart was involved, and for the rest of my life, I was going to make sure no one ever hurt you again. I was going to make up for everything we had done to you, and whatever plans she had to destroy your life were over because I was going to protect you along with my brothers. She was enraged and angry. Tried to claw my eyes out, but I walked away from her, not taking her threats seriously. She raged that I would regret choosing you and not her."

"So you knew she was sick with cancer?"

"I knew she wasn't well, but she even lied to her doctors at the hospital because when I looked up her chart there, they had no record of her cancer and its progressive state. She said she had been ruined because of the money she'd lost and continued to harp on her gambling story. I didnt care enough because I didn't want anything else to do with her. I should have. I don't think she would have lost it like that that night if I hadn't been cold and condescending. I could have stopped it, and I didn't. For that, I'm sorry, Tori."

"She was gone before that," Tori resolved. "If she hadn't worked with you, she would have found another way to hurt me or even killed me sooner."

Shawn took her hand and kissed her palm. "I can't regret working with her, because I would have never come to find what my heart truly desires." He placed her hand on his chest. "Tori, my brothers and I truly love you."

She was all smiles the rest of the ride and couldn't wait to get him in her hotel room and tear his clothes off.

Six hours later, it was nearing one in the morning, Shawn was lying on her groin, rubbing his hands over her stomach and up to her breasts.

"Thank you," he said softly.

Sexually sated from a very strenuous lovemaking session, she didn't open her eyes, enjoying his afterplay over her body. "For what?" she asked.

"Loving us."

Opening her eyes to see him looking up at her, she smiled.

"You make it easy by spoiling me," she admitted.

"And we'll keep doing it, Tori."

"I'll never get sick of -" She gasped because his mouth dipped down between her slit.

Shawn loved his newfound sexual attraction to the female body, and she loved being the one he adored.

When she rolled out of bed in the morning, realizing Shawn was gone, Tori huffed because she hated waking up alone.

That would mean you would move in with them if you don't want that to happen, she surmised.

Checking the time, she saw her nine o'clock meeting with her niece was coming up, and she needed to get out of bed. She knew she wouldn't be able to get her hair done before the repast, but when she contacted her hairdresser, she was glad to arrange an appointment in her hotel suite on Sunday. Tori needed to keep occupied, and she knew the day after the repast, she would have been tempted to take her whorish butt off to their house, use the choker to get access, and demand they please her.

Yet she knew that just physically pleasing her wasn't all they wanted; was Tori really ready to have a life of their love and dedication to all of them?

ALL OF THEM?

Any other woman would jump at the chance to be spoiled and happy, and the old Tori would have too, but this new Tori was terrified that maybe she was being greedy. Perhaps she was a nymphomanic whore, and her sexual appetite would never be sated.

Tori spent the rest of the day gathering supplies for the repast and decided she would try to spend the night alone, away from the brothers. Of course, all she thought about was them and could only think of them when she lay down in bed, missing their touch, warmth, and comfort.

The only good thing about the day was that she didn't get any more strange phone calls. Perhaps it was Norman who had been bothering her, and she was glad that all the horrible things in her life were now in the past.

After a restless night, she awoke and dressed to get to the church early for the funeral. She would leave her car there and then go to the graveyard with the family. Upon their return, she'd drive a block over to where the repast hall was. The church owned it, and since attendance was expected to be small, the service wouldn't be long.

People from the hospital board, a couple of hospital units, and some staff sent flowers, but fewer than 50 people attended the church service for her sister. This was the church where Malea and Scott got married, and almost everyone knew Scott, but hardly anyone knew her sister. The Cosgroves and Malea's supervisor showed up and offered their condolences.

Malea had been alone in her fight with cancer, and Tori felt like she had failed her sister by being involved in her own life, especially after the brothers had come into her life. All three of the Carter Brothers showed up to the funeral dressed in matching black suits. Everyone's eyes were on them as they paid their respects to the open casket and then came over to where the family was seated. Tori was at the end, so she was the last one; each one of them hugged her.

She noticed each brother pressed an envelope into Scott's hand and into his children's hands before coming to hug Tori tightly.

Duncan was the only one who whispered something. "Don't you dare feel one ounce of guilt."

Tori almost collapsed because she knew he had perfectly read her mind, and he held her longer than necessary until she could steady herself.

No one spoke on behalf of the family, but Scott had assigned someone at the church to read all the cards and notes of condolences from others. When they were on their way to the graveyard, Tori asked, "Why didn't anyone want to speak?"

"There was nothing to say," Scott said. "We all agreed we'd keep what we felt to ourselves. Let the public think what it wants. Their mother was never involved in their lives, not like you, Tori. She gloried in their achievements, but Malea would always have me handle things. It was like she wanted the title of a wife and mother, but not the work."

"Why didn't you say anything to me about this?"

"We didn't want you to think you were overshadowing her and stop what you were doing," her niece expressed. "Momma would tell you what she did for us, but in truth, it had always been Daddy doing everything."

Tori would have pulled back because she would have felt like she was trying to outdo her sister.

Scott reached over and took Tori's hand in comfort. "We appreciated all you did and have done for us, Tori. I told the kids never to say anything to you about it because I didn't want things to get worse at home. Blame me, not them or even her. I loved her, and I married her, and at any time I could have left her, but I didn't. Your help kept me a better father and a better man. I have no regrets."

"Thank you, Scott, for trying to make me feel better." She saw her nephew take out the envelopes the Carter Brothers had given him. "What did they give you?"

The envelopes were sealed shut, and both niece and nephew ripped them open, then squealed in delight.

"Money!" they said simultaneously.

Scott took out his envelope and saw there were gift cards and money in it. "This is going to be very helpful as I get ready to sell the house and try to find another place to stay."

"I can look with you. Maybe Monday," Tori suggested.

Her niece reminded her, "Don't you have your doctor's appointment in the morning for the baby?"

"Oh yes," Tori flushed. "I almost forgot."

"We wanted to come. Is that okay?" her nephew asked.

"We leave on Tuesday morning and would love to see the baby since it's your first ultrasound and you shouldn't be by yourself."

Tori was elated because she didn't know which brother to ask without offending the others. This was the perfect excuse to send them a message explaining why she didn't invite them. She'd figure out all the other doctor's visits as the pregnancy went on.

"It's fine. I'd love for you to join me," Toir answered. "Afterwards, we can do some mid-year school shopping and then lunch."

"Is it true you slept with all three of them?!" her nephew blurted out.

Her niece hit him. "That's rude!" she reprimanded her brother.

Tori sighed and admitted. "But it's true."

They were all awkwardly quiet for a long minute before her niece asked, "Is that why Shawn divorced you?"

"I divorced him, but not because I was sleeping with his brothers. It's a long story for much older adults," Tori explained.

"And none of our business to ask about or spread," Scott warned his kids.

The rest of the ride was spent listening to her niece and nephew talk about what they planned to spend their money on. The envelopes had definitely lifted their spirits.

After the repast, Tori was exhausted from the day and glad, because once she fell into bed, she slept the whole night. Since the next day was Sunday, she ordered breakfast and finished her work early.

Her arm was doing much better, and with all the space in the front room, she had been stretching daily and doing some form of exercise to stay in shape, including using the hotel's gym and pool. Today was a good workout day, and she made her way down to the private gym. The stitches were almost dissolved and didn't itch as much.

Hardly anyone was in there, but Tori was shocked to see Shadow sitting at one of the walking platforms as if waiting for her.

"Are you waiting on me?" Tori questioned.

"Today, yes, I am," the teenager huffed impatiently, dressed in a dark purple hoodie and black jeans with purple sneakers.

"Do you ever wear anything other than that?"

Shadow answered, "It's comfortable. Have you used the choker for access yet?"

"No. I don't plan on going over there or back to that island."

"You're just going to see them from afar? How's that going to work?"

"Why are you in my business? What do you need to use me for?"

"I'm nosey," Shadow admitted.

Tori huffed and started walking briskly on the machine next to Shadow. "My life is none of my business."

Shadow got up and started walking on the machine she had been sitting on. "They aren't usually there during the noon hours. You could walk right in and see what they've done."

"What's that supposed to mean?"

The teenager smiled wickedly and stopped walking. "Oh, you're curious. Are you doing this because you think everyone is going to call you promiscuous? A slut? The Carter brothers' whore?"

Tori stopped walking and faced Shadow. "You don't understand. There's too much, and I don't want that." Lowering her eyes to the ground, Tori couldn't stop herself as tears formed in her eyes and ran down her cheek because she wanted to scream at everyone and tell them to fuck off so she could be happy.

"But you need it," Shadow stated quietly and started to walk away. "Just go and stop putting off missing them. You're only hurting yourself. You love them, and they love you. Have fun. Fuck everyone else."

When Tori looked up, it was to see that the young woman had disappeared entirely from the gym. Tori hadn't heard any retreating footsteps or a door open. *How did Shadow do that?*

Getting back up to her room, the hairdresser had arrived, and Tori was glad to be occupied getting her hair done for the rest of the day. Late that night, Tori ran a hot bath and stayed in it until the water grew cold. Trying to pleasure herself was difficult because her orgasms didn't feel as fulfilling. After all, it wasn't the real thing.

You could be having the real thing if you swallowed your pride and stopped worrying about what other people were thinking!

Tomorrow was her doctor's appointment, and then she was going to have lunch with her niece and nephew before they packed up and left. Scott was going to drop them off early in the morning to accompany Tori.

She waited until she got up the next morning after an awful night of restless sleep to text all three brothers.

No need to come to the doctor's appointment with me. My niece and nephew insisted on accompanying me, and it would be awkward trying to explain our situation to them. I'll send you any doctor's notes and results as soon as I'm done.

Tori waited a moment before putting her phone down and was a little disappointed she received no response, but saw that all three had read the message. Perhaps she had doomed herself, and they didn't want to wait.

Maybe they had found someone else and had spent these past few days enjoying her.

You did this?! You were only their whore! You pushed them away by keeping your distance. You stupid, manipulative whore! So selfish for only thinking about how you feel while not caring about how they feel!

The knock on the door startled her, and she was glad to welcome her niece and nephew.

"Let me fix my face, and we can get going?" Tori said, quickly going to the bathroom so they wouldn't see she had been crying.

After running the water on high to cloud her crying and throwing cold water on her face, Tori applied some makeup, twisted her hair up, and came out to the front room.

"Are you okay, Auntie?" her niece questioned worriedly.

"I'm good. Let's go," Tori insisted, hurrying them out of the room.

When they arrived at the doctor's office, it was still early in the morning, and she must've been the first appointment on the schedule because the waiting room was empty.

To her surprise, Tori realized this was one of the buildings she had bought for Shawn, and that Dr. Chance Jefferson's practice was brand-new, on the other side of the medical office.

"Mrs. Carter," the nurse greeted her as she entered, handing her a clipboard.

Tori corrected. "It's Ms. Song. Good morning."

The nurse apologized. "Dr. Jefferson moved his morning clients to the afternoon because he said it was going to be a roomful when you arrived."

"No, it's just me and these two," Tori said. They're my niece and nephew. They wanted to see the baby if that's alright."

"The more the merrier. Finish filling out that paperwork, I'll call you back for a regular appointment to check on you, and then we can bring them in when it's time for the ultrasound with the doctor."

Tori was glad the nurse would allow everyone in the room. She sat down and quickly filled out the paperwork, but she kept looking at the door, waiting for it to open and for at least one of the brothers to walk in.

You told them not to come! Why would they?

She looked at her phone and saw they still had not replied to her message. This was not like them.

Because they already found someone new!

The outside door opened, and two young people entered, about the same age as her nephew and niece. One was a female, dressed in a full-length blueberry fleece coat, light-skinned African American with the most intense brown eyes, and soft, thick lips with a resting wicked smile. The young man looked exactly like the young woman, except he was dressed in the same style coat, but it was beige.

"Ms. Song," the young woman said as they walked up to Tori.

Tori stood, wondering how this female knew her name.

"How can I help you?"

"I'm Edward Carter," the young man said. "And this is my

sister, Eadie Carter. Shawn is our father." He extended his hand and then nudged his sister to do the same.

As she shook their hands, Tori was shocked but instantly saw the resemblance to the Carter family.

"We're sorry to surprise you like this, but when we found out about you and the baby, we had to know more. Our father came to us yesterday and insisted we join you," Eadie said.

Edward cleared his throat and shot his sister a hard look just like Duncan would have. Eadie rolled her eyes.

Eadie continued speaking, "And also to confess, I've been the one calling and not leaving a message and not talking. I'm here also to apologize. I should have told my father about my curiosity, but I just had to, I guess, hear your voice and know if it was true."

"Was what true?" Tori questioned.

Eadie blushed furiously, looking too embarrassed to answer.

Edward answered for his sister, "Whether we had a sister or brother, or was it a niece or nephew?"

CHAPTER 25
The Truth Comes Out

At the same time Edward had made his inquiry out loud, the nurse came out to call Tori in.

Tori heard her niece and nephew gasp at the implication, but she was still shocked to see Shawn's children standing before her, asking who the daddy was.

Feeling flustered, Tori said, "Let's get through this appointment, and we can all go to lunch and talk about this." She turned to her niece and nephew to introduce them to Edward and Eadie.

"The doctor will see you now," the nurse urged. "We can call everyone in when it's time."

Tori was glad to get a minute away from everyone's looks to get into the exam room. After changing and answering general questions, the doctor came in.

"How are you feeling?"

"I'm having a very rough day."

"It's expected in your situation," he said casually and started her examination. "I'm glad you came. I didn't think you would."

"Why?" Tori asked, trying to relax as he took a culture from her and then checked her cervix.

"I thought you'd be busy or they'd keep you from me."

"I don't think they care who I see or me in general. Just the baby."

The doctor frowned as he tapped her leg and moved back so she could sit up. He handed the cultures to the nurse, who sealed them, then left the room to bring in the young people.

Dr. Jefferson washed his hands and then came over to her. "Tori, I know sometimes a woman's pregnant brain can go off the deep end. Don't let it cloud the truth. And I won't sit here and tell you how they've given me the side eye as if I was trying to steal you away from them whenever they saw me come into your room at the hospital. That middle one gives me the fucking chills. I don't care who you've slept with or are still sleeping with. I care about you as a patient and the life you carry. You have the choice to be whatever you want to be in their lives. It's all up to you, but if you have a chance to be happy, then be it because every woman deserves a stress-free pregnancy."

"Thank you," Tori said gratefully.

The doctor pulled the ultrasound machine screen down and placed a sheet on Tori's legs so he could lift her gown. By this time, all four of the young people had entered and crowded around her to see her and the screen.

"Are you going to tell the sex too?" her niece asked the doctor.

"It's too early," Dr. Jefferson said after he coated Tori's stomach with the gel and then put the monitor on her. "Usually, we wait until the third month to do an ultrasound, but with Tori's injury, I want to make sure everything is fine around the uterus, but it might give us a chance to see a little something."

Tori suddenly wasn't so miserable, but just as excited as

everyone else in the room. A whole minute went by, and everyone seemed to be holding their breath until the doctor suddenly tilted his head and pressed a little harder on Tori's stomach. Tori looked up at the screen and then back at the doctor's concerned face. All she could see was gray blobs.

"What's wrong?" Tori asked, concerned.

"I don't think it's concerning," he said, then turned the monitor around and moved lower on her stomach. "If you don't mind this."

Tori looked back at the screen and gasped, as did everyone else.

"Triplets?!" Tori exclaimed.

Her nephew cursed while Edward passed his sister twenty bucks.

"I told you it was multiples!" Eadie said proudly.

"You made a bet?" her niece asked disgustedly.

"Uncle and Father are going to fall out about this one," Edward said.

"No, they won't," Tori said, getting control of the room. "What you've seen you will keep to yourself—all of you. I'll tell them on my own. Promise."

All four of the young people promised.

Tori looked back at the screen and then at the doctor. "Can I have four printouts?"

> Give me some time to wrap my head around things. I will contact you when I'm ready. Doctor says I'm healthy and things are fine.

She sent this text as soon as she finished dressing, then joined the young people in the lobby.

Edward and Eadie, along with her niece and nephew, kept Tori's mind off the impending pregnancy. At lunch, they discovered their colleges were only thirty minutes apart and made plans to see each other by Christmas break.

Tori was glad they were all getting along, and she was happy to meet Edward and Eadie.

"Why do you call him Father? And not Dad or Daddy?" Tori questioned.

Edward responded, "Our mother wanted us to call him the donor, but Uncle Kevin told her that wouldn't be allowed, so Father agreed."

"I thought they had an amicable arrangement."

"They did until we went off to college, and suddenly my mother wanted more from him because I guess we weren't around, but when he didn't return her affections, she became bitter," Eadie spoke. "We were well aware they had married for an arrangement. Her parents were harsh and demanding. They also passed a month before we graduated, which could account for our mother's sudden change in her feelings. It was like she was locked away from the world until they passed, and she just expected Father to enjoy the ride she wanted to give him."

Edward cleared his throat at his sister again.

"She asked Eddie," Eadie pouted. "I think she deserves to know everything."

Edward admonished, "But no reason to be vulgar about it, E."

Eadie changed the subject. "But when Father came to reprimand me about using Edward's phone to call you, I saw it all over his face. I knew you were different. And when we came home and saw how Uncle Kevin and Duncan were, I knew you'd changed them."

Her brother agreed. "Uncle Kevin has stopped drinking

completely, and Uncle Duncan said more in an afternoon than he's said to us his entire lifetime."

"And Uncle Kevin laughed," Eadie gushed. "I'd never heard him laugh."

Tori blushed. "I'm sure they're excited about the baby... well, now they'll be even more excited about the babies."

"It's not just that," Edward said. "It's you, Ms. Song. It's definitely you."

Tori filled her mouth with food so she wouldn't have to respond.

Afterward, she took everyone on a small shopping spree for things they needed after school, then dropped Edward and Eadie back at the hospital, where their car was parked.

"It was an honor to meet you, Ms. Snow," Edward said, shaking her hand. "We'll be leaving for school tonight."

Eadie hugged Tori. "I hope to see you at the house for Christmas. I know Father said they're giving you time, but I really want to spend the holidays with you and them together."

"We'll see," Tori said stiffly.

Tori took her niece and nephew home, gave them long hugs, and then left them to drive back to the hotel. Since her niece was going back to college, Tori had already lined up interviews and chosen a new assistant, but she was too depressed to send out the employment packet.

Looking at her phone, she saw all three brothers had seen the text message, but none had responded.

They found someone else! Tori was determined to sink into the hot bathwater with rose oil.

That would be the only thing she could imagine since they hadn't responded.

Any woman would be lucky to have the opportunity she had pushed away. Tori pulled her knees up to her chest and cried the rest of the night until the water grew cold, and she crawled into bed.

Tori woke the next morning and forced herself to get out of bed, get dressed, and get to work. After she sent out the employment packet to her new assistant, she cleaned up her email and then checked her phone.

No response had come from any of them.

Get mad! Get over there! Demand they give you attention! Or demand you aren't going to be their whore anymore! She'd make that decision when she got over there, but right now she was mad they were ignoring her.

Tori looked at the time. It was going on noon. Going to her bag, she put the rose ring on her right ring finger and the other rings on her left finger. She intended to hurl each ring at them after she told them she wasn't going to be their whore anymore!

She put on a black maxi dress, the long fur coat, and the hat. It was getting winter cold in Detroit, and going out half-naked was a death sentence, but the fur kept her nice and warm.

She only grabbed the choker and her purse, got her car from the valet, and drove to the house - THEIR house.

Reminders of the island immediately flooded her senses, and she was positive she was making the right decision, confronting them and letting them know she wasn't going to take being their temporary whore.

She wanted more - she needed more, especially if she was going to carry their children!

No one looked home, but she remembered their cars were probably parked behind the big brown iron-plated gate.

Once you go in, how do you know you won't ever walk out? she asked herself.

Deep down, Tori knew she didn't want to walk out. She wanted this life with them, but only if they really wanted this.

She couldn't do this alone or without all of them on board - forever.

Looking down at the choker, Tori wondered if Shadow had told her the truth.

As soon as she stepped close to the door, the lock clicked, and the door opened all the way for her as if the house had been expecting her.

She walked inside and saw a cubby hole filled with shoes. She wasn't sure whether that meant someone was home. Taking off her boots, she stepped past the foyer into the house.

With bare feet, the rug felt incredibly soft under her feet, and just as Shadow had said, no one was around.

But that didn't mean no one was home.

Tori remembered the house on the island, and, just as they had said, it was just like it, except the design was older. She walked into the kitchen, but there was no solarium off it like the one in the house on the island.

Going up the stairs, the second floor held five bedrooms. She immediately knew Eadie and Edward's room. The third room was the largest on the floor, and she gasped, seeing that a nursery had been set up, but there was only one bed in there. Looking around the room, she knew two more cribs could be accommodated, and she had to force herself not to grin.

The other two rooms were guest rooms, but she knew these could be the kids' rooms as they got older.

At the end of the hall was the wall where she knew the secret entrance was.

Reaching up to the wall light, Tori pulled on it, just as Kevin had, but it didn't budge. With the choker in her hand, she tried again, and the door automatically came all the way open. Tori decided not to go up there and close the door back by leaning on it.

Instead, she made her way up to the third floor. She remembered them telling her this was where they slept. The first room, she could smell Kevin as soon as she opened the door. His room was painted green, with a private bathroom with only a shower, toilet, and sink. There was nothing extravagant about the room, but he had kept it nice and neat.

The second room was Duncan's. Pretty much the same, but everything was brown. He didn't have a private bathroom, and she noticed a large bathroom across the hall from his door. Across from Kevin's room, she saw that the bedroom door was partially cracked, but no one was in there.

Tori went over to the clothes hamper, pulled up the shirt Shawn had worn to the funeral, and smelled it. His scent made her close her eyes and remember every time he'd touched her body.

Damn! She missed them.

He didn't have a private bathroom, but his room led to the floor's bathroom. Coming out of his room, she looked at the last door, wondering what it was. If the second floor had five bedrooms, would the third floor have the same?

She went to the final door at the end of the hall and tried to open it, but it was locked. Waving the choker at the doorknob several times wouldn't open the door, and she pressed her ear to the door to see if she could hear anything.

Nothing! *Was this the other woman's room?* She jealously wondered. *Was there a bed in there that they had shared with another woman?*

Going back down to the second floor, she looked at the secret wall again.

She was silly to think she'd get locked in. Using the choker again, she opened the wall and started up the two flights of stairs.

The first room door was open, but Tori was shocked by what she saw. The room was still the same, but *HER* bedroom furniture was inside. Had they stolen out of her storage?

Were they insane? Were they planning on kidnapping her again?

Going to the next room, it was open, and all her craft supplies were in there. The piece she had been working on at the island was even there as well, with no damage. There was one more room after that, which was set up like her office.

They'd stolen her items out of her storage and brought them here!

How dare they?!

A bump in the house was heard, and she stormed down all the stairs to find out who was there and confront them about ignoring her and stealing her belongings!

Shawn, Duncan, and Kevin were coming inside, all bitching at each other, each carrying a box from her storage with her kitchen items.

"You're stealing my stuff?!" she exclaimed.

Shawn almost dropped his box while the other two looked ready to pull out whatever weapons were possibly on them and use them.

"Tori, what the hell?!" Shawn exclaimed.

She tossed the choker down at their feet.

Duncan put down his box and picked up the choker. "How'd you get it off?"

"Does it matter. You can give it to your next whore because I'm not going to be used by any of you, anymore!" She started taking off her rings, but Kevin dropped his box and came over to her. "I refuse to be some temporary slut while you go find others to impregnate!"

"Tori, stop," he ordered, putting his hands gently over hers to stop her actions.

She hit his chest and pushed him away. "You can't tell me what to do! None of you can. Not anymore. Now that you have someone new."

Shawn looked at his brothers, confused.

"I don't care who she is!" Tori went on. "I just came to return your stuff and tell you..." She had to take a deep breath because she didn't like feeling like this. It was almost similar to when she had come to sign the divorce papers, but this hurt worse, and they all stood there looking at her just like that night, except Beck wasn't here.

"I'm not jealous. I'm just being sensible," she said, sucking in a sob. "I know I've pushed you away, and you had every right to find someone other whore." Tori looked down and tried to take the wedding ring off again, but her finger wouldn't let it go, and the more she tried to twist it off, the harder it was to get past her knuckles.

"There's no one, Tori," Duncan said, slowly moving towards her left side.

Shawn added, "There will never be anyone, Tori."

Kevin tilted her face up to his. "There will always be you, Tori."

She looked at each one of them and let the breath out. She didn't know how long she had been holding.

They were waiting for her. She had control over them, and in that moment, she knew they would wait forever for her.

"I feel so stupid," she admitted.

Shawn moved to her and hugged her. "Tori, we were moving all your items here because the storage facility couldn't move your items to another similar container because they were full. So we moved them here and paid them not to inform you until the end of the month."

"We were giving you time," Kevin explained.

She saw Kevin look at Duncan, who nodded up the stairs.

Shawn took her hand and led her up the stairs. "Have you seen the whole house?"

"Pretty much," she admitted.

"How'd you figure out the choker opened everything?

And how'd you get it off?" Kevin insisted on following behind them.

"Beck had a friend," she admitted. "They figured it out."

"Of course," Duncan growled as they all took to the third floor.

"I only came to see if it was true," she admitted as Shawn led her to the end of the hall. "And to give you all this." In her bag, she pulled out the three sonograms she had the doctor print out. "I made Edward and Eadie keep it a secret."

"They told us you made them swear to keep their mouths closed, and we didn't bother them. We were going to wait for you to tell us," Shawn said, taking the picture she handed him along with Kevin and Duncan.

All three of them stared at the picture for a long moment before looking at her.

The doctor had indicated all three fetuses.

Kevin was first to react, yanking her up in his arms and swinging her around. "Fuck, yes!"

She was startled by his response, but just as he set her down, Shawn drew her in his arms, hugging her so tight she thought she was going to break, before Duncan pulled her to him and kissed her passionately.

"Thank you," he said softly.

They all looked at each other proudly, and suspiciously she asked, "This wasn't the plan? To get me pregnant?"

"Nah, Tori," Kevin stated, with a salacious wink. "You brought that dream on yourself, driving us crazy with your needs and your baby-making sex fantasies."

She blushed. "I should admit I did know I was pregnant before I was kidnapped."

Kevin's demeanor changed. "Oh fuck, you were going to leave us!"

Shawn approached her with remorse, softly cupping her face. "I could have hurt you and the babies, Tori."

"I was angry," she explained. "I was going to leave and just focus on whatever good I could continue to remember about you all."

"And let Beck's brother raise our children?" Duncan growled. "I think the fuck not!"

"I should have told you, and for that I'm sorry, but you did kidnap me, so even then it was hard to-"

"What about the Plan B I made Kevin give you?" Shawn asked worriedly, cutting her off.

"I seduced him not to give it to me," she admitted.

Kevin snorted as both his brothers looked at him. "What? You know I fucking love baby-making sex. I could not turn that shit down. And y'all just still pissed she talked to me first."

Shawn pulled her into his arms. "We're sorry, Tori. Even more so because we could have caused so much harm to you."

"But we didn't, and I'm fine," she resolved.

"Although," Shawn responded in a very professional doctor's voice. "Those garbanzo beans you loved to snack on could have increased your fertility levels."

Duncan jabbed him in the stomach.

"Were you really coming to tell us to fuck off again?" Kevin asked, looking very bothered. "What were you going to do? Run away with our kids?"

"I didn't know what I was going to do," she flushed. "I was jealous and angry because you didn't respond to my text message. I wasn't going to leave, though. I really do want to stay here in the city and work on my project and raise the babies with their fathers."

All three smiled, and she loved how they seemed to brighten at the prospect of becoming fathers. "I don't know the sexes yet, or who their father is specifically."

"It doesn't matter," Duncan declared. "We're going to raise them together, Tori. And you'll never have another worry for the rest of your life if you stay."

Kevin explained, "Shawn said we had to give you your space, especially since you were going to see the doctor and he'd know we'd been up in you."

Tori opened her mouth to say something, but then couldn't think of how to respond. In a way, Shawn was right, and Tori would have ignored that logic if any of them had come around. The doctor would have seen and known. "I don't know whether to thank you or be embarrassed that I didn't realize that."

"You said to give you time and space," Shawn reminded her again. "Each one of us just wanted to tell you to get over here and be with us, but since we couldn't, we didn't know what to say or how to respond. Do you want to stay with us, Tori?"

"I love you. I love all of you, and I'm just confused because this isn't normal."

"Fuck normal," Kevin growled and kissed her. "And we know you love us. But like Shawn asked, do you want to stay with us?"

"In what world would we make sense? Would I have to stay in these walls and hide from the world?" she questioned, looking at all of them.

"No, Tori. We'd make a world of our own, make you happy, and be damn the rest of the world," Duncan said. "Now answer the question. Do you want to stay with us? Be with us forever."

Tori's heart was going at a mach speed, and she could barely catch her breath. Walking up to Shawn, who'd ask the question first, she said, "Yes, Shawn. I love you, and I want to stay with you." After kissing him, she turned to Duncan and repeated the words. "Yes, Duncan. I love you, and I want to stay with you." When she turned to Kevin after kissing Duncan, the oldest brother's smile made her heart do a double flip. "Yes, Kevin, I love you, and I want to stay with you as well."

Kevin gave her a deep, mindless kiss until she heard a door open.

Turning around, she saw the door at the end of the wall open, and Shawn took her hand and guided her inside.

In the center of a soft mauve decorated room was the largest bed she'd ever seen in her life - A California king-size on steroids. It went the whole length of the room.

Enough for everyone?

There was a huge private tub/jacuzzi - enough for three to four people and a large shower.

There was a massive wardrobe in the corner, and Tori opened it to see that it wasn't for clothes. Every sexual device she could imagine was in this closet, and all of it looked as if it had never been used.

Quickly, Tori closed the wardrobe and turned to them with a wicked smile on her lips. Kevin sat on the edge of the bed with a pillow over his lap. Duncan was still standing at the doorway, and Shawn was standing near her.

"The rooms upstairs will be all yours," Shawn explained. "The closet in this room has a set of stairs that also leads down to the nursery, and Duncan's working on the camera and speaker system to have up in your rooms and on this floor."

Tori knew she was going to be spoiled, and so were all her babies.

"Kevin ordered the bed," Shawn continued. "The night we came home from the hospital."

She looked at all of them and then smiled. "Well, it'd be a waste if we didn't use it as much as possible."

Each of her men smiled, and she went to Shawn to help him out of his clothes.

"Not so fast," Kevin said in a very stern tone.

Tori turned to face him. "Did you want me to start with you first, Kevin?"

"No, I want you to take that coat off," he ordered.

Very ready to get something started, Tori dropped the coat and purse at her feet and took off her hat as well.

Kevin looked at Duncan and Shawn before looking at Tori. "Come here," he ordered.

In her most seductive walk, Tori neared him, liking how he gripped the pillow, holding it close to his groin, but she knew underneath his shaft was swelling, just like she could see Duncan's bulge, and she knew if she turned to Shawn, he too was aroused.

The sexual power she had over them turned her own, and she could feel her own body warming up fast.

"Shawn, take her clothes off," Kevin ordered.

She loved this game!

Shawn came over and took off her dress, which was the only thing she had on. He licked his lips as if he were looking at the most delicious steak, and she could tell he couldn't wait to eat on her.

Yet when she moved to press her body to him, Shawn moved behind her, guiding her so she was inches away from Kevin.

"Tori, didn't I warn you not to demean yourself ever again?" Kevin said sternly.

She had to wait for the lust fog to clear up a bit before she understood what he was saying. "What?"

"You're not a whore, a slut, or anything else you want to call yourself negatively, and I warned you never to call yourself that again, didn't I?" Kevin said.

"I only did it because I was angry and jealous. We really aren't going to have this conversation here. Now?!" She looked at Duncan as if he could help out, but he only crossed his arms over his chest after closing the bedroom door with him inside to show her she wasn't going anywhere.

"There's no conversation," Kevin said and patted the

pillow on his lap. "Lay over this pillow and take your punishment."

She snorted. "Punishment? You're going to spank me like I'm a child! I'm a grown ass woman!" Yet she found herself stomping her foot in a tantrum to make her point. "Even my father didn't punish me! You have lost your ever-loving mind, Kevin Carter." She turned to Shawn. "And the fact that you are standing there and will let him do this to me-"

"Tori, we can't have you thinking you're nothing to us," Shawn said in a very calm but firm voice. "Today is the last day you're going to call yourself a whore. You're our woman from this day forward."

"I'm pregnant!" she cried. "He could hurt the baby."

"Kevin is not going to hurt the baby," Shawn said. "There's the pillow."

"I'm not letting him spank me!" she cried. "Duncan!"

By this time, the middle brother had his shirt off, and he only folded his arms and leaned against the door, nodding towards Kevin.

Tori glared back at Kevin and stomped her foot again. "I won't agree to this, Kevin."

"The longer you prolong your punishment, the longer you prolong your pleasure, Tori," Kevin said. "Now you can either lie here and take your licks, or we'll find another way to punish you." His eyes looked over at the wardrobe.

She was almost inclined to see what he would take out and use. Lawd, she could feel her juices running down both sides of her thigh.

Stepping up to him, Tori groaned as Kevin pulled her down and situated her across his lap so her stomach was on the pillow, but it also left her rear high in the air. She looked at Duncan, pleading with his eyes, and he only shook his head and looked down at the ground.

Was he smiling?! That son of a bitch! All of them! They all were sons of a bitches.

Tori gasped, feeling Kevin's large palm feel over her naked rear cheeks. He had the nerve to rub on them as if warming them up, but damn if her body wasn't tingling all over.

The hard slap caught her off guard, and he followed it with another one, which hurt more. Tori burst into tears.

She'd never been hit in her entire life, and she sobbed loudly.

"I was going only to give you two, Tori," Kevin said, but his other arm was firmly over her back, so she still couldn't move off of him. "But since you argued and had the nerve to ask my brothers for help-"

Tori screamed, feeling three more swats, but then he paused one more time, rubbed her rear, and then gave her a final one.

That last one hit different, and she cried but gasped at the same time.

Shawn dropped to his knees behind her and started planting kisses all over her rear. He then parted her cheeks and slid his tongue all the way down to her perineum and then back up, doling more kisses all over her backside.

Kevin leaned over and kissed her tears away, raised her face so he could press his lips on hers, and Tori greedily took his deliciously long kiss.

Duncan came over from the door, taking off his clothes on the way, and pulled Tori from Kevin's lap. Picking her up and holding her in his arms, he doled sweet, rewarding, soft kisses, further stirring her arousal.

"Tori, we want you to have a bonding ceremony with all of us," Duncan said. "My partner has a villa in Canada. We can go up there and spend a honeymoon together."

Tori's bottom was sore, but her sexual need for them overpowered any pain, and Tori was ready to have them all - now!

She responded to Duncan's offer with a smile. "Only if I can change my name to Carter so we can be one big happy family."

"Fuck yes!" Kevin said in relief, taking off his clothes and kissing her cheek.

"And I can have you all as much as I want!" she declared.

"Any time or any day," Shawn swore, kissing the top of her feet. By this time, he was undressed as well.

"Tonight?" she asked. "Can I have all three of you after a shower?"

Duncan kissed her forehead and carried her into the bathroom, showering her with kisses. "You can have whatever you desire, Tori. Forever."

Shower, lovemaking, possibly dinner somewhere in there, and more lovemaking.

It was going to be a long night, but a beautiful, happy, spoiled life to come for her, and Tori would love every minute with the Carter Brothers.

THE END 12052025 1209AM 206028

Author's Bio

Award-winning Detroit author and founder of Motown Writers, Sylvia Hubbard, has independently published more than 65 dark-romance and intriguing-suspense stories over the 25 years she's been in the literary business. As an avid blogger, podcaster, social media manager, and digital strategist, Sylvia has received literary recognition for her literacy work and has had nine #1 Bestsellers. She is also a speaker, literary encouragement doula, and busy mompreneur expert.

Connect with this author on Instagram, Threads & TikTok at: @SylviaHubbard1

Companionship books to Her Substitute Husband... His Brothers

- Red Heart - where Kevin works
- Delilah's Desire - the electrician on his honeymoon is Dag
- She Works Hard for the Money - Beck Hardy, construction manager

- Black's Innocence – Tyler Black, lawyer
- Sin's Iniquity – Sinclaire Bowman – lawyer

Honorable Mentions from other stories in The Literary World of Sylvia Hubbard

- Private school in Chicago | Restaurant in Detroit
- The Bellinis – a prominent Italian Family moving their HQ and Family from Chicago to Detroit, intertwined into several stories.

Author Request: Please take a moment to write a review and support this author and then share that review to your reading friends. Bad or good, please let this author know how you felt and which brother you liked.

And don't worry, I have bigger sisters so you can't really say anything that would hurt my feelings. I'm a middle child, GenXer, so I'm pretty tough.

Visit my website for more books and subscribe for more updates to come.

Books – sylviahubbard.com/books
Subscribe – sylviahubbard.com/subscribe

Happy Reading and Thank you again for your Support. Your Author,
Sylvia Hubbard

www.ingramcontent.com/pod-product-compliance
Lightning Source LLC
LaVergne TN
LVHW040215110826
845146LV00005B/1297

* 9 7 9 8 9 9 5 3 3 4 9 0 3 *